D1713080

SMALL

P R O F E S S I O N A L

MURDER

a spriz mystery

by

NED AVERILL-SNELL

# AUTHOR'S NOTE

*Small Professional Murder* is a work of fiction. Any resemblance of its characters to actual persons is unintentional.

The "actors union" in this novel also is a fictional character whose actions and policies are not intended to portray any actual labor union or other real organization.

The small professional theatre organizations described in Perry, Monticello and Palatka are my inventions, but those cities are real, and you should visit them.

The Monticello Opera House is a real and wonderful place. Reese's Bar-B-Cue is made-up, which is a damn shame.

Sadly, the small professional theatres listed as casualties of the recent recession are all too real, or were.

The Galilee Repertory Theatre is fictitious, as is the small Florida city of Galilee. Neither is based on a real place, but both are composites, collages of parts from places I have loved.

N. A-S.

For mom, who has read so many mysteries she can tell whodunit by looking at the cover.

# I

*The Dragon had stolen a family not his own.*
*A mother and two boys.*
*The Dragon kept them in his rocky, steamy lair*
*Where no one could hear them cry.*
*They cried in pain*
*They cried in fear*
*They cried for rescue from the Dragon.*

NEVER BEFORE had Spriz seriously contemplated taking her own life. But this production meeting had just crossed into Hour Three, and a messy death was looking better by the minute.

For most plays, the director was the culprit in adding hours to the weekly production meetings in the cramped conference room. Gary, the director of this production, had been jobbed in from Cincinnati and seemed a pleasant enough fellow. He had even remembered Spriz's name without a reminder—a first in her experience. Spriz had seen dozens of guest directors come and go from Galilee, and though she liked Gary, he seemed too low-maintenance to make it in showbiz. As the director, he should have been doing most of the talking, and he wasn't.

When Galilee Repertory Theatre was working on a

premiere of a new play, the playwright was sometimes invited to production meetings (always a mistake) and could wind up being the squeaky wheel that took hours to grease. Spriz had noticed that playwrights pretty much showed up at meetings and rehearsals whether they were invited or not (they usually weren't). But *Deathtrap*'s author was long dead, and thus no impediment to a speedy meeting.

No, the bottleneck this time was not the playwright or the director, but a man who was probably the least important person in the room—or would have been, had the propsmistress obeyed her gut and played sick that day.

In her six years at GaliRep, Spriz had accumulated something like two hundred and eighty hours of unused sick time. She had every intention of taking the days off eventually. During difficult productions, she daydreamed about various painless diseases that could keep her home reading fantasy novels and watching Netflix for seven weeks. Somehow, she always wound up at the theatre, even when she really was sick, which wasn't often.

Spriz's adopted Daddy believed that people lied to themselves too much to really know when they were sick, and that only a doctor could say for sure whether you were truly ill or just "feelin' puny," as old Hoosiers liked to say.

Stampeding bison could not drag Spriz to a doctor now. A few months after she landed the props job, and with it her first-ever health insurance, she was bullied by the thickheaded good intentions of the artistic director into getting a checkup. Upon learning that Spriz had been adopted as an infant and knew nothing of her true family medical history, her new Primary Care Physician ordered her to undergo every test known to medical science in order to "set a baseline" for her care.

The trivial fact of Spriz's left-handedness inspired the doc to fish for schizophrenia, alcoholism, dyslexia, Crohn's disease and ulcerative colitis. The slightest hesitation in responding to one of his bizarre queries instigated a neurological workup. He ordered a blood film to look for sickle-cell anemia, a disease almost unheard of in people with Spriz's pigmentation. When the insurance company got the pre-certification call for that test, an adjuster phoned the doctor and politely ordered him to cut the crap.

When she told her friend Tommy—her only friend, really—about the tests, he clicked his tongue and said, "I'm surprised he didn't tell you to turn your head and cough." Spriz didn't understand the joke, and didn't ask. Her reflex was to avoid embarrassing admissions, even to Tommy, at all costs.

She endured three and a half of the tests and then stopped. The CT scan (with contrast) had been the final straw. Just before her body was to be inserted into the contraption, she yanked out her own I-V, scooped up her clothes, and marched to her Jeep in her hospital gown. Later she gave the gown to the costume shop, in case GaliRep ever decided to do *One Flew Over the Cuckoo's Nest* or *Wit*.

The doctor never followed up. Spriz took this as his tacit admission that all the tests had been unnecessary in the first place, especially since she was then still in her twenties and, despite being bony and underweight for her frame of five feet eleven and one-half inches, healthy as a horse.

She had been told she resembled a horse, with her long face, the hard corners on her jaw, her chocolate eyes and her long, caramel hair that fell in scattered strings and twists about her shoulders—a mane and tail in one, and both in need of a comb.

As tall girls will do if self-conscious, Spriz slouched invariably. She had been told she would be more than six feet tall if she'd just straighten up, but that was not an honor she coveted. Spriz had spent her life perfecting the trick of making herself invisible, and she had gotten good at it, despite her stature. She had never owned a pair of heels.

Now thirty-three years old and suffocating in a "conference room" barely big enough to hold its single table and ten chairs, she dearly wished she were dying right then of some disfiguring disease that everyone could see, something that made bits of flesh peel off and slide down her face so there'd be no questions when she got up and staggered away from this interminable meeting.

Andreo—his whole name, even in the program, was Andreo—had been commissioned to compose original music for the production. On the rare occasions when composers were hired, it was usually to spice up Shakespeare or Shaw, to give a classic a few original notes to set up a tone consistent with the director's *vision*. For modern plays like *Deathtrap*, far less effort was applied: A few apropos tracks from the popular canon were simply burned onto a CD to be played before and after the play.

But besides being a mediocre composer of joyless, tuneless, rhythm-free music, Andreo was concertmaster of the Galilee Symphony Orchestra. GaliRep's artistic director and the public relations people at the little semi-pro symphony had arranged this cross-pollination to germinate much-needed press for both organizations. "THE PLAY'S THE THING: VIOLINIST MAKES SWEET MUSIC FOR *DEATHTRAP*" was the headline on the joint press release.

Andreo had never before attended a theatrical production meeting. No one at the table was entirely sure whether Andreo had ever seen a play. So Spriz figured he might be due some slack for making a rookie mistake and assuming the meeting had been called for the sole purpose of talking about his music.

Producing artistic director Conrad, who usually played the role of referee in these meetings, had made his own rookie mistake. In an effort to ingratiate himself, he had opened the meeting by asking Andreo to share his thoughts about the play and his music.

That was two hours and eight minutes ago, and they were still talking music. And if they ever finished talking music they would still need to give the floor, in turn, to Ana Maria the stage manager, Maisy the costumer, Sheila the set designer, sourpuss Karl the technical director, Lawrence the lighting designer, Carlos the sound designer, and last and most certainly least, Suzanne "Spriz" (rhymes with showbiz) Prizzi, procurer of every candle, armchair, pistol, Bible, wine carafe, Confederate dollar, china plate, Coke bottle, leg lamp, switchblade, Persian rug, pulpit, credenza, sword, treasure map, poison pill and jester's skull to appear on the GaliRep stage for six years and counting.

Conrad had just tried to steer Andreo off the subject of how atonalism represented a "death trap" for harmonic structure and onto the more practical matter of scheduling, and had backed into an ambush.

Andreo rolled his eyes skyward and inhaled sharply. "Seeex weeks? Seeex weeks my friends, to compose two an' a half hours of music, she cannot be done!"

"Two and a half hours?" Conrad asked, genuinely confused. He wisely elected not to question Andreo's calendar math just yet. The first rehearsal had been held yesterday, and opening night was not six weeks away, but in four weeks and three days.

Andreo stabbed a meaty finger toward Ana Maria, down-table from him. "Her. Zat girl. She say ze play last two an' a half hours, apprrrroximately. I tell her I need to know exakly how long, but she refuse to say."

"We can't know exactly how long the play runs until previews, Andreo, and really not even then—it's never exactly the same twice," Conrad said carefully, maybe too carefully, worrying that Andreo might feel he was being spoken to like a child, because he was. "And we don't need music under every minute of the play. We really just need what we call 'curtain music': A few minutes before the play starts, a few minutes at intermission, a few over the bows at the end. Maybe a few more to cover scene changes if they go on too long." He shot director Gary a quick, hard look that said, *But that won't be necessary, will it?*

Ryan Mountain was a lawyer and a theatre lover, and was thrilled when named to GaliRep's board a few years ago.

Like everyone else on the board, Ryan had been brought in for his "invaluable expertise in the for-profit sector," which was the board's nice way of saying that Conrad and the rest of the regular staff were harebrained artists with the business savvy of second-graders and even less legal sense.

Tucked away in a sleepy arts oasis near the Gulf of Mexico, GaliRep operated under the actors union's Small Professional Theatre designation. SPTs are the little, regional not-for-profits that pay the actors (barely), live hand-to-mouth on grants and fundraising, exist in a perpetual state of hanging-by-a-thread, and have midwifed most great American theatre talent in the years since Broadway unconditionally surrendered to tarted-up circus acts from British producers and Walt Disney.

Ryan knew his board membership was the little company's way of getting free legal advice, but he didn't care. He loved the theatre, and this was as close as he would ever get to stepping out under the lights himself. He would tell them anything they wanted to know, *pro bono, in dulci jubilo.*

From his first day, Ryan had been urging Conrad to make two changes: 1) Expire unused sick days every December 31, and 2) Pay more attention to contracts, to make sure they spelled out each party's obligations to the letter. He kept reminding Conrad about his failure to add the boilerplate phrase "and other duties as needed" to the new box office manager's contract. Now they were stuck with a box office manager who refused to put tickets into little envelopes for the will-call window because his contract did not require him to do so, and he had a paper-cut phobia.

Conrad's pat counters to Ryan's pleas were: 1) When they used to expire sick days every year, employees felt obligated to use them up and always left him shorthanded for the Christmas show, and 2) He only worked with "experienced theatre artists" whose job descriptions had not changed in centuries.

"When you write a contract for the actor who will play Hamlet," Conrad explained, "the contract does not need to specify that his job is to say Hamlet's lines and not Gertrude's. The costumer knows her role is to borrow or make as many costumes as are required—her contract does not have to say how many. Theatre people know their jobs."

Even reading upside down, Conrad recognized the contract Andreo had just produced from a creamy folder, and as soon as he saw it, he recalled lawyer Mountain's furrowed brow, followed by the image of the exact words the contract used to spell out Andreo's end of the deal, words Conrad only now understood to be woefully vague.

"Composer will write, arrange, and record musical accompaniment for the play *Deathtrap* by Ira Levin. Music to be ready in time for technical rehearsals beginning one week prior to opening night, November 11." Conrad had a photographic memory, an asset when he was an actor learning lines, now a curse when there was so much he witnessed every day that he dearly wished he could forget.

"Mooseecal accompammunt for ze play!" Andreo recited, jabbing a fat finger at the precise clause. "For ze play! Not a part of ze play. Not some of ze play. FOR ZE PLAY!"

Andreo apparently believed he had been hired to adapt *Deathtrap* into a five-singer, unauthorized opera, or perhaps a ballet. And that's what he expected to be allowed to do, and for which he was about to demand that opening night be postponed a few weeks so he had enough time to do it in.

The composer's interpretation of the agreement was not only inconsistent with Conrad's, but diametrically opposed to it, as Conrad had expected Andreo to do no actual composing whatsoever.

Over too many drinks at the outset of this sad conspiracy, the symphony's music director had assured Conrad that Andreo was not only talentless but also lazy, and would almost certainly pull from a drawer ten minutes of music he composed years ago, slap a new title on it and present it to GaliRep as new work. Andreo had no incentive to do otherwise: Few people had ever heard his compositions, which were both entirely unmemorable and virtually indistinguishable from one another.

Conrad thought he knew what he was getting, and he was okay with it. The arts editor for little Galilee's one daily newspaper routinely ignored theatre, other than sending a critic on opening night, but he adored the little local symphony. This collaboration would give that old twit no choice but to finally spill some decent ink on GaliRep, if only by association.

And Conrad knew his subscribers. A lot of 'em attended the theatre just to look smart to their friends. They'd never risk appearing uncouth by complaining that their unsophisticated ears were unmoved by the work of Central Florida's only semi-famous Italian atonalist.

But as an insurance policy, Conrad had stuck Andreo where he could do the least damage: on a play where no one would pay any attention to the music, helmed by a milquetoast director jobbed in from Ohio who was looking to build his resume and wouldn't rock the boat over something as trivial as bad curtain music. Conrad had big plans for the *Measure for Measure* he was directing himself in the spring to close the season, and he had no intention of letting that tone-deaf dago anywhere near it.

Conrad was looking down at the table and massaging his bald head with all ten of his fingertips, struggling to reconcile Andreo's incisive grasp of English legalese with his near-total inability to speak English of any sort, and Spriz was distracting herself by trying to remember how to tie a proper noose, when Gina, the new assistant stage manager for the show on the mainstage, hustled in and whispered in Spriz's ear.

As Spriz quietly rose from her chair and mumbled that she had to run to the dressing rooms, she heard Daddy's voice in her memory, chuckling, "Praise Jesus, a disaster!"

As she was gently closing the conference room door behind her, she could hear poor old Conrad wading into the soup: "Here's what 'for the play' means to *me*, Andreo…"

.

# 2

"I WILL NOT EAT THIS SHIT!"

Spriz heard the ejaculation long before she reached the dressing rooms, and even from a distance knew instantly who had issued it and in which dressing room she would find him.

She tapped gently on the door. "Brandon? It's Spriz, can I help?"

"YESSSS." The reply was deep and authoritative, and amplified for the back row. Spriz had her hand on the old wooden door, which thrummed at the word like the back of a guitar.

She entered and found Brandon Wishart at his dressing station, a section of a long counter with a mirror above it, wall to wall. He sat facing the mirror, habitually looking deep into his own grey-blue eyes instead of toward whomever he was speaking to. His section of the counter was the one nearest the door, where it always was, where he always demanded it be.

Three younger men along the counter were busy applying makeup and crepe facial hair. Wishart had already finished making up his face and was sitting in his dressing robe, waiting until the fifteen-minute call to dress. The curtain would rise on the 8 p.m. performance in seventeen minutes exactly. Ana Maria ran a tight ship.

"I WILL NOT EAT THIS. I WILL NOT EAT THIS SHIT. I ABSOLUTELY WILL NOT," the veteran actor intoned, with perfect enunciation. These were the very same words poor, terrified Gina had heard five minutes ago, when she smartly recognized she was over her head and made a bee-line for Spriz.

Wishart had cleared some of his stage makeup and other paraphernalia to one side of his dressing area—intruding deep into the territory of the actor to his right, who five weeks into the show's run was well past caring about Brandon's sense of entitlement and pretty much everything else—and had set before himself a pewter plate holding a peeled pear half, a single marshmallow and a Hawaiian sweet roll.

"You know you're not supposed to take your props off the prop table unless you're about to carry them onstage, Brandon," Spriz said, with calm authority. "Now how can I help you?" She offered her assistance to the fussy actor with a deft blend of impatience and affection. She and he had shared this same dance before. His bellicose eruptions and lethal gripes were inflected with a dog-whistle charm that only she could detect.

Newbie actors thought he was mean to her, and disliked him on her account, as well as for many other reasons—not that they had ever shown her any particular kindness themselves. To them she was invisible, as she was to most people, most of the time. But when this old ham complained to her, she saw a twinkle in his eye that neutralized the venom in his stinger.

He saw her—he could *see* her—and he liked her. She liked him. She suspected that the crisis of the moment was legit, but she knew that in the past he had sometimes cooked up phony emergencies when he missed her. Or so it seemed to Spriz.

Brandon Wishart was a miracle of the illusive power of stagecraft. His age was anywhere from fifty-five to seventy, depending upon the relative age and attractiveness of the person to whom he was speaking. His heels were raised two inches by lifts in his shoes, and under his costume he always wore a compression shirt that squished his belly fat up onto his chest to simulate pectoral muscles. He had no hair except what he kept in his makeup case, an amazing array of wigs and pieces for every character on stage and any mood offstage. He had painted deep shadows on his neck and under his cheekbones to slim his flabby face, and "popped" his eyes with expert application of liner, shadow and highlight. A smudge of rouge on his high cheekbones gave his ashen skin the youthful glow it must have had naturally when he played Romeo, about two hundred years ago.

Were you to see him roll out of bed in the morning (and no one did, not anymore), you would see a short, fat, bald, hunched-over alcoholic with a sickly cough and stage makeup packed so deep into the creases in his forehead that it persisted through multiple washings.

But on stage, something happened to Brandon Wishart. Under the sharp beam of the ellipsoidals and the softer glow of the fresnels, his feet high on a deck serving as a broad pedestal, his sloppy spine and shoulders squared up into the powerful posture he'd practiced in front of mirrors since childhood, his adrenaline spiked by the sea of hearts beating in the seats, he transformed from a sad old sot into a Greek god, a towering figure of masculine authority. His regal brow, broad nose, commanding chin, and angled jaw—all makeup-enhanced— recalled a granite bust of Andrew Jackson. He could be a retired Olympic athlete of forty-five—from the tenth row back, he could make forty.

Those who knew the offstage Brandon Wishart were awestruck by his appearance on stage, no matter how many times they saw him perform. The patrons in the seats did not know they were witnessing a miracle. They accepted what they saw: a vigorous man of distinction, a matinée hero, a beloved and beautiful star.

Offstage, no one liked him, except Spriz. He was vain and selfish and needy, and he treated his fellow actors with cruelty on his bad days and indifference on his good ones. He was a mean drunk, and drunk often, though never on stage. He routinely reduced backstage crew to tears over trivial complaints. He delighted especially in demeaning young actors, giving them unsolicited direction, reminding them of their relative inexperience at every turn, and stealing scenes from them with undisguised pleasure. The more openly a rookie admired him, the crueler he was.

Despite his acting prowess, his most refined skill was his near-psychic ability to identify a person's vulnerable spots and twist a knife there. If you were sensitive about your muffin top, or were afflicted with a cold sore, or had always been shy about your dyslexia, you would find yourself on the receiving end of an ugly joke about your malady on the day you met Brandon Wishart.

Most people made up their minds pretty quickly to avoid the man's company. Even those who'd worked with him for many years didn't know much about him, nor were they willing to risk their self-esteem by attempting to learn more. The man was a monster.

But no one could deny his ability, or tried to. He was a complete actor. He could pass for forty in the right light, yes, but he could as easily twist his body into Scrooge's, or splay it into Lear's. His voice did whatever he asked of it, from Othello's terrifying rumbles to Willy Loman's impotent squeaks, and when the moment required it, he could call forth a vocal fury that rattled the rigging above his head and made the audience check their fillings with their tongues.

All of this he could do with such pure, heartbreaking truth that actors sharing the stage with him were known to forget their lines, the name of the character they were playing, and the title of the play they were performing and simply stare at him, mouth agape, until another actor's elbow bumped them back onto the rails.

"THIS is the SHIT they are serving us on STAGE now!"

The play coming up at 8 p.m. was an adaptation of Charles Dickens' *Great Expectations*. Wishart played all the father figures, including Pip's benefactor Abel Magwitch and Joe Gargery, the kindhearted blacksmith.

For an early scene in which Pip shares a meal with Joe, Mrs. Gargery and their brood, the director had nixed the idea of miming invisible food, and she didn't want to see phony plastic food on stage that the characters didn't actually eat. She insisted that the actors have real food on their plates, ideally food with an indistinct shape and color so that the audience could imagine it was whatever they wanted it to be, in keeping with her Expressionist concept for the production. The set and costumes were similarly shapeless and colorless, ink blots on which the audience was invited to imprint its Dickensian subconscious.

Spriz understood immediately that she needed to find a small set of food items that were cheap, easy to store, and required no preparation, and that one of the foods would have to be moist so there'd be no need for the extra fuss of a beverage. Easy enough. But then she was going to have to get the actors to approve her menu, and that job was going to be a complete freaking clusterfuck, especially with Brandon Wishart in the cast.

If a proposed food item was approved by any five of the six actors in the scene, the sixth had a problem. Allergy. Lactose intolerance. Gluten sensitivity. A "texture thing." Some foods were rejected for posing too high a risk of getting stuck in front teeth where the audience might see. Some were nixed because of their halitosis potential, especially by those actors who would give or receive kisses later in the story. Lots of suspect claims that certain ingredients "gum up the voice" were made by actors who did not know that Spriz the invisible propsmistress was often in the room when they were snacking and knew full well the sorts of reputedly voice-destroying crap they consumed when they thought no one was watching.

Wishart rejected everything out of hand, and did not always feel obligated to cite a reason. "No no, that won't do at all, please find something else, if you would, dear." Wishart's go-to suffix "dear" perverted a tender word into a dirty needle, dripping with disease and ill-will.

As tech week loomed, Pip and the wife and children of Joe Gargery were tiring of the conversation. They all had long since approved enough options—Wishart alone was prolonging the search.

Spriz would always be proud of her solution. After watching a rehearsal, she pointed out to Brandon that it was really his scene—he had the most lines—and if at any point he stopped talking long enough to eat, he'd kill the pacing. She knew he was proud of his ability to keep a play moving, a skill he found woefully lacking in young actors. If he played the scene as though always on the verge of eating—picking up a roll or a cup and gesturing with it as he spoke—the audience would trick itself into believing they had seen him eat. Audiences were stupid that way.

Wishart loved the plan, and the acknowledgement of his ownership of the scene. She bought enough canned pears, marshmallows and Hawaiian rolls for tech week and the run, put most of the rolls in the freezer, gave Gina written instructions to put one of each food item on each plate—with a special note that Wishart's food was going to return manhandled but unbitten—and got back to the job of locating or making the eleventy million other props this Victorian nightmare required.

Now here Wishart was, bitching about the food he was not required to eat and had in fact never eaten throughout six shows a week, for five weeks now.

"You don't eat the food, Brandon," Spriz said calmly. "So I'm not sure I understand the problem."

With a theatrical flourish that showed he had been waiting for this precise moment to pounce, Wishart lifted the pewter plate, pivoted in his chair to face Spriz, and held it before her, a few feet in front of the buckle on the weathered brown belt holding up her paint- and glue-stained jeans.

"Sniff," he said calmly.

"Brandon, I don't want to sniff, and what does it matter, you don't have to eat it!"

"Indulge me, dear. Sniff."

Without moving, Spriz sniffed the air in front of her. "It's fine."

"Closer."

Spriz rolled her eyes, and with a sweep of her left hand she deftly corralled her loose hair behind her neck, her fist a ponytail holder. She bent at her waist and lowered her face to just a few inches above the plate. She almost sniffed, but she stopped herself. She knew if she did, she might get dizzy and fall down, which would be embarrassing.

She had caught a face full of the alcohol fumes rising from the plate. The pears had fermented. They probably wouldn't make anyone sick, but they might make an actor woozy enough to miss a stair or drop a line, and Spriz guessed that the parents of the child actors playing the Gargery kids might have a few questions if junior came home high on pear huff.

Still bent over, she lifted just her face, which was now even with Wishart's, and smiled slyly. "Thanks. I'll take care of it." She straightened up, released her hair and took the plate from Brandon with both hands. The old thespian dismissed Spriz by returning to his mirror. "See that you do, dear."

Spriz turned and left in search of Gina just as Ana Maria arrived at the dressing rooms to issue her fifteen-minute call. She'd make further announcements at ten minutes and at five, and finally she'd call "Places!" to inform the actors that the show was about to start, with or without them.

A half-hour later, while they listened to his gripping

graveyard scene on the monitor speaker in the green room, the young bucks from that dressing room would gripe to other cast members that the old fart had made a big stink over nothing, for his own sadistic amusement—it wasn't even his problem.

Spriz didn't know for sure, but she liked to think he was looking after his castmates' wellbeing but had concealed his intentions. He had a reputation to maintain, after all.

# 3

TRAPPED.

The two-story downtown building had been many things in the ninety years since it was constructed. Built as a cigar factory during the Florida boom in the 1920s, it sat vacant through most of the Great Depression. It was remodeled as an appliance store after the war, and when that failed in the 1960s, it was remodeled again, briefly, as a bar & grille downstairs, offices up. A grease fire chased away those tenants but left the building more or less standing, empty and boarded up for nearly a decade except for the two years it housed a storefront church, the Galilee Church of Christ the Redeemer. After an exposé in the *Galilee Star* revealed the redeemer to be a craps table, the city seized the little cigar factory for unpaid taxes and fines. And then let it sit.

Weeks before the building's scheduled demolition, the city council voted to lease it for a dollar a year to a small actors' collective, hoping a theatre would draw nighttime patrons to the blighted downtown's bars and restaurants. It did.

The structure was perfectly serviceable for cigar-rolling,

selling stoves and slinging suds. But it was inadequate in every imaginable way as a theatre space, and forty years of inexpert jerry-rigging had only made it more of an albatross.

Like most small stages designed in and for the 1970s, GaliRep's mainstage house had no proscenium arch or grand curtain, and the "stage" was just a broad, bare floor flanked by rising seating banks and a lighting grid above. Tall, black velour drapes on sliding tracks were positioned as needed to create wing space and selectively mask off or reveal backstage areas, depending on the set design. It was a utilitarian space, but marvelously flexible—a big, black, empty box into which artists poured their dreams and nightmares so an audience could peek in safely from the top.

But even with the flooring that divided the two stories removed to create a mainstage house with twenty-two-foot ceilings, the lighting grid was too low, and hot lights often hung perilously close to flammable scenery. Of the 147 seats, a half-dozen had views obstructed by support poles or other immovable objects, and Sheila always struggled to design sets that did not exacerbate the sightline problems.

The building's antediluvian wiring and main power supply stunk. For many years the theatre went dark in June, July and August because there was insufficient current for both stage lighting and the air-conditioning demands of summer nights in Florida. A minor upgrade in the '90s enabled the theatre to operate year-round, but during summer shows they still stationed a volunteer with a flashlight and a walkie-talkie close to the main service box, just in case a circuit breaker needed to be flipped back on in the middle of a performance.

There was no space for a rehearsal room. Rehearsals took place on the mainstage, as did auditions, usually on the set of another show in the middle of its run, and coordinating the scheduling of the shared hall was an ongoing catastrophe. The audience restrooms were too small and too far from the seats, and the dressing room toilets were so close to the stage that actors were forbidden to flush during a performance. And the tiny conference room made staff members long for death.

Worst among the charming old building's deficiencies was the logistical flaw the staff fondly called "The Mousetrap" in honor of the longest-running play in history: From the backstage area—which included not only dressing rooms and the green room but also the costume shop and, in the basement below, Spriz's prop room—there was no route out of the building except by strolling right across the stage. If you were backstage when the show began, you were there for the duration, or at least until intermission.

Over the years, multiple swings had been taken at correcting the problem. Twice—once in the '70s and again in the '90s—architects had been invited to join the board so that the company could finagle a free plan for adding an exit someplace backstage. But every door attempted ran afoul of the original building design. Here a doorway could not be cut because of the fragility of an ancient load-bearing wall, there a door could not go because it would open closer to the property line of the adjacent building than zoning would allow.

Some enterprising actors in the '80s (young Conrad, sporting a luxurious ponytail, was one of them) cooked up an ill-conceived and entirely unauthorized plan that involved cutting a hatch in the ceiling of an upstairs hallway and running a retractable ladder from the roof to an alley below. They got the hatch cut, but were denied both the funds and the permit for the ladder. The hatch was a godsend, though: It had been used ever since to facilitate rooftop smoke breaks.

By the time Spriz had disposed of the spoiled pears, cleaned the Gargerys' pewter plates and redecorated them with fresh food (an extra roll would understudy the pear until Spriz could hit the store tomorrow), quietly restored the plates to the prop table backstage, gently quizzed Gina to learn how the pears had spoiled (actors illicitly snacking from the Tupperware bowl in the fridge failed to close the lid), talked Gina down from a guilty crying jag, and told Ana Maria the whole sordid tale for retelling in the nightly performance report, the backstage clock read 8:04. The show had started. The Mousetrap had sprung on Spriz.

She didn't mind. There was no place she would rather be. Her apartment was comfy, but it had picked up a serious infestation of actor roommates, three of them. They were okay, but so boisterous and talkative that they overwhelmed the quiet Spriz. She was used to being invisible—she enjoyed it, actually—but didn't like feeling invisible in her own home. Like many actors, all three chain-smoked. Being a theatre rat, Spriz was used to cigarettes, but being a non-smoker herself, she felt even more left out, and outnumbered.

But her apartment wasn't really her home anyway. The properties room was home, and sanctuary, and playground.

It was less a room than a cage, a 909-square-foot chicken wire enclosure carved out of a corner of the basement directly beneath the costume shop and next to the water heaters and junction boxes that hummed night and day and smelled of hot insulation.

An ancient freight elevator with a wooden pull-down gate ran from the far end of the basement up to a hallway behind the stage, enabling Spriz to deliver big tables or mattresses without wrestling them up the winding staircase.

There were no windows on the basement, no natural light, and year-round the still air stuck at 81 degrees—tolerable, by Florida standards. Spriz liked to pretend it was a secret chamber deep inside one of the pyramids.

A small padlock secured the wide, chicken wire door. Spriz dutifully locked it when she was not there, though where walls are made of chicken wire, a padlock on the door is mostly a suggestion. Spriz never worried about theft much. She was certain that besides a handful of trustworthy people—herself, Tommy, Conrad, Maisy, Ana Maria and Karl—no one else knew where the prop room was, or cared. The actors seemed to believe that props magically appeared when needed, pulled from thin air by an invisible props faerie and dropped into their ready hands on-cue.

Though the walls were wire, you couldn't really see anything inside from the other half of the basement except the backs of row after row of wooden cases and steel shelving units. But once you opened the padlock, took one and one-half steps straight ahead through the darkened doorway, reached for the string that would be six inches in front of your nose, and pulled, seven evenly spaced bare bulbs snapped on, and suddenly you were orphan Nell in her grandfather's Old Curiosity Shop.

A combination toy store, antique mall and junk emporium, the L-shaped enclosure was stuffed with stacks and racks of wonders, anywhere you looked.

Shelves neatly arranged by period and style held row after row of china, glassware, cups and cutlery. A hundred bottles of every imaginable shape, size, color and purpose lined the tops of the shelving units: antique brown medicine bottles, wine bottles with corks, vintage Coke and Orange Crush bottles, gallon moonshine jugs, etched crystal decanters, Schlitz and Blatz bottles, liquor flasks, milk bottles in three sizes, scientific Pyrex beakers, and brightly colored seltzer dispensers.

Books and magazines were crammed into the bottoms of the cases, their weight intended to prevent the overloaded shelves from tipping. They included a matched set of fat lawbooks and the complete 1947 Encyclopedia Britannica, except for volumes Ka-Kl and V. When bored, Spriz often pulled a random Britannica volume and enjoyed exploring the world as it was when Daddy was a child, when most things were black & white and national borders were very different on some continents.

Studded jewelry boxes sparkled from a glass dessert cart. Silver serving platters were filed in a large cubbyhole, on their edges like record albums. Old radios, walkie-talkies, televisions and telephones had their own department. Most of the electronics actually worked, though they never needed to work when used on stage. Spriz's Daddy had taught her how to replace vacuum tubes and repair wiring.

A Radio Flyer wagon. A Flexible Flyer sled. Stuffed animals, a dozen different types of playballs netted up in a rope hammock, a wooden rocking horse, and a '50s tricycle—candy-apple red—in mint condition. Barrels, casks and wineskins. A crib, a rocking cradle and a baby carriage. Vases and vases. Three folding, fake Christmas trees with lights and ornaments glued on. Plastic houseplants in pretty pots. Chairs in logical groupings, carefully stacked all the way to the rafters for efficient use of space. Desks, wardrobes, bureaus and beds. Three upright pianos, including a player piano. Lifelike rubber fruit and plastic pork chops.

Long, sticklike items were bundled up together like Roman *fasces* and strapped by a loop of clothesline to the bottoms of the low rafters overhead: oars, flagpoles, walking sticks, baseball bats, Queequeg's harpoon, an Irish shillelagh from *Juno and the Paycock*, fishing poles, caveman spears with foam faux-stone spearheads, Death's plastic scythe, and an ornate bow and quiver of arrows—tipped by realistic rubber arrowheads—from *William Tell*, the 1804 play that inspired the opera, just one of Conrad's many money-losing attempts to "give the people something they've never seen before."

Assorted unwieldy objects were hung from the rafters with hooks or bungee cord, such as army canteens and antique steel milk cans. Kerosene lanterns in several sizes and styles hung there, each converted to battery power by a tiny bulb that flickered like a flame. Since the rafters were only seven feet above the floor, these items presented a dangerous obstacle course for the skull of the nearly six-foot Spriz. She could run it with her eyes closed.

She had spent six years arranging and rearranging this space, and finally had it exactly the way she wanted it. She knew precisely what she had and where it was stored, down to the last spoon. There was no map, directory or catalog, except in Spriz's shaggy head. Had Spriz taken her life during the production meeting as she had dearly wished to do, no prop would ever be located again. They'd just have to raze the building and find another cigar factory.

Every prop had history. Every piece was first made, bought or stolen for a particular show, and then stored afterward in case it was ever needed again. Over time, props simply accumulate, like sedimentary layers. Some props get used over and over again, especially chairs, glasses and rugs. Other props get their one shining moment on stage, then go into storage and are never seen again, except by the propsmaster. Eventually a propsmaster runs out of space, and begins to weed out those objects that never seem to be needed, and those that have been seen too many times.

Spriz hated having to thin the herd. She felt she was letting her props down, like whoever marooned those poor misfit toys on that awful island in *Rudolph*. That scene still made her cry.

She'd gone to Conrad to suggest plays for future seasons only because those plays featured starring roles for props she felt needed time out of the basement. She'd been begging him to do a Noël Coward play so she could dust off that rosewood cane settee that had lain upside down (to protect its crushed-velvet upholstery) and under a set of wicker rockers since before she came.

Now and then, regretfully, when she had no choice, she purged things that were just taking up space, as long as she could find them a good home. A few lucky local actors she deemed worthy had furnished whole apartments with her castoffs.

After you turned right at the bend in the L, you could see the tall steel cabinet in the back corner of the room, the deepest place in the pyramid. It was the weapons cabinet, and it had a lock that meant business.

Nothing in it was lethal. The replica muskets, period rifles and shotgun all had sealed barrels. The handguns had chambers made the wrong size for real ammo of any caliber, and could be loaded only with special blank rounds that made a satisfyingly scary BANG but held no projectile. The saber blades had rounded edges, the knives were dull and either rubber or spring-loaded, and the foils and bayonets all had blunted points.

Still, the contents of the weapons cabinet were expensive, the blanks contained real gunpowder, and even if a stolen prop gun was incapable of firing a projectile, a miscreant could easily bluff with one to hold up a bank or mug an old lady. Spriz regarded the contents of this cabinet with deep respect, and kept it locked at all times.

In the other back corner sat Spriz's command center, a huge desk-slash-workbench. On its right side rested the underpowered computer the company had given her, which she used to locate and order the few objects she did not already have. Spriz was an unbeatable eBay bidder; if she wanted it, she won it, and always for less than her budget.

Sometimes she climbed out of the basement and into the blinding Florida sun to hit antique malls and thrift shops for props she needed. But Galilee was a little city stocked with limited variety, and Spriz could track down the perfect poker-chip caddy or tea pitcher much more efficiently online. Besides, Conrad was notoriously stingy about reimbursing for gas.

When a show's rehearsals started before she had managed to procure every prop required, she often delivered the best facsimiles she had on hand, "doofers," to the stage manager so the actors had something to practice with. "Doofer" is a propstalk contraction of "It'll do fer now." It was not unusual for a doofer to be promoted to actual prop, either because the actor fell in love with it or because Spriz couldn't find anything better by opening night. No one else minded, but Spriz cringed when that happened.

On a shelf beside her computer sat the inkjet printer she played like Yo-Yo Ma to craft all manner of paper props: family photos, grandpa's last will and testament, convincing beer labels to disguise the cans of soda water the actors were actually drinking, and Beatrice and Benedick's love letters, splendidly hand-written thanks to Microsoft's Lucida Calligraphy font.

To the left of her computer, she had erected a plastic shield to protect it from what she did on the left side of her workbench. The wooden surface there was pitted, cut, stained and, in places, burned. It was dusted with the overlapping haze of so many different colors of spray paint, Spriz called it her nebula. Along the back were mason jars and coffee cans crammed with an X-Acto knife handle and assorted little blades for it, woodcarving tools, pencils, rulers, tiny screwdrivers and paintbrushes.

Above, cubbyholes and shelves held scraps of sandpaper and steel wool, hot-glue guns, a soldering iron, clamps, files, Q-tips, cotton balls, a can of acetone, paper towels, furniture polish, tie line, a small acetylene torch, Sharpies, wire, white glue, yellow glue, clear glue, super glue, rubber cement and Bondo. She had three pairs of scissors in differing sizes, all made for lefties. Her big swing-arm lamp had a magnifying lens she could pull into view to work on tiny details. Tiny details don't count for much on stage, but Spriz took pride in her work.

Here she made things, and fixed things, just as she'd watched Daddy do in his shop her whole childhood. Here there was no day or night. Here she could be privately invisible without the awkward reminder of other peoples' indifference.

On a little shelf above her nebula, she had placed an old Bakelite-cased AM/FM radio she repaired after it had been destroyed nightly by Stanley Kowalski in *A Streetcar Named Desire* for six weeks. The director had chosen to update the play from the late 1940s to the late 1960s so Stanley could be a Vietnam vet suffering from post-traumatic stress disorder. Spriz knew better than to put an FM receiver in a 1940s apartment.

The radio was perma-tuned to the local FM Public Radio station, and was always switched on. Radio waves could not penetrate the heavy foundation of the cigar factory, but in an uncharacteristic moment of helpfulness, Karl had shown her how to wire the old set to an exposed iron vent pipe to engineer an effective antenna.

Cellphones didn't work in the basement either. Atop the tallest building in little Galilee, on a clear day, holding your phone as high as you could and standing on your tippy toes, you were lucky to get two bars on your signal-strength indicator, which was only one of the many reasons Spriz didn't bother to own a cellphone. Cellphones worked about half the time in other parts of the building, but the basement was the Dungeon of No Service.

An outmoded landline office phone with speed-dial buttons for Conrad, the costume shop and other offices sat next to Spriz's computer. It almost never rang, and when it did, Spriz usually ignored it. Everybody knew that the only way to ask Spriz for something was by email.

She was passing her time in the Mousetrap by starting to pick out objects to put on the *Deathtrap* main character's desktop: blotter, pencil caddy, framed photo, book, and a wooden doofer for the pistol—the actors would not be permitted to touch the real prop pistol until tech week. She had not yet decided whether she'd escape at intermission or stay until the show was over when she heard a tiny voice coming from the open chicken wire door.

"Spriz? It's Gina."

Spriz came around the corner. "Gina? I didn't know you knew how to get down here!"

"I know you're friends with Tommy," Gina explained. "I asked him how to find you. I hope you don't mind my coming down."

Squat and curvy, Gina was capped off by a magnificent spray of shiny black curls that arced from a black scrunchie on the top of her head almost to the tops of her shoulders, and bounced when she walked, like a fountain of springs. She was wearing the traditional show-night Ninja uniform of an assistant stage manager: black chinos (hers a size too tight), black shoes, black t-shirt. Spriz pegged her at a year out of college.

"No worries," Spriz said. Then she worried Gina would be able to tell she didn't mean it. "Don't you have to be backstage now?"

"It's twelve minutes until intermission. I've got nothing to do until the changeover. I kinda wanted to ask you about something."

"I'm working, Gina. Is it important?" She tried to say it nicely, but not so nicely that Gina wouldn't get the hint.

"Oh, gee, I'm sorry, it was after hours so I didn't think… I figured you weren't here to work, you just got trapped, and maybe you'd be okay with some company to pass the time, especially since it's my fault you got trapped. I'm sorry, I'll go. Sorry. Bye." She turned and started for the stairs.

Spriz felt like a heel. She was picking low-hanging fruit for an easy show that was still a month away. She just didn't like unexpected company. Or expected company, really. "Hang on. I have a minute."

"Really? You sure? I'm sorry."

"It's okay, Gina." Spriz tried to smile. "Come on in."

Spriz led Gina back to her workbench, and noticed for the first time that although she had at least fifty chairs, she only had one put out for sitting on—hers. She deftly lifted an elegant mahogany dining chair from its stack and set it down opposite her rolling task chair. She turned the volume on the Bakelite radio down to a whisper.

"Thanks," Gina said as she sat down. "I really appreciate this." Then Gina looked around for the first time, and suddenly began waving her hands in front of her as though she were about to be hit by a schoolbus. "Ermagherd! This place is AWESOME!" she squealed.

Spriz felt an agreeable whiff of pride as she started to sit—followed immediately by panic, as Gina jumped up and began moving about the room, pawing the props and PICKING THEM UP.

"OH EM GEE, is this REAL?" she giggled as she pulled a fake shrunken head off a hook. "Ewww!" Before Spriz could grab it from her, Gina had set the head down in the wrong place. While Spriz was restoring the head to its hook, Gina pulled a baby doll from a shelf. "I had one just like this!" She dropped the doll on a rolling cart when she looked up and spotted a gorgeous cobalt-blue wine bottle atop a shelf unit. "OOOH!" It was too high for her to reach, so she lifted the toes of one foot onto a low shelf and began to climb...

"GINA!" Spriz scared herself with the sharpness of the command.

Gina stepped down, clasped her empty hands in front of her, tilted her head downward and turned her big, baby blue eyes up at Spriz. She looked like a little girl who had been caught climbing onto the kitchen counter to steal a cookie.

"I'm really sorry Gina," Spriz said, embarrassed. "It's just, I sorta have a system down here, y'know? You can look at anything you want to, just let me please pick it up for you."

"That's okay," Gina replied sheepishly. "It's not what I came down here for." Then she smiled. "But it is *so cool* down here! Lucky you."

Spriz smiled back. "Thanks. Don't tell anybody. What's on your mind?"

"Oh, um, well," Gina said as she settled her round bottom in the dining chair. She paused to prepare, and then spoke calmly: "Is it me or is that old man a total turd?"

"Brandon?"

"Yeah, *Bran*don."

"Well, he's sorta hard to take sometimes," Spriz confessed. "But there's lots of actors like him, Gina. Most are nice, but if you stay here you're gonna meet lots of actors like him, and you're gonna need a thick skin."

Tears brimmed in the baby blues. "Why *me?* Why do I need

a thick skin? I didn't tell *him* he was bad at *his* job! I didn't threaten HIM with getting HIM fired!"

"Brandon said he would get you fired?"

"Aw Spriz, it was terrible!" The tears were rolling now. "He called me stupid, right in front of everybody. He said I was hazardous to the health of the actors, that somebody better fire me before an actor dropped dead from poison on stage!" She sniffed, trying to compose herself. "I wish I poisoned *him*."

Spriz didn't want to believe it. But she did. It was hard sometimes to like the man, and impossible to defend him. She handed Gina a paper towel. "Do you know if he actually went to Conrad, or even Ana Maria, Gina? I know what he said was terrible, but it sounds to me like he just wanted to scare you. I'm not saying that's better. But I don't think your job is in danger."

"Maybe." Gina tried on a weak smile. "I guess. What should I do?"

"Nothing," Spriz said firmly. "There's nothing you can do, and anything you try will make things worse. The way you handle people like that is to be good at your job. Do your job, Gina. Learn your job. Do it better than anybody, so that when some jerkface pulls crap like that, everybody will just laugh at him, because they know how good you are. Do your job."

Another voice suddenly rang out from back at the doorway, startling Spriz. "Somebody's not doing her job? Fire her, Spriz! Fire her bony ass *now!*"

"Hiya Tom!" Gina suddenly looked as if she had never cried in her life.

Like most people, Gina was crazy about Tommy, even though it was he who had invented her new nickname, "Gina Glow Tape." One of the assistant stage manager's duties was to stick tiny strips of pale-green, glow-in-the-dark adhesive tape anywhere an actor might trip or bump during scene changes: on stairs, chairs and so on. Actors followed glow tape like runway lights to navigate on and off the stage in the dark. Some actors, especially older actors, especially Brandon Wishart, requested so much glow tape in so many places that during blackouts the set looked as though it had been splattered with bioluminescent lime yogurt.

Tommy had come down here many times, but Spriz had never before had two guests at once. She felt the chicken wire walls closing in. She was concerned about how much oxygen the basement held. "Oh god, what do *you* want?"

"I felt bad about sending Gina-pants to you unannounced. Thought I should check on things. I hear sometimes people come down here and never return. Heard you hide the bones in the pianos."

"You're safe," Spriz volleyed. "I'd never eat you, I'd get cancer."

"Don't knock it 'til you've tried it!"

The sex joke was for Gina's benefit—Tommy didn't say things like that to Spriz when they were alone.

Tommy was out and proud and that was just fine with Spriz. He had spent the better part of four years trying to get a bead on Spriz's sexual orientation, and could never nail it. For all his sassy bravado and apparent lack of inhibition when he was around other people, he respected Spriz so much he could not bring himself to ask.

Spriz could tell he was curious, but was glad not to hear the question because she honestly did not know the answer—she pushed such things out of her mind, and out of her heart. There was too much else that needed doing.

And with that little agreement in place to keep them from annoying each other, Spriz and Tommy were as close as an old married couple, and their time alone together was quiet and gentle. A heavy smoker at all other times, Tommy never smoked around Spriz. It was the only time he didn't feel like it.

A former actor and current costume shop assistant, Tommy was on the short side of average, and always a little overweight, which bothered him. He cultivated a masculine-Bohemian thriftshop wardrobe. Today it was a tweed sportcoat, sneakers and a scarf—he was the love-child of Harry Potter and Mister Chips. His strikingly handsome face was lit by fierce green eyes under sharply arched brows that always seemed to be making comment. Spriz thought he was the most beautiful person she knew.

"Spaz giving you the 'Do Your Job' speech?" Tommy asked Gina.

"Yes," Gina answered. "And it helped. Thanks Spriz."

Spriz worried she was blushing. Being invisible, she didn't get much chance to give advice. She'd heard Daddy give that speech a hundred times. She hoped she'd done it right.

"Can I ask you something?" Gina asked Spriz.

It was Spriz's least-favorite question. "What?" She tacitly reserved the right not to answer.

"What kinda name is 'Spriz'?" Gina asked. "Does it mean something?"

Tommy snorted. "It's her email."

"Huh?"

"The email address they gave me the day I started here," Spriz explained. "S Prizzi at GaliRep—s-p-r-i-z-z-i at galirep-dot-org. Tommypants there made it 'spriz,' and I've been Spriz ever since."

"It rhymes with 'showbiz'!" Tommy declared proudly.

"Prizzi?" Gina puzzled. "You're Italian! My mom's Italian, well, Brooklyn, but her mom and dad are from Tuscany. It's why I've got big boobs." She giggled and stuck out the tip of her tongue between her shiny teeth as she thrust her ample bosom forward. Then she pouted. "They're a pain, really. They always get in the way. I wish I was flat-chested like you. You don't look very Italian. Was your mom Italian or just your dad?"

Spriz wasn't hurt. She knew she had little up top. More than one busybody had told her that her slumped posture was tenting her t-shirt over her little breasts, exacerbating the problem. "Stand up straight, sweetie, and your girls will stand up too, and we'll all applaud!" a plump saleswoman at Dillard's had told her the day she'd summoned up the blood to go buy a dress for Conrad's wedding. It was still the only dress she owned. She'd only worn it the once. And Conrad's marriage didn't last two years.

"I'm not Italian," Spriz corrected. "Not far as I know."

Gina puzzled again. "Prizzi's not Italian?"

Spriz inhaled. "Thirty-two years ago in Chicago, somebody dropped me on the step of a rectory, rang the bell and ran," Spriz explained. She was surprised she was being so forthcoming. Tommy knew everything about her—almost everything—but Spriz barely knew Gina. Why was she making so free with the bio? Maybe it was because they were on her turf. Maybe it was because Gina had cried. Anyway, Spriz was talking, and not feeling bad about it, and that felt a little good.

"A very nice couple adopted me and took me to southern Indiana. She died when I was little. After that it was just Daddy and me, right up until I came here."

"What brought you here?" Gina was leaning in as though she were about to learn where Hoffa was buried.

Spriz paused, looking for the most inoffensive way to dodge the question.

And then all the lights went out.

And then they heard screams coming from the stage.

# 4

THEY HELD THEIR BREATH so they could hear.

The screams stopped after only a moment, replaced by muffled cries coming from up the stairs. The basement itself was perfectly quiet. Spriz had never heard it silent before—no radio, no hum from the junction boxes, no purr of sewing machines and sergers from the costume shop overhead. Dead quiet, and dead dark. She felt as though she were underwater, drowning, and hearing the water-baffled calls of witnesses on the beach crying for a lifeguard to rescue her.

More screams suddenly came, louder and more anguished than before, followed again by quieter sobs and whimpers.

Gina broke the spell: "Ohmygod ohmygod... What do we do?"

Spriz said, "We go upstairs," and headed purposefully for the chicken wire door. Tommy tried to follow in the direction of her voice. Behind herself, Spriz heard a hard object bang against a metal surface, making it ring like a gong.

"Ow, fuck!" Tommy said. His forehead had found a hanging washtub.

"Just stay put!" Spriz warned. She reached beyond the door

for the flashlight Conrad had officially stationed just outside it three years ago, after the time he entered the room alone and banged his head on a striped barber pole, a shovel blade and a cricket bat before finding the light pull.

Spriz switched on the flashlight with her thumb, and pointed the beam across the ceiling to illuminate the hazards. Tommy and Gina quickly made their way to her, and all three hurried up the stairs, Spriz in front, lighting the way.

The mayhem in the mainstage house reminded Spriz of newsreel footage she had seen of London after the Blitz.

The only illumination came from three usher-operated flashlights darting about the huge room, and from the cellphones of audience members who were trying—and failing—to raise 911 on the meager signal.

The flashlights danced across a disaster site on stage: Two of the tall flats making up the walls at the back of the set had fallen straight over, covering almost half of the stage floor. A wooden bridge that had been suspended thirteen feet off the deck had snapped free of its wires, and as it fell, it had pulled along with it the wooden staircase attached at one end. Bridge and stairs now formed a mangled heap of twisted sticks and cable on top of the upstage ends of the fallen wall flats.

Instinctively, Spriz started counting the actors standing on the apron beyond the debris. Still in their shapeless Expressionist costumes, they were easy to find as the wandering flashlights happened by them. There was Lanford, who played Pip, and there were the kids who played the younger Gargerys. Sally Faye, who played Miss Havisham and Mrs. Gargery, was hugging and comforting pretty Dana Monroe, who played the haughty Estella and who was weeping and shivering.

The more actors she located, the more worried she became about the one she didn't see.

She heard Ana Maria somewhere near the stage, calling out

both forcefully and calmly—a skill common to stage managers and Marine sergeants—to the audience, ordering them to please remain in their seats until the lights came back on. With the power out, Ana Maria was denied the preferred voicebox of stage managers, the "god mic" up in the control booth through which she could project announcements into the big speakers arrayed around the stage, such as reminding the audience to switch off their cellphones.

Spriz darted around the fallen flats, and shined a light on Ana Maria's face.

"Get that out of my face *please*!" Ana Maria barked. "Who is it?"

"Sorry," Spriz said as she angled the light up to her own chin. "It's me. Where's Brandon?" She turned the light back toward Ana Maria's face, but indirectly this time to avoid blinding her.

Beneath the hard expression Ana Maria pulled when in charge of a crisis, Spriz saw her bottom lip tremble. "Lobby."

Brandon Wishart lay on his back on the lobby floor's blood-red carpet, a chair cushion pillowing his head. Conrad stood over him, lighting Wishart's wan face dimly with a tiny flashlight on his keychain. In the soft spill of the keychain light Spriz could make out volunteer house manager Connie, kneeling beside the injured man, holding his hand and saying the Lord's Prayer quietly.

Spriz heard an ambulance siren in the distance, and turned toward the sound. She saw streetlamp light coming through the windows at the far end of the lobby. The power outage was restricted to the cigar factory.

Conrad heard Spriz give a little sniff, and turned the keychain light up to her face just as Spriz aimed the brighter beam of her big steel torch at Wishart's.

The old man had lost his wig, and his bald head reminded

Spriz of a baby's head, so smooth and round, except for the two wide strips of double-sided wig tape and a bloody divot where part of the top of his skull had been crushed.

Spriz knew he wasn't dead—she had seen dead people, and you could always tell right away. But his breathing was shallow and irregular, and his wound didn't look to Spriz like the kind people survived. She thought she saw him twitch; he was probably seizing.

Conrad watched Spriz's face in the dim yellow glow of his keychain light. He'd never seen her cry before. He wanted to go hug her, but something stopped him. Conrad knew Spriz liked Wishart. She'd stood up for him once when Conrad wanted to fire him for ruining the esprit de corps in a show he was directing. She turned her face up into the light, and her eyes asked, *What happened?*

"They pulled him out from under the flats downstage," Conrad explained. "They said the walls started to go, then the lights went out, then they heard the bridge fall and everybody started screaming. When the screaming stopped somebody heard a moan under the flats, and I guess when somebody pointed a light at where his hand was sticking out from under, everybody started screaming all over again. When I got there, the people from the front row were pulling him out. One of the guys evidently was an Eagle Scout or something, made sure he was breathing and didn't need a tourniquet or a brace anyplace, and then helped us move him out here to wait for help." The sirens were close now. "Connie called 911 from the box office phone. I guess that's them."

Lights spinning, a white ambulance van pulled right up onto the sidewalk outside the lobby doors, and two EMTs jumped out and rushed into the lobby, each lighting his way with a halogen Maglite. They located the patient by Spriz's beam, and jogged to the injured man's side.

Without being told, Spriz, Conrad and Connie backed away and watched as the EMTs got to work. As they were starting an

I-V, Conrad tried to put his arm around Spriz, but she shrugged him off. She had stopped crying.

Two patrol cars in quick succession jumped up onto the sidewalk behind the ambulance, and four of Galilee's Finest marched through the lobby doors and began to take charge of the scene.

Within minutes, the EMTs had wrapped up the old man's head, loaded him onto a gurney, slipped him into the back of the van and sped away.

Then the lights came back on.

In a daze, Spriz wandered back into the house and over to the place where they had extricated Brandon, and saw his wig in a heap near the front row. She picked it up. She'd keep it safe, and bring it to him in the hospital when she visited.

She looked up, and saw tangled, broken airplane cable where once a very realistic bridge had hung. She turned to look into the seats, where she saw some people sobbing, some sitting and staring blankly, in shock.

She heard a familiar sniffle behind her, and turned around to see Gina, her face soaked, big wet tear spots on her black t-shirt. She was trying to speak, but nothing was coming out. She managed to squeak out a teeny "i'm sorry," but Spriz couldn't understand the words.

"Gina, what?"

In a small voice, quivering, Gina tried again: "I'm sorry. I'm sorry. I didn't mean it. I'm sorry for what I said about him, Spriz, I'm sorry. I'm so so so sorry. I didn't mean it. Oh my god Spriz. Oh god. I'm sorry Spriz. I didn't mean it. I didn't mean it."

Still repeating her sorries, Gina threw her arms around Spriz, squeezed her hard, and wept. Spriz stood perfectly still, silent, her arms at her sides, and looked up again at the broken cables.

The hanging wires reminded her of the chicken wire door on the prop room. Had she remembered to lock it? Of course she had. But once the disease of doubt took hold, there was no cure but to check. She gently slipped out of Gina's embrace and hustled down the stairs, an old man's furry vanity in her slender hand.

# 5

THIS IS WHAT HAPPENED, as near as anybody could figure.

The bridge was suspended by four steel airplane cables tied to two of the exposed girders that supported the roof of the cigar factory. Sheila wanted the bridge to appear rickety and dangerous, so Karl hung it from the ceiling, instead of mounting it on poles, so it would swing a little when the characters crossed it, adding to the atmosphere of spooky peril a Dickens story requires. He used cable stronger than required for the weight, if carried by four lines. Karl did not fool around when it came to safety, or much else.

One of the old girders was jagged in a spot a person couldn't see when twenty feet up on a ladder tying cable. The sharp little nub may have been a blister caused by the bar & grille fire in the '60s. The swinging motion caused by the actors crossing the bridge several times a night had rubbed one of those thick airplane cables back and forth across that tiny nub. Incrementally, over the course of five weeks, the tiny flaw had sawn through most of the thickness of the cable.

When the cable finally snapped that night, the upstage-left

corner of the bridge dropped. The bridge canted, and the low corner banged a wall flat.

On the backswing, the corner of the bridge slammed into the wall of the theatre, demolishing a wall-mounted dimmer box and causing such a serious ground fault that the old building's circuit breakers all flipped at once. As it was October, no volunteer had been stationed at the breaker box.

Ana Maria wisely insisted on assessing the damage by flashlight before permitting the power to return. A full seven minutes passed before she dispatched an usher to the other end of the building to snap the little switches back to their ON position.

The tops of the wall flats were lined by huge ornate moldings simulating stone cornices. The cornices made the flats top-heavy on the downstage side, but the flats were connected together so that they held each other up, like the sides of an open box. The falling bridge had banged the flat free of the screws that held it to the others, and the weight of the cornice pulled it forward onto the stage. Having lost the flat that was holding it up, the flat beside the first one fell, too. The side flats had separate bracing behind them, and remained standing.

By the time the flats hit the deck, the force of gravity had overcome the remaining three airplane cables, and the bridge fell straight down, pulling its staircase down on top of itself, which torqued and crumbled as it collapsed into a mangled heap.

The only characters on stage when it happened were Pip and his uncle, Joe Gargery. They were standing in a pool of blue light downstage, a "special," for a lovely monologue in which old Joe, his arm around young Pip, passes Pip his treasured blacksmith's hammer and begs Pip not to go to London to become a gentleman, but instead to stay and become a blacksmith, and be his son. This monologue reliably brought the audience to tears.

According to the report of the investigator who interviewed

Lanford (Pip), he and Brandon both turned their heads upstage to look when they heard the bridge start to go, and then saw the flats headed right for them. Lanford froze just as the lights popped out. And then he felt the man whose arm was around him give him a hard shove, off the stage, into the seats, and out of harm's way.

In the matter of Brandon Lyle Wishart, 73, most recently of Galilee, Florida, the county medical examiner's determination was: Accidental Death. The investigation was closed, as was *Great Expectations*. Both were halted prematurely.

# 6

EMRGNCY PROD MTG @ 10.

That's what the email and text from Conrad said. Spriz had expected an emergency meeting, but not on the morning of the day of the funeral, which was scheduled for that afternoon.

Hair still wet, she flew into the tiny conference room three minutes late and saw every member of the production team seated there, except two. Spriz caught the end of Maisy asking what the *Deathtrap* cast was doing today.

"Home learning their lines, on their honor," Conrad replied. "What else can they do, the stage is still covered with crap."

"Where's Andreo and Gary?" Ana Maria asked as Spriz took her usual seat, between Maisy and Carlos.

"Andreo and Gary aren't invited today," Conrad replied. "We don't need them for this. This is just family." He stood and coughed into his fist.

"Preview for *Deathtrap* is four weeks from tonight," Conrad began. "We need to decide what we're gonna do. I have to tell you, we took a huge hit on *Great Expectations*. We lost a whole weekend of ticket sales, and we have to reimburse the subscribers who didn't see it yet. I talked to Kami Carroll at the local actors union office, tried to see if there was an Act of God loophole we could squeeze through, but she says we have to pay the union actors for the final week come the rapture, and the favored-nations clause in the non-union actor contracts says we have to pay them if the union actors get paid."

He put his hands on his hips and gave the group a hard look. "And even though the police found no wrongdoing or culpable negligence, the insurance company is doing its own investigation, and our rates will almost certainly go through the roof. Those bastards will find *something* to screw us with, they always do." Karl stared straight down at the table, and shifted in his chair, the bill of his tractor cap pulled low over his eyes. In six years, Spriz had never seen him without his cap, indoors or out. The rumor was he showered in it.

"Do the math, folks. That's a lot of money going out and no money coming in," Conrad continued. "That, and we've got no lead for *Deathtrap*." Brandon Wishart had been cast in the role, and he would have been great in it.

"I guess the only good news is that I have been told the police are releasing the stage today, so we can finally strike *Great Expectations*—what's left of it. So, question one: Do we push ahead with *Deathtrap*, or do we cancel, give everybody an unpaid two-month vacation, and all come back in December for *Steel Magnolias*?" Question two: If we push ahead with *Deathtrap*, who do we get, and how soon can he start? I know we don't usually cast this way, but I am asking for ideas."

Everyone felt the pall in the room. A man was dead, and his play had died with him. Now they were looking for a donor, a transplant to save the life of the next play. It was a weird dream from which they all wished they could wake up.

After a few moments, Maisy piped up: "Steve Candelora?"

"Booked in Orlando," Conrad replied. "He opens in Richard the Third in two weeks. Called him this morning."

"Steve Candelora as Richard?" Ana Maria asked,

incredulous.

"He wishes," Conrad sniffed. "Clarence."

"Tom Peters!" Carlos suggested. Carlos and Tom were friends.

"Not in this lifetime," Conrad avowed. There was history there.

Spriz started, "Shouldn't—" then thought better of it.

Everybody turned and looked at Spriz. She didn't usually offer opinions unless the subject was props. She didn't think it was her place.

"Spriz?" Conrad asked gently.

"Well," Spriz said, a little more boldly, "Gary's directing, shouldn't he choose his own leading man?"

"Gary doesn't know anybody local," Conrad explained, "and I'm not paying transportation and housing, and besides, it'll take too long. If we find him somebody, Gary's just gonna be happy not to lose the gig, trust me. He's got no union contract guaranteeing he gets paid come hell or high water."

They all sat quietly, stumped, scared. There were only so many top-drawer leading men within commuting distance of Galilee. And they were down by one.

"OK," Conrad said. "Think on it. I will too, I'll make some calls. Tomorrow morning we'll meet again, same bat-time, same bat-place. And if we don't have a lead by then, I'm pulling the plug on the mainstage, and we all go home."

It was Conrad who had conditioned his staff to call their one and only stage the "mainstage" as if it shared the building with a second stage—which it did not. The cigar factory was barely big enough for a single theatre, let alone two. Companies with more money and bigger facilities often operated a smaller, second space for riskier fare that couldn't draw a crowd sufficient for their larger house.

A promising college tackle in his day, Conrad had been converted to the religion of positive thinking by inspiring coaches. When a knee injury sidelined him, he turned to acting, as athletes sometimes do after having enjoyed a taste of stardom on the field. The setback never dimmed his faith in the power of visualization to bring dreams to fruition. He truly believed that calling the big house the "mainstage" was a spiritual prerequisite to conjuring up a second stage and raising the company a notch in the cutthroat hierarchy of regional theatre. Conrad was a man of faith. But today, he simply could not summon the can-do spirit.

"Last one out," he concluded, with a rueful smile, "please hit the lights."


The funeral was a sparse affair. Wishart had "pre-planned" and paid for his own arrangements years ago, after a prostate scare. So there was a casket—open, with the divot in Wishart's bald head masterfully filled in by the mortician's art—and there were flowers. Mourners, however, were in short supply.

Seated with Tommy, Spriz wore her only dress, the one from Conrad's wedding, an inappropriate, flower-print shift. Tommy wore a black tux he'd scored years ago at Goodwill. He told Spriz it was his only dark suit, but he really wore it so she wouldn't feel she was the most unseemly person in attendance.

The arts critic for the *Galilee Star* gave the eulogy, even though he had never met the man and knew nothing of him but what he had seen on stage. He used the occasion to announce that his paper was starting an actors' scholarship fund in Wishart's name, in memory of all that the man had done to mentor young performers, and of course to celebrate his "selfless sacrifice" in the rescue of Lanford, his scene partner and protégé.

Most of the GaliRep regular staff were there, Karl the notable exception. Lanford alone represented the *Great Expectations* cast. The other actors had quit town within hours of hearing the show was closed, as if they had already lined up filler jobs elsewhere and could not stay for the memorial. They all felt they should attend, but since they'd all hated the man, they couldn't escape the awkward feeling they'd be hypocrites for doing so.

Finding no emotionally palatable resolution to this internal conflict, they grabbed Plan C and took a powder. Most had gone directly to the city of their next gig, even though their housing would not yet be made available to them, and planned to spend the free vacation staying with friends and resting up for rehearsals that would start in a week or so.

Spriz thought Lanford looked a lot older at the funeral than he had on stage. Though twenty-nine years old, Lanford had a baby face, and was both small-boned and short. He had leveraged these advantages into a steady career playing children. His specialty was portraying teenagers who had to mature by the end of the play, as they so often did in the many *bildungsromans*, coming-of-age stories, written or adapted for the stage. As he had in *Great Expectations*, Lanford would loosen up his body and lighten his voice for the early scenes, then incrementally stiffen his frame and deepen his voice as the character aged. It was very effective.

But as the Big 3-0 loomed and the lines in his face hardened, the compact actor knew his extended adolescence was coming to an end, and he worried that work might soon be harder to come by.

Brandon Wishart had seen a hundred puppy-dog actors come and go the same way, knew all about the ugly surprise that was waiting for little Lanford, and took every opportunity to publicly lament the fact that this pony was about to lose his one trick. "*Quelle tristesse* that when you're too old to play children, you'll still be too short to play adults," Wishart had told him. "Perhaps they'll let you sweep the stage, dear. Or sell tickets!"

Company lawyer Ryan Mountain came to the service. He had been a huge fan, and had done the deceased's tax returns, free of charge, for several years. A handful of others attended, all over sixty. Spriz didn't know any of them. Tommy chatted briefly with two and reported back that they were all actors who had worked with Brandon back in the day in other towns.

What they didn't tell Tommy was that they had hated Brandon, every one of them. In making his arrangements, Wishart had given the funeral director contact information for these actors and requested that they be notified, when the time came.

They all interpreted this courtesy as his final fuck-you from the grave. But they came because, having made no secret of their animosity toward the man, they felt they'd be labeled petty for refusing the invitation. They spent most of the funeral and reception off to themselves, smoking hard, recollecting old slights that still stung.

Over the course of the afternoon, Spriz overheard variations of the same joke told three times by three different mourners: After fifty years of being chewed by Brandon Wishart, the scenery finally bit back. She wondered if the joke had spread from person to person like a virus, or if all three jokers had come up with it independently.

"Where's his family?" Spriz said quietly to Tommy at the reception, shaking her head. "Where are his kids, his grandkids... His ex-wives? Brothers and sisters? He's not even *from* Galilee, they're burying him here just 'cause it's where he happened to die. This is all so *sad*."

"Life of an actor," Tommy replied. "Working actors die alone. Unless they have really good friends."

In 73 years on Earth, Brandon Wishart had accumulated fewer than twenty people willing to pay him their final respects. And of those, a quarter did so only out of spite.


After the reception, Spriz and Tommy changed into work clothes in Spriz's eggplant-colored 1996 Jeep Cherokee in the funeral parking lot. The deep-purple Jeep was the only car she had ever owned. When Daddy took her to the wholesale lot with the $3,200 she had saved up waiting tables, she fell in love with it the moment she saw it, not least because she knew it was the ugliest car on the lot and no one else would appreciate it as much as she. Her Daddy might as well have taken her to the dog pound instead.

She didn't name the little truck, but when Tommy came along, he named it, after Sonny's ex: Cher. Like her namesake, the truck had a lot of hard miles on her, and not all her parts were factory-original, but she still looked fabulous.

They talked about what to do next, and decided that they might as well keep working on *Deathtrap* until told to stop, if for no better reason than a lack of anything else to do in Galilee. Spriz still had a few props and doofers to pull for the show's short list, and Maisy had told Tommy to straighten up the shop, a Maisy between-shows ritual.

Spriz on the way to her basement and Tommy on the way to the costume shop, they both had to cross the stage to reach their destinations. On any other Thursday afternoon they would expect to have to sneak past a rehearsal in progress. Or when the stage was not being used for a rehearsal, they would have found it lit dimly by only the "ghost light," a single bulb on a tall pole with a round, heavy base, which served to prevent accidents by ensuring that the theatre was never left completely dark. But today, Spriz and Tommy happened upon Karl, mid-experiment.

The yellow police tape had been pulled away from the set, and for the first time in two days, Karl was allowed access to his stage to strike the wreckage that debased it.

While the others were at the funeral, Karl and Sandy, the master carpenter, had cleared the bridge and stair debris off the flats and carried one tall flat, the second one to fall, into the wings. Later they would truck the flats to the scene shop, a warehouse across town—there was no room for a scene shop in the cigar factory, and Karl enjoyed not having the AD or any other busybody over his shoulder while he worked. Only the first flat to fall, the one that struck Brandon Wishart, remained on stage.

Karl had twisted a screw-eye into the top of the flat, and knotted about forty feet of black cotton tie line to it. He had tied a roll of gaffer's tape to the other end, and after a few circular windups, expertly lobbed the line up and over the bottom part of a ceiling girder. Karl and Sandy had gently pushed the flat back into its upright position, and Sandy was screwing its bottom rail back into the stage floor, when Spriz and Tommy came through.

They stopped and watched, curious. After a moment Karl noticed them and barked, "Clear the stage!" He motioned for Sandy to run up to the control booth behind the top row of seats.

"We work here just like you, Karl," Spriz affirmed. She was a little afraid of Karl, and so went out of her way to speak to him as if she was not. "Whatcha doin'?"

"Watch an' you'll see," Karl replied sourly. "You and your special li'l friend can get up in them seats and keep your mouths shut an' you can stay." Spriz and Tommy climbed up to the tenth row, and took seats. They felt like they should have popcorn. What was he up to?

The wall flat fully vertical again, Karl had cut the roll of tape from the tie line and was keeping the flat upright by holding the line taut in his hand.

He walked downstage, then looked up at the booth. "Where's that special?" he yelled impatiently.

"Comin' Boss!" Sandy hollered in his soft Piedmont drawl. Sandy knew how to operate the light board, but it was going to take him longer to find the right cue in the computer that controlled it than it would have taken Ana Maria, who had gone home after the funeral. Though a member of the production staff for the show, stage manager Ana Maria was not a full-time permanent staff member of GaliRep. She was a "jobber," paid only for the hours she spent on a given show, and the one after that, and the one after that, and offered no fringe benefits.

If you visited GaliRep most afternoons, you'd think the place was humming with dozens of employees, but most would be jobbers—though regrettable, it was the only way most small theatres could get a show up and not charge a hundred dollars a seat.

Despite her meager pay, Spriz counted herself lucky to be on staff with Karl, Maisy, Conrad, the box office manager, an education director, and a handful of fundraisers and office workers. The house manager and ushers were volunteers. All of the actors, the directors other than Conrad, the stitchers, the scene painters, most designers, Sandy, Ana Maria, Gina, and a handful of other helpers were jobbed in.

Tommy was technically a part-time staff member with no benefits, but thanks to Maisy's demands he worked overtime many weeks, and was paid his regular rate—Florida minimum wage plus fifty cents—for every hour. Maisy had been in Conrad's ear for a year to put Tommy on salary so she could work him 80 hours a week in crunch times without dinging her budget. Tommy was all for it. Despite the certainty of unpaid overtime, he'd still come out ahead. And though he enjoyed the game of bitching about her, he adored Maisy, head to toe.

After two minutes, Sandy took the worklights out and the stage went dark. Then a pool of pale-blue light bubbled up at the front edge of the stage: the special for the "be a blacksmith" monologue. Karl first stepped to the center of it, then moved one step left, splitting the exact center of the circle of light with an imaginary scene partner.

"Say what you will, son of a bitch knew how to find his light," Karl mumbled to no one. And then he dropped the tie line.

Tommy and Spriz saw the cornice slowly begin to arc downward out of the inky darkness, and heard the floor splinter as the screws tore out of it. They jumped up in unison, and Tommy yelled, "MOVE!"

But then they noticed how slowly the flat was falling, even with the weight of the cornice pulling it. It was like watching a feather fall, or the Space Shuttle lift off. As it passed the halfway point, it was picking up speed, but not much. After about four seconds, it made contact with Karl's tractor cap, bounced softly once, and came to rest on his head.

Karl was standing under it, fully erect and unhurt. The falling flat would not have cracked an egg.

Spriz smiled. "Since when did you start building canvas flats, Karl?" she called down from the tenth row.

"Since that woman started drawin' twelve-footers, whattaya think?" Karl hollered back, as he raised the flat with one hand, stepped out from under it, and let it fall softly to the floor. "Din't want to see no seams, didya?"

Karl preferred to use what some people called "Hollywood" flats, which were faced with a thin, smooth plywood called lauan and then painted. Hollywood flats were hard and heavy, but they were cheap, quick to build and hard to destroy. Karl had dozens of standard 4' x 8' Hollywood flats in storage, and a few precious 4' x 10' flats, all of which had been painted over for countless shows.

But that woman (Sheila), in some artsy-fartsy attempt to express the oppressive scale of the period or whatever, had designed the walls for *Great Expectations* twelve feet high. Lauan plywood came in eight-foot sheets from the Galilee Lowe's, or in expensive ten-foot lengths by special order. To make a twelve-foot Hollywood flat, you had to face it with two pieces of plywood—a full eight-foot sheet plus a four-foot half-sheet—and then disguise the joint somehow, which was usually done with wainscoting or tape.

Since this was supposed to be an exterior wall, and an Expressionist one at that, wainscoting was out. Depending on the paint treatment and the lights, no matter how carefully you made them, tape seams tended to show, and over a long run, tape seams tended to pull open, especially on a very tall flat that might flex a bit with the extreme temperature changes between when the hot stage lights were on and when they were off. Sheila had specified gray texture paint to simulate stone, and Karl knew tape seams painted that way would look like hell, and get worse over the run.

So Karl and Sandy built themselves some old-school canvas flats, which neither of them had done since college. They stapled together lightweight 4' x 12' frames of one-inch sticks, reinforced them with triangular corner blocks, then pulled muslin—a cheap cotton canvas available on wide bolts—over the front and around to the back, where they stapled it in place. With a Hudson sprayer, Sandy saturated the muslin fronts with a solution of water and white glue. As the glue dried, it pulled the muslin tight, and when fully dry, it left a glossy surface for paint. Coated with texture paint, the flats made a convincing stone wall, as long as no one poked the soft canvas from behind and gave away the trick.

Big as they were, the flats were extremely light, and when they fell forward, they became parachutes, and took their time falling. But no one at the theatre that night had actually seen the flats fall. The wall was just beginning its collapse when the lights went out, and when the lights came back, the flats were on the floor.

"How did nobody notice the flats were muslin?" Tommy said as he and Spriz made their way down to the stage.

"Well, none of y'all seem to know where the scene shop is, so you din't see us build 'em," Karl said, sounding as though he felt neglected when in fact he had always made it clear to the staff that they were very specifically not invited to visit the scene shop, ever. Conrad made the mistake of stopping by once, unannounced. Karl called a break and drank coffee alone in his tiny office until Conrad took the hint and left.

"Sandy and me did the load-in our own li'l selves. The backs of the side flats went behind the drapes, and nobody ever walked behind the back flats to see they was canvas, there weren't no room for a crossover, thank you Slick Willy!"

"Slick Willy" was a refrain of Karl's. When the Americans with Disabilities Act of 1990 took effect, GaliRep responsibly made all the required accommodations in and around the lobby, such as special stalls and toilets in the restrooms. But the company pretty much ignored the act when it came to requirements for the stage and backstage areas.

In the spring of 2001, some wonk from the U.S. Equal Employment Opportunity Commission in D.C. took his kids to Disney World on spring break, and discovered the little city of Galilee and GaliRep's website when Googling (thank you Al Gore) the title of his favorite play, *The Lion in Winter*, which was then playing. He dragged his ungrateful family away from the sunshine and carnival rides for a four-hour drive to see a three-hour matinée about family arguments in a dark theatre, and after the show, he peeked behind the curtains and jotted a few notes. A week later, little GaliRep was slapped with the first of several fines.

Karl was already the technical director back in '01, and as he had for many shows, for *The Lion in Winter* he built platforms right up to the bottoms of the risers that held the seats. After GaliRep got caught with its ADA pants around its ankles, Karl was forced to start leaving thirty-six inches of bare floor between the front of his sets and the seating banks, for easier wheelchair access to the restrooms.

As far as Karl was concerned, the gubmint had robbed him of three feet of real estate by eminent domain. And he would not take it lying down. He had always left at least four feet between the back of a set and the back wall of the theatre, enabling actors to cross behind and thus make entrances and exits from any side of a set. Now he built most of his sets one foot away from the back wall so that they could cover the same footprint they always had and still leave the mandated gimp lane in front.

This passive-aggressive protest caused no end of trouble for directors and for Sheila, who struggled to find creative solutions to the problem that actors could only enter from one side of the stage. In many plays, after exiting from a door situated on the far side of a set, actors were trapped over there in a tiny, dark cavity until they had another entrance, and a chance to exit again on the side where the dressing rooms were.

Karl blamed the whole thing on Bill Clinton, because he wanted to. Once Conrad had tried to explain to Karl that the ADA was enacted before Clinton took office, and was signed into law by George Herbert Walker Bush, but Karl just laughed. No Republican would have done that to him. For a while, Sheila tried designing shallower sets that left room for wheelchairs in front and a crossover behind, but Karl just backed them up to the wall anyway, leaving double the room in front. That woman might be content to live under communist rule, but he'd die before he let them tread on Karl Gilly.

Spriz, Tommy and Karl were standing in the blue special and studying the fallen flat while Sandy sat dutifully in the booth, awaiting instructions. Sandy could barely take a piss without Karl's say-so.

"Karl," Spriz said carefully, "the medical examiner ruled it an accident. There was a whole investigation, like CSI."

"All the doc knows is he got head trauma and a wall fell on 'im," Karl growled. "So he puts two an' two together. He don't know a flat don't weigh nothin'. He never even came in an' saw the wall. I was in the booth watchin' the whole time the cops was here, an' they never even touched it, they just looked at it, scribbled some notes an' went for donuts."

"What if the cornice hit him?" Spriz asked Karl.

"Too far downstage" Tommy interjected.

"Downstage got nothin' to do with it," Karl spat. He reached under the flat to put a calloused palm on a cornice. Spriz and Tommy heard a *crunch* before Karl withdrew a fat hunk of the Styrofoam that had been masquerading as rock. Foam was not only light and soft, but also cheap; no doubt Karl planned to scrape off and discard the cornices so he could slide his new 12-foot flats into storage.

"More questions, Sherlock?" Karl sneered to Tommy, because he didn't much like either of 'em, but he liked the tall girl better than the pansy. "Painted foam's heavy enuff to pull 'er over, but it's soft enough it could fall on a baby an' not wake 'im up. Anyways the cornice din't hit 'im. Too far downstage."

Tommy frowned.

"Bridge missed 'im too," Karl continued, covering all contingencies, pointing to the rigging upstage. "Bridge an' staircase dropped way upstage of 'im, foam dropped just past 'im, he fell 'tween 'em, nothin' but a cotton sheet on top of him, safe as a kitten."

"What are you planning to do?" Tommy asked Karl. "Will you tell Galilee PD?"

"Nah," Karl said, looking away. "Won't bring him back, even if anybody wanted him. And 'tween you, me an' the lamp-post, I got reasons not to get them looking too close at me. Water over the bridge anyways. I jes' needed to be sure."

Spriz bent over and lifted the flat up over her head with one hand. "There's no blood," she said. "I saw him. There was blood all over the top of his head. Why is there no blood on the flat? Or on the floor here? The police never lifted the flat?"

"I told ya already, they never touched it!" Karl snapped. "Probly thought it was real stone and too heavy. Galilee PD is 'bout as useful as a screen door on a submarine."

Spriz suddenly remembered the preposterous pile of hair she'd dropped on her workbench when she went down to check the padlock that night. "C'mon!" she said as she grabbed Tommy's hand and pulled him toward the stairwell.

Still bathed in blue light, Karl looked down at the floor and shook his head slowly. He kicked a stray screw off his stage and under the seating banks, and sniffed. "No way did my wall kill that man. No way."

# 7

NOT A DROP OF BLOOD was on the wig. After inspecting it closely with the magnifier on her swing-arm lamp, Spriz tried to hand it to Tommy for a second opinion, but he quickly raised his palms in protest and said he'd take her word for it.

"What do we do?" Tommy asked. "Do we tell the police?"

"There has to be something they know that we don't," Spriz replied. "They're not stupid."

Tommy arched his left brow, as only Tommy could.

"They *might* be stupid, but we don't know that. And if the wall didn't kill him, what are we saying? A different Act of God killed him? Or he was... murdered?" She felt silly saying the word. It sounded like a line from *Deathtrap*, which Spriz found silly when she read it.

"Okay, but what else then, Spriz? The whole thing is nuts, but something bashed his head in. If it wasn't the wall, it was somebody who wanted the old man dead."

"And that's my problem," Spriz countered. "He's a broke old actor with no friends. His life touches no one else's. You were at the funeral. No one had a reason to mur— to kill him. He didn't matter to anybody. Why bother to kill somebody who doesn't matter?"

"Why bother doing a complete and thorough investigation of the death of somebody who doesn't matter, you mean?" Tommy said. "And everybody hated him, Spriz. Everybody. You know that."

"Enough to kill him?"

"Some people have impulse-control problems," Tommy shrugged. "A guy in Texas shot a drive-thru girl for stiffing him on ketchup packets."

"It was pitch dark when they pulled him out and carried him to the lobby… Maybe they hit his head on something moving him? Plenty of stuff to bump between the stage and the lobby."

"Maybe," Tommy conceded. "But it's thin. They were moving an old man they knew was hurt. They would've used kid gloves. Four guys carried him. If they crashed his head on the doorframe, you'd think at least one of them would have copped to it—it's not like they did something wrong. Besides, if he wasn't already hurt, why'd they have to carry him anywhere? Why didn't he tell them not to fuckin' touch him, like he did to me once in a fitting?"

Spriz looked at the brown wig sitting in a heap on her workbench like roadkill. She picked it up and held it against the tangles of her own hair falling in front of her shoulders, noticing for the first time that her hair was the same color as Brandon Wishart's wigs, which were made from real human hair. He had once told her so, as though it were something to be proud of. It occurred to her now that his hair could have come from her relatives, whoever they might be, and if their hair was Wishart's hair, somehow that made him… what? Her cousin, twice-removed? "What do I do with this now?" she said, presenting it to Tommy.

"Eww, throw it away. He's past needing it and no one else wants it!"

"Where's the rest of his stuff?" Spriz wondered aloud.

She wanted to check the dressing rooms. But first: Conrad.

"Who was Brandon's next of kin?" Spriz asked Conrad, who was seated at his long desk, buried in paperwork, a phone handset pinched between his ear and shoulder. Tommy had split off to go straighten the costume shop before Maisy came in and pitched a fit.

Conrad looked up. He hadn't noticed Spriz in his office until she spoke. He'd often wondered how someone so tall managed to be so stealthy. He also wondered how someone so shy could be such a pest when she really wanted something.

"Oh Spriz, can we talk about this later? I'm on hold."

"Who else would know?" Spriz asked.

Conrad sighed. "Nobody else. Sit." He hung up. He'd known before he dialed that getting anybody at the theatrical equipment rental place in Orlando on a Thursday was a longshot, and he'd already heard "Sultans of Swing" four times through. He wanted to ask for more time on the past-due balance. He'd email later. They would ignore his email, but when they called in another week to ask why he'd been ignoring their letters, he could honestly claim he'd gotten back to them and they'd dropped the ball, not him. That would buy him another ten days. He was good at this. This was his job.

Spriz pushed aside the papers Conrad had stacked in his guest chair, and sat.

"He didn't have any," Conrad said matter-of-factly.

"How can that be?" Spriz asked. "Isn't he required to have one?"

"He's required to have an emergency contact, and for that he always gave the main number of the actors union office in New York. I always thought it was a joke, but it's what he put, so I followed through anyway and called. They said they were sorry to hear. What else was there to say? The guy I talked to didn't sound like he recognized Brandon's name. He didn't even ask me how it happened." Conrad rubbed his bald scalp. "Man pays his dues for fifty years."

"What about his pension, his life insurance? He had to have beneficiaries," Spriz asked.

"Apparently it's not a requirement for the pension," the AD explained. "And he turned down the life. Pension money just stays in the fund, for the other actors. The fund counts on that happening sometimes."

They sat quietly for a few moments, neither knowing what to say.

Then Spriz had a thought: "His apartment?" she asked. "Who's cleaning out his apartment?"

"Spriz, you need to get out of that basement and spend more time getting to know the actors. Come to the cast parties, willya? These are actors, regional theatre actors, they don't live like people."

Conrad sighed. "He was on the road three-six-five, Spriz. We had him here one or two shows a season, but that's not a third of the year, and we're the only gig in town, it would be a waste of money for him to have an apartment here when he was working elsewhere most weeks. He used actor housing anywhere that offered it. Where there was no housing he stayed in the cheapest motel he could find. Actors like him, they get their mail forwarded to the theatres they work in. They don't have apartments. They don't have homes."

*Or families*, Spriz thought. "Where did he stay in Galilee?"

"The Star-Lite. Not the very cheapest, but walking distance. He could go out for drinks after the show and not risk a DUI getting home. He didn't own a car anyway, just rented one when he needed it, so he liked staying close to the theatre. Drove the same way he lived."

"Does the Star-Lite have his things? Did anybody claim them?"

"There weren't any things. Virgil called to offer condolences after he heard from one of the other actors. He said Brandon had paid up through Sunday, through the end of *Great Expectations*, and asked if they should send a refund to his widow or someone. I said keep it, there's no widow. It can't be more than a hundred dollars or so anyway. Virgil said the man never left anything in his room while he was at the theatre. He'd told Virgil he'd been robbed once in a motel in Miami and learned his lesson. Not so much as a toothbrush."

Another long silence intruded. Conrad was eager to get back to bailing the sea out of his dinghy, but he waited patiently for another question. He hoped Spriz would leave with her curiosity satisfied, and not come marching back in another hour with another question.

Spriz broke the silence. "Okay. Okay. Well, I'm going to get together his things from the dressing room and keep them in props until we can figure out what to do with them, or hopefully somebody comes asking. I'll bring up the rehearsal props for *Deathtrap* in a bit."

"No, Spriz," Conrad said quietly. "Put 'em back on the shelves, please. I've taken another look at the numbers since this morning. We're not doing *Deathtrap*."

By the time Spriz had crossed the stage again on the way from Conrad's office to the dressing rooms, Karl and Sandy and the wall flats were gone, the stage had been swept, and the space was lit only by the lonely ghost light, a long loop of glow tape hung across a lip beneath the bulb like a shoulder sash.

Glow tape required charging by exposure to light in order to give a few hours' radiance, and Ana Maria had taught Gina her trick of always keeping a lasso of tape under the shine of the ghost light to ensure that charged-up tape was at the ready when an actor made an unexpected demand for a fresh strip on a doorknob or table leg.

Walking past the ghost light, Spriz thought the pale green ring, hanging at an angle and well below the equator of the ghost light's single bulb, made the whole thing look like the planet Saturn with its pants down. She found the image strange and sad, the way this whole day had been.

Brandon Wishart's street clothes were neatly folded and piled on the chair at his dressing station, his shoes on top and upside-down so as not to soil the clothing. His makeup, tissues, towelettes, coffee mug and wristwatch were arrayed exactly as he had left them to make his final entrance, and exit. The dressing room was otherwise clear, and newly clean. Wishart's ragged belongings stood out against the gleaming white of the bare counter and walls.

Spriz just stood behind the chair, staring at the artifacts.

"I washed his street clothes," Maisy said, startling Spriz. Maisy was leaning on the doorframe.

Maisy was black, five-foot-nothing and a hundred pounds soaking wet. Her long, natural curls were drawn ferociously taut to her scalp, bunched into a fat bun at the back of her head and tightly tied in a blue satin ribbon. A magnificent denim apron pocked with pushpins and sewing needles, and tricked out with pockets carrying tape measures, markers, seam rippers, thread and chalk, mostly covered her simple cotton shirt and pants. She was a fine designer and the most efficient shop manager the American stage had ever known, and she was afraid of nothing and no one on this Earth.

"I took them off the rack when I struck the costumes," Maisy explained as she stepped into the room. "I washed them with the last show laundry and put them with his stuff. Didn't know what else to do. I was hoping somebody else would know."

Spriz started gingerly packing up Brandon's detritus into his makeup case, a brown Sears tackle box Spriz could tell was older than she was. "I'm taking this stuff down to props while I try to find his family," Spriz explained. "Hopefully I'll be able to send it to someone who wants it."

"Good luck," Maisy sniffed. "I can't imagine many folks

want souvenirs of that man." She caught herself, and apologized quietly with "Rest in peace," her hand over her heart. In her head, she recited a silent prayer.

Spriz kept packing, quietly.

"Don't forget the satchel," Maisy said, pointing underneath the counter with her toe. Spriz pulled the chair back, and in the dark space beneath the counter she found an ancient, brown leather bag on the floor. She pulled it out and set it on the bare counter to the right of Wishart's station. It was heavy, and flanked with zippered pouches packed nearly to bursting.

As Spriz put the final few items in the tackle box, Tommy danced into the room, pleased with himself.

"Clean?" Maisy asked him.

"Go see," Tommy answered proudly. "Eat off the cutting tables if you want."

Maisy shrugged. "Well, now I got a clean shop and clean dressing rooms, after you get that last pile out of here." She didn't bother to hide the obsessive-compulsive tendencies that served her so well in her job. She watched Spriz latch the tackle box. "Now we can finally put both feet in *Deathtrap*, God save us."

Spriz turned to face Maisy. "No, we can't, Maisy. Sorry."

"No!"

"He just told me," Spriz said with resignation. "We're laid off after today. He's gonna email everybody tonight, say not to come in. He's talking to Kami Carroll at the union, trying to work out how to cancel the actor contracts without paying any penalties. If he can get some things ironed out, he says he'll bring everybody back for *Steel Magnolias* in eight weeks. But Maisy, he did say he thinks he can keep the benefits going through the layoff."

"Well thank God for *something!*" Maisy's ten-year-old son was epileptic, and took expensive anti-seizure meds daily.

"It's gonna be okay," Spriz reassured Maisy, weakly.

"Easy for you to say," Maisy huffed. "They can't afford to

fire *you*, they owe you six years of sick time."

Maisy sighed heavily, then picked herself up smartly—despair was a sin, and worse, it was counterproductive. "Well Tommy, you're on the clock for another two hours, let's go find you a way to earn it. Maybe there's pieces of thread in the bobbin compartments again."

As Maisy turned away for the dressing room door, Tommy turned to Spriz and gave her his "Rescue me, for the love of God!" face.

"Maisy!" Spriz yelped. Maisy turned in the doorway, surprised.

Spriz sputtered, "I need Tommy. The Properties department makes formal request to the Costumes department for temporary interdepartmental transfer of assistant Tommy Q. Gustafson—"

"Q?" Maisy interrupted.

"He made the Q up," Spriz explained.

"I made it up," Tommy confessed.

"His middle name is Evelyn," Spriz said.

"My middle name is Evelyn and you are SO DEAD, Suzanne!" Evelyn warned.

Maisy said, "I don't think you can trans—"

"Raise your right hand!" Spriz said quickly to Tommy.

Tommy raised his right hand, and smiled. "What do I do with my left?"

"Never mind! Repeat after me: I, Tommy Evelyn Gustafson…"

"I, Tommy Stop Saying That Name Gustafson…"

"Do solemnly swear to uphold the right honorable office of deputy assistant propsmistress…"

"Do solemnly swear to uphold the whatever you just said…"

"And to preserve, protect and defend the props…"

"That too…"

"So help me God."

"So help me God. High five!"

They high-fived. Spriz told Tommy to grab the satchel, and quickly scooped up the tackle box and street clothes herself.

She pulled Tommy through the doorway, almost knocking Maisy down. As they made for the stairs Spriz called over her shoulder, "Take his pay out of my assistant budget!"

Maisy yelled down the stairwell after them: "YOU DON'T HAVE AN ASSISTANT BUDGET!"

# 8

TOMMY HELPED SPRIZ DIG OUT her biggest dining
table—a heavy oak number with lion's feet—and stand it up in
the long part of the L of the prop room. The table was so wide,
and the room so narrow, that they could not walk around the
table, but had to crawl over or underneath it to get from one
side of the room to the other.

Spriz positioned the clean clothing, shoes, tackle box and
satchel in the center of the table. She and Tommy methodically
removed and examined the satchel's contents, one item at a
time, like forensic pathologists extracting vital organs through a
Y incision and studying each one for signs of injury or
pathology.

Most of Brandon Wishart's vital organs were pretty
unremarkable: pants, shirts, underwear and socks, a thin sweater
and light jacket, shaving gear, toothpaste and toothbrush,
Polident, nail clippers, Flomax and Lipitor, brush and comb. In
the pouch crammed with his socks, they found an expired
passport—he had been to the UK, and to Ireland, and to
Mexico, but all very long ago. In another pocket they found a
rolled-up reversible belt and two decks of cards, the solitaire

equipment he routinely deployed to avoid socialization during rehearsal breaks.

In a secret fold in the bottom of the satchel's main compartment, Wishart had carefully hidden his brown leather wallet from dressing-room mates he didn't trust. Spriz found it right away; she knew her satchels. The wallet held a Florida driver's license, actors union card, Social Security card, Medicare ID, $265 in cash, and his last paystub from GaliRep, showing gross pay of $1,000 for two weeks' work, with deductions for taxes, union dues, pension and insurance.

"No credit cards?" Tommy asked. "No debit card, no checks?"

"I think he lived cash-only," Spriz explained as she explored a pocket-within-a-pocket they had overlooked. "One payday I gave him a ride to the theatre's bank. He cashed every paycheck he got at the source. No bank account. He probably couldn't get a credit card without a bank account anyway."

All along one side of the satchel was a broad, zippered pocket: pay dirt. In it, Spriz and Tommy found an oaktag accordion folder packed with papers: pay stubs, contracts, photocopies of audition monologues (*refreshers for a failing memory*, Spriz thought), copies of tax returns going back five years, at least a hundred little receipts for meals and lodging from all over Florida, and a single photograph, a Polaroid of an attractive, fortyish woman sitting on the arm of a sofa, perhaps at a party.

There was no writing on the Polaroid to identify the subject, or the place, or the year. Spriz could tell the thick, square little photo was taken on Polaroid SX-70 film with an SX-70-type camera—her stores included vintage cameras spanning more than a hundred years, from an early Eastman folding "pocket" bellows model, to plastic Instamatics from the 1960s, to modern SLRs. She even had a Brownie. Pick a play set in the twentieth century and she could hand you a camera that suited it.

Polaroid stopped making SX-70s in the 1980s. The film was still sold for many years after the cameras had been discontinued, but based on the film type, how faded and yellow the photo had become, the style of the dress and the fabric on the sofa, Spriz guessed that it was taken at least thirty years ago, perhaps longer ago than that. *Who was she?* She was pretty.

The satchel was empty now, its guts splayed at its sides in careful piles.

"Okay," Tommy said. "Maybe it's too late to ask, but what the hell are we looking for?" He started flipping through the tax returns as though he knew what he was doing. He noticed Wishart's adjusted gross income at the bottom of the first page of his Form 1040 for last year: $19,750. A teenager's wages at seventy-two years old. Tommy had made almost that much himself, and he had worked only part-time much of the year.

"I dunno," Spriz replied. She had hoped to find something that would lead them to the old man's people: address book, family photo with names, cards and letters... But there was nothing, nothing but a very old photo, which was useless.

She stepped back to survey the whole dissected corpse on the table, and suddenly a wave of sadness, *lonely* sadness, washed over her and made her shiver.

"Tom?"

"Yeah Spriz?"

"This is it. This is all of it, everything that man owned in the world. His whole life is right here on this dining table."

They stood quietly for a few moments, looking at the sum of a life in a dozen tidy piles. Tommy returned his attention to the tax forms, hoping to make a discovery that might cheer Spriz up. Spriz started going through the receipts.

"Hey," Tommy asked, "who is Ryan Mountain, Esquire?"

"He's on the board," Spriz replied. "What did you find?"

"He signed these," said Tommy, leaning across the table to show a signature to Spriz. "He's the paid preparer, he did the old man's taxes. Maybe he knows more about him than we do."

Spriz made a checkmark in the air with her finger. "Okay, we need to talk to him. But look at these." Spriz had started dividing some of the receipts into five piles. "All of these are from in or around just five different cities."

She dropped the unsorted receipts on the table and reached down to a bottom shelf to retrieve Volume F of the 1947 Encyclopedia Britannica. She opened it to a beautiful full-color plate of Florida, complete with a huge pink flower blooming in the center of the state and tiny black alligator shapes in Lake Okeechobee. The type in which "Orlando" was printed was much smaller than what Spriz had always seen on modern maps.

A little orange-growing city of 1920s bungalows packed around an Army airbase left over from the war, the Orlando on this map had not yet begun to see all the land to its south gobbled up by dummy corporations fronting for a man with a mouse and a dream.

She traced her finger in a long, lazy circle, from Galilee through the other cities on the receipts: north to Perry, then west to Monticello, back east to Starke and Palatka, southwest again to Galilee, north again to Perry, northwest to Monticello…

"Gigs," Tommy said.

"Gigs," Spriz echoed.

Tommy picked up a pile of little receipts. "Where the hell is Starke? Why does it sound familiar?"

"Here." Spriz pointed to a spot on the map between Jacksonville and Gainesville. "And it sounds familiar because that's where they will lock you up someday." Starke was well known as home to the state prison, and little else.

"He worked *there*?" Tommy asked. "They have a professional theatre?"

"We're gonna find out," Spriz answered. Then she dropped to the floor and crawled under the dining table, encyclopedia in hand, to get to the end of the prop room where her command center was stationed. As Tommy came to join her, carrying the receipts between his fingers to keep the piles separate, Spriz propped the encyclopedia open on her workbench, pressed the spacebar on her keyboard to wake up her computer, and waited while it reacquired the Internet.

"If we look for theatres in these towns," Spriz explained, pointing to the map, "we'll find out where he worked this year, probably places he's worked off and on for years, just like here. If we find the theatres, maybe we'll find somebody who really knows him, who maybe knows where he has an ex-wife or son or daughter stashed. But the lawyer first."

She opened Google, entered the search term

```
ryan mountain attorney galilee
```

and hit on the website for Mountain's firm. She found the firm's main number at the bottom of its home page.

It was late on a Thursday, but she took a chance. Snapping her desk phone's handset out of its cradle to make the call required a little effort. She had spilled glue on her phone once, and the handset had been semi-stuck ever since. No one was sure whether she'd done it accidentally or on purpose, including her. Mountain wasn't in, but Spriz asked the service to page him with the theatre's number and the prop room's extension, and to flag the page urgent.

Then she started searching with the city name from one pile of receipts:

```
perry florida theater
```

A long hit list appeared, all movie houses in Perry and surrounding Taylor county.

"Try 'theatre' with an 're'," Tommy suggested.

Googling "perry florida thea*tre*" turned up the websites of two stage companies. One was a community theatre, a place in which Brandon Wishart would not have been caught dead, even in the audience. The other was the Perry Playhouse, a small professional theatre. Spriz tried a new search:

```
"perry playhouse" "brandon wishart"
```

The top hit was a link to a year-old newspaper review of *Blithe Spirit* at the Perry Playhouse, which featured effusive praise for Wishart's performance as Charles Condomine. One down.

They worked the other cities. For Monticello they found Wishart in a cast list on a theatre's website, and for Palatka they found another newspaper review that put Wishart and a local theatre company together.

Tommy and Spriz got sidetracked reading the reviews, and an hour passed unnoticed. The arts critics in these little cities had worn out their thesauruses coming up with superlatives for Wishart's work. One wag called him "Florida's favorite leading man." The actor was as unreservedly adored onstage as he was detested offstage, and the proof was here in print and on the Internet, testament for all time. Better than a marble headstone.

"Spriz?" Tommy said softly. "That's not all of it, that stuff over there on the table." He pointed to Spriz's computer screen, on which appeared the headline, "A Lear to Rival Olivier's."

"This is his life too."

Spriz smiled.

Starke was a dry hole. Nothing they searched for turned up a stage company. Looking at the receipts more carefully, Spriz noticed that the dates were too close together to encompass a gig. The first and last receipt for the most recent year were only six days apart. And he had three years of them, three consecutive years in which he had apparently spent six days each year in Starke, staying at the same motel and eating once or twice each day at the same barbeque joint.

Spriz said, "So he works most of the year in SPTs in Galilee, Perry, Monticello and Palatka. And after that he spends less than a week in Starke for… fun?"

"Starke doesn't sound like a lotta fun to me," Tommy said.

Spriz's desk phone rang, making her jump—she hadn't heard it in years. She yanked the handset out of its sticky cradle and answered: "This is Spriz."

"Spriz?" Ryan Mountain puzzled. "I know this is Galilee Rep, but I'm not sure where this extension goes."

"It goes to the basement, Mr. Mountain, I'm Spriz, I do props. I'm sorry to bother you, but you knew Brandon Wishart, didn't you? I saw you at the funeral today."

Mountain sighed. "So sad. Just awful. He was a… a difficult man. But what an actor. And nobody deserves to die like that. Nobody." He let out a deep sigh. "Funny, you saw me but I guess I didn't see you. You sound like a young woman, and I don't remember seeing a woman under fifty there today."

Spriz smiled. From within a handful of people mostly dressed in black, he had not even seen the girl giant in the ugly flower-print dress.

Mountain puzzled some more. "I apologize, but I'm not sure I recognize your name. Spriz, is it? Don't they call you Suzanne in the program? Or is that someone else?"

"No, that's me," Suzanne replied firmly. "I do the props, just me. My name is Spriz." He didn't remember he'd been introduced to her once, a few years ago, at a meet-and-greet kicking off the season. Apparently she not only was invisible, but also erased memories. Her powers were extraordinary.

"Call me Ryan, Spriz," the lawyer said pleasantly. "How can I help you?"

"Well, we have his things here, his clothes and papers and whatnot, and we saw you did his taxes. We're trying to find his next of kin or somebody so we can send his things and his money to them. Do you have any idea who that might be? Or where?"

"Sorry Spriz, I don't. All I know is what you see in his returns, his income and his expenses. We barely spoke, just a couple of phone calls. He dropped off his papers at my office when I wasn't in, and I mailed him a copy after I filed the returns. That was the sum of our interaction." It was a regret.

"Yeah, speaking of his expenses," Spriz queried, "he has a bunch of receipts here for meals and a motel in Starke, near the state pen, but we can't find a professional theatre there. Can you think of a reason he'd save receipts if he wasn't working there?"

"Actors in my experience are pretty good at finding ways to justify expenses," Mountain chuckled. "He might have been researching a role I suppose, maybe he was going to play a convict. That, or he was just padding his deductions. He tried to slip a lot of padding past me over the years. I didn't hold it against him. Made me laugh because, at his age and with his income, padding his expenses was hardly worth the trouble. He paid practically no taxes anyway."

"Could he have a will someplace?"

"I wondered the same thing myself, so yesterday I made some calls, checked with the state and a few other states he may have lived in. It doesn't look like he had a will. And why would he? You have his things. From what I saw of his financials, I'm guessing his things aren't worth writing up a will over. People who have no property don't bother with a will. Especially if they have no issue."

"Issue?"

"Offspring," Mountain said gently. "Kids."

"Oh. Okay. Well okay Mr. Mountain, Ryan, thanks... You sure you don't know where he has any family, or close friends?"

"No Spriz, but if I think of any, I'll call back. But hey, it's nice to finally meet you. I've noticed your props in shows. They're wonderful."

Spriz thanked him, but she knew it was a lie. Nobody noticed the props. Usually, that was good: When the audience didn't notice the props, it was because they accepted the props, because the props fit perfectly into the play. Props were only noticeable when they were wrong. Good props design, like a good propsmistress, was invisible.

After hanging up, Spriz returned slowly to the dining table and the estate of Brandon Wishart. She began silently repacking the satchel, taking care to restore every item to the precise compartment from which it had been extracted. She added the folded street clothes and shoes. She carefully smoothed the wig from *Great Expectations* and put it with his others, in a gallon Ziploc freezer bag in the tackle box.

"Spriz?" Tommy asked, watching her. "Spriz? What happens now?"

Spriz turned suddenly, stood straight up to her full six feet and then bent her face down toward Tommy's, her expression taut and determined, her loose hair backlit by the bare bulb behind her head.

"Here's the deal," she declared. "We're unemployed for the foreseeable future. I have a full tank of gas and almost fifteen-hundred dollars in my checking account, and if I really, really need it, the loan of Brandon's two hundred sixty-five in cash. I'm taking this satchel and this tackle box and I'm gonna go visit those theatres and I'm gonna find somebody who cares enough about this man to inherit his stuff. I've got nowhere else to be. How about you?"

Tommy's handsome face broke into a broad smile. "Tommy! Spriz! Cher!" he cheered.

He thrust his fist up into the rafters, just missing a copper kettle.

"ROAD TRIP!"

# 9

*The Dragon raised the two boys in his own image.*
*One boy became a dragon, the other remained a boy.*
*The mother remained a mother, with a mother's burden.*
*The mother wept beneath the Dragon's claw.*

AFTER RESTORING VOLUME F beside Volume G, they loaded Wishart's belongings into Cher's wayback and then hurried over to Tommy's apartment so he could throw some clothes into a bag. They had no idea how long this expedition would take, and no reason to hurry back until they ran out of money.

Spriz didn't need to stop by her apartment. She had grabbed the green Publix shopping bag of fresh clothes and toiletries she kept under her workbench for overnights in her prop room when she had too much work to do to sleep at home. She threw in the prop room flashlight from Conrad, because Daddy had conditioned her never to embark upon an overnight journey without one.

She wondered how long she could be gone before her actor roommates noticed, or if they even would. She trusted them to feed Osric, the formerly stray calico who had adopted her.

Sometimes the ungrateful kitty seemed to prefer the actors.

Only sporadically employed, they were home more than Spriz was, and easy marks for a warm lap and a good stroking. But Osric spent his nights in Spriz's never-made bed, and nowhere else. Spriz had cut a hole at the base of her bedroom door. The landlord could keep her security deposit. They always did anyway.

The mid-October early sunset had slipped away before they finally got on the road. Spriz disliked the Interstate, and was fond of proving that despite the stoplights one could actually navigate Florida more efficiently on the old U.S. highways and local roads that still crisscrossed the state.

Interstates 4, 10, 75 and 95, and the Florida Turnpike were always clogged with confused tourists and perpetually bottlenecked by construction delays and by rubberneckers gawking at the countless daily fender-benders—and worse.

The Florida stretch of Interstate 95 had been ranked "Deadliest Highway in America." Interstate 4, the road to Disney, the one that never left the state and ran only 132 miles end-to-end, Tampa to Daytona Beach, came in third. On January 9, 2008, there was a seventy-vehicle pileup on I-4 near Polk City, caused by a blinding stew of morning fog cooked with smoke from a scrub burnoff. Four commuters perished.

Because Cher presented the same aerodynamic profile as a brick, she did not achieve a dramatically better MPG on the highway than off. As with every Jeep Cherokee built from 1984 through 2001, at highway speeds her stone-age engine and bumpy tires made a deafening roar and thrum, and the many air gaps in her rugged yet sloppily constructed frame let shrill whistles invade the cabin. Conversation was impossible. Hearing one's own thoughts was a challenge.

On the back roads, Cher was a tolerable ride, and her high, tint-free windows let in the glorious Florida color unfiltered— lush greenery in the daytime, cheerfully tacky neon at night. The local roads were not only plenty fast, but more scenic and more delicious than the highway, peppered as they were with roadside stands offering boiled P-nuts and freshly picked fruit, and mom & pop joints serving real Florida barbeque. You couldn't get that at any of the generic national burger-mongers installed at every Interstate exit.

Over the dark miles to Perry, Spriz and Tommy joked, and they teased and they sang. The radio stayed off; it was poorer company than they were for each other, and there wasn't much radio to hear in the deep Florida forest. In the woods at night, Spriz couldn't help imagining Swamp Cabbage Man—Florida's Bigfoot—leaping out into her headlights from the treeline, after all the silly stories she'd been told. But there was nothing at all swampy about this high, dry, stony part of the state.

Theme park fans and Miami partygoers rarely see the real Florida, especially the northwestern region just below the panhandle. It's not on the route from anywhere to the theme parks, and it's on the opposite side of the state from I-95, the main road by which Yankee snowbirds come down. The area is hilly, and densely pine-forested, with nary a palm tree in sight. Every undeveloped patch of grass is claimed by cattle. The roads are black and narrow, and only lit by streetlights within little strips of towns, which are few and far between. If not for the heat and the palmetto bushes scattered about the pine scrub, and the lizards and the giant prehistoric birds, the place might pass for parts of Massachusetts.

Sad fossils of tiny motels and offbeat eateries along the state highways serve as capsules of a time before The Mouse, when Americans drove down simply for the sunshine and a soak in one of the region's sweet, cool springs. The beautiful place itself was a draw. No plastic wonderlands or drops from dizzying heights were required to attract visitors. The scented air itself sufficed.

Tommy and Spriz rolled through the night, around and over the knobby hills, stopping a few times in the darkest places to switch off the headlights and clamber onto the roof of the little truck to gaze at a billion bright stars and planets in a black sky free from the light pollution of Galilee's strip malls. They watched two meteors burn across the heavens. Each time the mosquitoes found them, they got back on the road.

Inevitably the conversation worked its way to Scott, Tommy's ongoing is-he-straight-or-isn't-he crush. Scott was a very pretty and marginally talented actor who worked at GaliRep for one or two shows every season, during which he would flirt shamelessly with Tommy at every opportunity while avoiding ever being alone with him, and making a great show of his heterosexuality at all other times. Scott had driven Tommy straight up a wall for three seasons running.

Spriz always said the same thing whenever He Who Shall Not Be Named was named: Forget him. Move on. Start liking people who like you back. But Scottie was an itch Tommy couldn't scratch, and Spriz had come to believe that Tommy enjoyed the drama of the non-affair more than he hated its absence of requital. She listened patiently, just as he always listened to her.

Farther down the road, Tommy decided that because their trip was A) Embarked upon impulsively, B) Impelled by a good cause, and C) Highly unlikely to succeed, it met the conditions of a quixotic quest, which compelled him to start calling her "Sancho." After the third time, she told him flatly, "You're Sancho. I'm Don Quixote."

"I called Quixote first," Tommy said.

"Didn't," Spriz replied.

"I called him by calling you Sancho. I'm Quixote by the axiomatic property of calling stuff."

"Don Quixote is tall," Spriz played. Wounded, Tommy clutched his heart.

"I sing better," Tommy recovered. "Don Quixote has more songs."

"It's an actor's role," Spriz said. "Peter O'Toole played it in the movie. He's not a singer."

"I'm an actor," Tommy declared. "And they dubbed Peter

O'Toole."

"No WAY!" Spriz cried.

"WAY!" Tommy responded.

"My Daddy showed me that movie. Why dub Peter O'Toole with another guy who sings just as bad as Peter O'Toole?"

"Why give Richard Kiley's part to Peter O'Toole in the first place?"

"Hollywood," Spriz huffed.

"Hollywood," Tommy agreed. Then he began to sing:

*To dreeeeeeeeam… The impossible dreeeeeam….*

Spriz joined him. She had a wretched singing voice, and she knew it. People with perfectly serviceable voices often play at claiming to sing poorly, but Spriz was the real deal. The tone she produced was more shriek than song, and she did not know one note from another. In school assemblies and during the anthem at the minor league ballgames to which Daddy had dragged her, she had mouthed the words, silently.

From the beautiful choir at Daddy's church, she had come to believe that singing was the best way to speak to God, and that when we sing, we let our souls shine through. She thought singing was the very best thing most people could do. But she did not sing, ever, period. Except alone with Tommy. And then she sang full-blast.

At the top of their lungs, cruising an empty, dark road in the wilds of Florida, they sang the one verse they knew, then sang three more they made up as they went along. The last verse, composed mostly by Tommy with the assist of a rhyme from Spriz, went like this:

*And the world, will be better for this*
*that two nerds, in a fabulous car*
*still drove, having no more employment*

*to reeeeeach! The un-reach-a-ble…*

*STAAAAAAAAR!!!*

They both nailed the high note, more or less.

They talked and they sang, but they were also comfortable together in silence. An hour could pass while both watched the murky scenery roll by and said not a word, though both understood they were sharing the experience intimately, more intimately than if they had discussed it.

But now and then when the conversation lulled too long, Spriz heard Tommy take a sharp breath, followed by the words "What if…" and she knew what was coming: another half-baked theory about how Brandon Wishart had died.

What if he'd already had an aneurism that was ready to pop—there'd been no autopsy—and the shock of the flat falling on him triggered it, and then he got bloody when they scraped his scalp on the texture paint pulling him out? What if a board or other heavy object had fallen on his head right before the flat fell on him, then bounced or rolled away? What if another object hit his head through the muslin, after the flat hit him? What if his toupée somehow exerted just enough pressure on his skin to stanch the bleeding until they pulled him out and it fell off, right where Spriz had found it? What if…

Spriz didn't argue with Tommy's deductions. She knew engaging him on the subject would only encourage him. She tossed off a lot of maybes and you-could-be-rights, and hoped he'd talk himself out—she really didn't want to think about it.

Sometimes shit just happened. Her Daddy worshipped JFK, and as a young man had cast his very first vote for the thirty-fifth president. For decades after the assassination he read every book, every exposé picking apart the Warren Commission's shoddy investigation. There were too many holes, too many impossible coincidences, too many unanswered questions—there had to be a cover-up… Somewhere along the way, he took a step back, looked at the whole picture, and arrived at an inescapable conclusion: Oswald acted alone.

Sometimes shit just happened. If it was unlikely, or hard to believe, that didn't make it any less true, and not everything true in this life was going to make sense. Spriz accepted that. No, she embraced it. She needed that aphorism to stop herself from woolgathering pointlessly about the circumstances of her own childhood and other aspects of her life and character that she feared defied analysis.

And frankly, she thought Tommy's theories not only failed to answer the essential questions surrounding the accident, but also sounded too dramatic, too much like the shocking revelations that came just before the last commercial break on a TV procedural. They only seemed plausible to Tommy because, well, because Tommy had been an actor, and in Spriz's experience actors often had trouble with the whole fantasy-versus-reality thing.

She had been accused of disliking actors, as backstage staff sometimes are. Techies and actors both come in all sorts, but generally speaking there is a cultural divide between theatre people who appear onstage and those who don't.

Actors tend to be more liberal, talky, uninhibited, and touchy-feely, and are more likely to be fabulously gay than are techies or members of the general population. Compared to typical actors, typical techies are somewhat more likely to be conservative, restrained, and straight. If they are gay, they're comparatively quiet about it, unless they're costumers, like Tommy. Sandy the carpenter was gay, but few knew, because the rules are different in a scene shop where manly men like Karl cut boards and pound nails.

Every company has those actors and techies who buck the norms. Few chemistry experiments yield more entertaining fireworks than the insertion of a single right-leaning actor into a communal dressing room.

Still, there is often a subtle, usually unspoken friction

between these distinct populations who have only one thing reliably in common: a love of the stage. Techies often feel actors are flaky and childish and technically inept, and they aren't always wrong. Actors sometimes fear techies: Some actors go into the theatre to hide from a world that does not accept them for who they are, and techies often seem to them to resemble the sort of people they're hiding from, the rough boys at school who bullied them for wearing an earring or pink shoes.

Some actors have a habit of treating techies like servants, and don't even bother to learn their names—Brandon Wishart was notorious for such behavior. And of course, the techies know they contribute just as much to making a play wonderful as the actors do, but the actors get all the applause and all the pictures in the paper. Techies claim that doesn't bother them, but deep down, it rankles a few, and the resentment sometimes finds expression in a condescending manner and bitter sarcasm.

But Spriz loved actors, she did, and she admired them, even though she sometimes regarded them as she would naughty children. They were tender, and funny and brave. They were like explorers, she thought: They wandered into dark and scary emotional territory normal people did their best to tiptoe around.

Conventional wisdom holds that actors are egotists, and how could they not be? Who but a person who thinks far too highly of himself would strut out under bright lights in front of a crowd and expect applause? Spriz knew better. Actors were amazing paradoxes—split personalities almost. They were egotists, to be sure, but they could also suffer from near-debilitating insecurity, even in the same instant. All at once, they could believe that they deserved nothing less than a standing ovation and also feel themselves unworthy of the audience's—or anyone's—love.

They often had come up under trying circumstances—a happy childhood is poor preparation for the stage—and found the first real love and acceptance they had ever known when they discovered the theatre and the broken people therein who make it hum. Lions on stage or when cornered, actors were mewing kittens inside, Spriz knew.

Fractured creatures themselves, actors held a deep and abiding empathy for people who were too mixed up to fit neatly into the round holes that make up the world outside a theatre. In fact, they preferred the company of such people, and Spriz loved them for that.

That's why Spriz could see all the menace Brandon Wishart was capable of, yet not believe he was a villain. *It's never that simple*, she thought.

If his fellow actors had not similarly granted Wishart the benefit of the doubt, it was only because he had poked them all in places so tender that their reptilian brains responded, overruling their more forgiving, human hearts.

When the long, dark road at last gave way to the streetlights of Perry, Tommy was asleep in the passenger seat, and the time was well past 2 a.m. The traffic lights in the old, tiny downtown were all flashing, and a thin mist hazed the streets, creating the illusion of a wintry night despite a temperature in the mid-60s.

Spriz hoped that following the main drag through town would lead to a motel. They'd crash for a few hours, and then find the Perry Playhouse in the morning. At most SPTs, Friday was a rehearsal day, and rehearsals began at 10.

Near the center of town, Spriz stopped for a flashing red light—not that it mattered. The streets were deserted, empty of both pedestrians and cars. After making a full stop, she began to move forward—then hit her brakes abruptly just before her front wheels reached the middle of the intersection, waking Tommy.

"Wha?" Tommy huffed, squinting against the streetlight glaring through Cher's un-tinted windshield.

Spriz threw Cher into Park, opened her door and got out,

and took a few steps toward a tall building on the corner to the left.

Tommy got out and came around to see what Spriz was looking at. "Are we there yet, mom?" he asked, rubbing his eyes. "Is this Perry? Why are we stopped in the mid...?" Then he looked up, and saw what Spriz had seen.

The third story of the building on the corner was a tall, flat box, with no windows in it—the classic profile of a theatre, its lighting grid and flyspace no doubt housed within the high box of faded red brick.

Spriz walked to the center of the intersection so she could see both faces of the building at the corner. On the far side she saw a broad marquee, empty of lettering, jutting out from the building's second story above a wide, recessed entrance. Through storefront windows on the near side, the streetlights spilled just enough light to reveal the red carpeting of an empty lobby. But the windows held no publicity signs or posters, just a small FOR LEASE sign taped inside and scribbled with a realtor's number in blue ballpoint.

"This is it!" Spriz said. "It has to be. But it's... *dead*. It's gone dark."

Tommy was already Googling "perry playhouse closes" on his iPhone. There were just enough signal bars in downtown Perry to carry the results.

"Last spring," Tommy reported as he read a newspaper story. "They went bankrupt. It says here most of their corporate funding dried up and subscriptions had been falling off for years. They cut ticket prices... did a lot of little shows, one- and two-character stuff, got some loans... but they didn't make it. They'd been operating right here in this building for more than twenty years. Used to be an old movie house, vaudeville before that."

Standing smack in the middle of an empty four-lane intersection, a red light flashing over their heads, Spriz and Tommy were looking at a corpse, the second they had viewed in the past twenty-four hours.

The nationwide economic collapse that kicked off in 2008 hit everybody hard, but it was devastating for regional theatres, especially in Florida.

Mostly not-for-profit organizations that ran close to the bone even when the economy was booming, small theatres had long survived on a precarious revenue stream comprising ticket sales, education fees (acting classes for kids, mostly), public and private grants, corporate sponsorships, and individual donations. At large theatres in New York and Chicago, the artistic director spent his day making art. In small regional theatres, the AD—along with a managing director, where the budget allowed for two at the top—spent half his day looking for money, and the other half looking for ways to cut costs.

When patrons started tightening belts, theatre seemed an easier sacrifice than other necessities. Even the most devoted theatre lovers, forced to choose between their season subscriptions and their car payments, made the only choice they could—though some die-hards considered buying both their tickets and a bicycle.

Local governments, under pressure to keep up services despite dwindling tax revenue, pulled up their grants. Corporations with dwindling profits dropped their arts sponsorships to stanch the red ink. And parents who were out of work, or afraid they might become so, decided junior's summer Shakespeare camp was a luxury they could sacrifice until the recovery arrived.

Already on the bubble thanks to litigation and other misfortunes, the thirty-two-year-old Seaside Music Theater in Daytona Beach was given the final shove into oblivion by the effects of the recession in October, 2008. Boca Raton's storied Caldwell Theatre Company had spent some of its thirty-seven years operating successfully out of a strip mall, but had more recently moved into a new, $10-million facility—right before the shit hit the fan. Five years later, the building was on the auction block, and the company for which it had been constructed dissolved. After twenty-four years, the lights went out at the big, nationally recognized Florida Stage company in West Palm Beach, crushed under its own debts. Orlando Theatre Project, then the oldest professional theatre company in Central Florida and founder of the still-successful Orlando Fringe festival, fizzled in 2009. The casualty list went on…

A month did not pass when someone or other from the Chamber of Commerce did not laud Conrad for keeping GaliRep lit while other small Florida stages were winking out of the heavens. The compliment made him queasy, just as he had felt at eighteen when the war in Vietnam was winding down but not yet over, and he was simultaneously thrilled that he had not yet been drafted but nervous about his low lottery number.

Soon after, the war was over, and Conrad was deployed to the battlefield of Doak Campbell Stadium at Florida State University, until the University of Florida Gators cut his tour of duty short by demolishing his left knee under a dog pile.

After seeing every one of his draftee buddies return home unscathed, Conrad came to believe he'd have been safer sneaking across the border into Cambodia than facing the Gators across the line of scrimmage.

Everyone at GaliRep had followed the news of the first few theatre closings with the sort of dazed attention one pays to a violent coup overseas. But after a few years, they became numb to the carnage, and turned away. A small theatre closing in a small Florida city was not a statewide story. No one in Galilee would know that the Perry Playhouse had gone belly-up until Spriz and Tommy brought the sad news home with them.


Named for a Confederate colonel, Perry is a city of seven thousand souls founded around one of Florida's many natural springs that have been sold to suckers for their reputed magical healing powers since Ponce de León.

An early settler of what would become Perry had a rheumatic wife, and the local Indians advised him to go soak her in the spring. It's possible the Indians were kidding, but whether by magic, science or placebo effect, the man's wife quit complaining, and America's first health & fitness scam was born.

In the early twentieth century, hotels went up in Perry to host winter tourists—including Theodore Roosevelt, so they say, although they say Teddy visited pretty much every hotel ever built in Florida, in violation of the laws of Time and Space.

The biggest resort hotel in Perry was built in 1910 over a springhead to feed its indoor swimming pool with Perry's magic juju water. It burned in '54, and the city markets its bare, crumbling foundation and empty pool as a "ghost town" attraction and historical site.

In the wee hours, downtown Perry was a ghost town too, and after another half-hour of driving that carried Spriz and Tommy well beyond the city limits, they gave up and pulled into a feed store parking lot to sleep. Spriz curled up in back while Tommy slept in the passenger seat, its back lowered to just above Spriz's feet.

A knuckle rapping sharply on his window jolted Tommy awake shortly before dawn. A weathered man in a short-sleeve button-down had his scowling face close to the glass. Tommy smiled weakly and cranked the window down while Spriz slowly woke up in back.

"This ain't no K-O-A campground, kids," the man growled. He was the manager of the feed store, which opened at 6 a.m. for early-bird farmers.

Tommy replied softly, "We're sorry, sir, it got so late and we were a little lost, and we just needed an hour's sleep. We're on our way to Bible college."

The old man laughed. "Sure you are." Tommy squirmed, not sure what to say next.

"Well, you can't sleep here, we're opening," the manager said. "But we got a ladies' and a gents' if y'all want to clean up some before you get back on the road to wherever you're really goin'."

Tommy and Spriz both thanked him as he turned away and walked back across the dark parking lot toward his store. They didn't hear him mutter to himself, "Sleepin' hippies in a purple truck. Sweet Jesus."

# 10

ON THREE HOURS' SLEEP, Spriz and Tommy washed up in the feed store restrooms, thanked the manager again, and then headed back toward Perry. They stopped at the first diner they saw, eager to treat the effects of sleep deprivation with fat and carbohydrates, an old theatre tradition.

Spriz ate three eggs over medium, four strips of bacon, wheat toast and buttered grits. Tommy had stuffed crepes and an omelet. Between them they downed a half-gallon of hot coffee as they watched the sun come up through the window beside their red leather booth. Tommy played "Paradise by the Dashboard Lights" on the jukebox, to the tacit irritation of the early breakfast crowd. He made it up to them by playing "Sweet Home Alabama" next. They were warming to him.

Once the grease had restored their mental faculties, they began to argue over what to do next. Tommy declared Perry a write-off, and was ready to try for better luck in Monticello. Spriz felt that since they had gone to the trouble of getting to Perry, they should at least make a good-faith effort to learn something before moving on. "We're here," she kept repeating. It was the best argument she could come up with.

As always, they compromised: They agreed they would track down the artistic director of the late Perry Playhouse. If the AD gave them a fresh lead—the name of a friend of Brandon Wishart, or hell, even a friend of a friend—they would follow it. If not, on to Monticello.

Tommy found the AD's name in the article about Perry Playhouse's demise, and Spriz found her address in the white pages chained beneath the diner payphone. Tommy plotted a course in Google Maps and they were off, with two more coffees, to go. Tommy held his coffee in his hands, while Spriz cradled hers between her thighs—'96 was the last model year for which the Jeep Cherokee came sans cup-holders.

They stopped in front of the AD's house at 7:47 a.m., worried they may have arrived offensively early. They stopped worrying when they noticed the FOR SALE sign on the lawn. A peek in a front window confirmed it: The house was empty, the AD was gone. "I *hate* this town," Tommy moaned.

Back in the car, a more targeted Google search turned up a press release announcing the former AD's appointment as a resident director at Indiana Repertory Theatre in Indianapolis. She'd landed on her feet.

"AD to resident director," Spriz said sadly as they pulled away. "Big step down."

"Bigger theatre, and she gets to direct plays and doesn't have to worry about where the money's coming from, 'cause that's somebody else's problem," Tommy replied. "Bet she cries into her pillow every night."

After a long pause, Spriz smiled. "Cold winters."

Tommy countered, "Pretty snow. Sledding."

"No pelicans," Spriz volleyed. "No gopher tortoises!"

"No flippin' Disney tourists driving rented minivans badly!" Tommy returned.

"No BEACH!" Spriz slammed.

"No gators! No sharks! No feral escaped pet pythons! No mosquitoes big enough to ride! No Stand Your Ground nutbags! No rest of the country watching the news about us and Jon Stewart making fun of us and everybody thinking we're all complete fucking idiots!" Tommy had spiked the ball.

Spriz sighed. "You win. Florida blows." She smiled slyly. She had let him win.

Florida was home, and that was the trump card. Tommy knew it—he was a Tampa native. Because Spriz would never know exactly where she had been born, she believed she had the right to select her own native soil. She had been raised in Indiana, but she had vowed never to set foot in the Hoosier State again. She wanted her ashes tilled into the sandy loam of the Sunshine State to fertilize some pretty hibiscus bush or Christmas cactus.

Tommy chuckled. "You got that right, baby. Evelyn wins every time!"

"People make fun of Indiana, too," Spriz corrected.

Monticello was just an hour or so north of Perry, up U.S. Route 27 past Lamont, then right on U.S. Route 19 where 27 splits off toward Tallahassee to become the Apalachee Parkway. Route 27 is the old Florida north-south highway, running 481 miles from Miami all the way to the state capital. Before the Interstates, Route 19 had been a major U.S. artery, carrying trucked goods and car-trip families the full 1,377 miles from Lake Erie to Central Florida.

The seat of Jefferson County, Monticello was named after the third president's Virginia home. Jefferson himself never set foot near the place, but surely Teddy Roosevelt must have visited, and there he would have learned that the twenty-five hundred residents pronounce it *mon-tih-SELL-o*, favoring an honest American sound over the namesake's hifalutin Italian accent.

In the land surrounding the city, you can still spot random Chinese tung trees, whose poisonous seeds produce an oil that was once a key paint ingredient. Jefferson County's economy thrived on tung orchards until synthetics and soybeans took over the paint business, and most of the county's trees have since been plowed under, killed by frost, or toppled by hurricanes. But a few indestructible "escaped" specimens survive, and they bloom every spring, as testament. They have selected Florida as their adopted home, too, and like Spriz, they're not giving it up.

The jewel in Monticello's crown is the Opera House downtown, built in 1890. Despite a promising and wildly popular start, the beautiful two-story brick theatre had fallen into disuse and disrepair after the railroad was rerouted around Monticello and started carrying Yankee vacationers and theatre patrons elsewhere.

But beginning at about the same time as GaliRep's founding in the cigar factory, the old Opera House had undergone a long and loving restoration, inside and out. Now it booked in musical acts and other traveling shows, but it also hosted in residence the Monticello Stage Company, a small professional theatre started a decade ago by refugees from the theatre program at nearby Florida State.

Always struggling to find an audience in the sparsely populated county, little MSC had escaped the fate of other small Florida theatres largely because the city let the troupe use the Opera House stage free of charge. The theatre in turn donated a quarter of its ticket revenue to the restoration fund. No one had yet decided how the arrangement might be altered once the restoration was complete, but no one gave it much thought, either—the restoration had been in progress for 40 years, with no end in sight.

Cher pulled in behind the Opera House at 9:50 a.m., just in time for Spriz and Tommy to catch the actors and staff before rehearsal got underway. They walked straight in through the stage door like they owned the place—there was no security like you'd find in any theatre in cities larger than Monticello and

Galilee. The stage door opened onto a narrow hallway Spriz instinctively followed in the right direction to arrive... on stage.

Spriz and Tommy stood in a far corner of the empty stage, their small audience in the seats before them comprising a dozen actors in rehearsal togs, the director, and the stage manager for the Monticello Stage Company, all staring at them in silence.

"Can I help you?" the director said tersely.

"We're very sorry to interrupt," Spriz said. She was suddenly shocked by the volume of her own voice, and the reverberations that returned to her ears. The acoustics in this place were amazing. As they hurried to the lip of the stage, she noticed the balcony, the deep-stained bead board wainscoting skirting the whole house, and the two elegant seating boxes capped with faux minarets. "Oh boy, this place is incredible," Spriz spurted, her small voice filling the theatre.

"Yes, we know," the director snapped as he stood with his arms folded across his chest and peered over his reading glasses. "We work here. Now how can I help you?"

"Oh, sorry, sorry," Spriz said as she and Tommy climbed off the stage into the shallow orchestra pit. "Sorry. We're here from out of town, and we were hoping to catch you before rehearsal started." She looked hard into the man's eyes. "It's important."

The director huffed, then spoke to his stage manager without looking at her. "Joan, call five please." Joan yelled, "FIVE MINUTES EVERYONE!" One actor muttered softly, "We can hear him."

The director walked into the pit, away from the actors who were funneling through the back of the house to go outside and smoke. They'd just snuffed out their final pre-rehearsal cigarettes not ten minutes ago, but a break was a break. Spriz and Tommy met the director at the piano. "What do you want?"

"Really," Tommy said, "We're really sorry to interrupt.

We're from Galilee Repertory Theatre. Our rehearsals start at 10."

"We start at 9:45," the director said through his teeth, "so I can let the actors go before rush hour." Tommy thought *there's a rush hour in Monticello?* but managed to keep it to himself.

"Sorry, I'm Spriz and this is Tommy. We're from GaliRep. I'm sorry to bring this up, but did you know Brandon Wishart?"

The director grimaced. "Ah, yes. I heard he worked down your way sometimes. How is the 'dear' old man?"

Spriz was dumbfounded. He didn't know? The Florida actor gossip grapevine was the most efficient communications system ever devised.

If a director balled you out on stage at noon, every actor in every other theatre statewide knew about it by five, and knew what the director had said, verbatim. Actors in Miami knew who was sleeping with whom at theatres in Jacksonville, and vice-versa. If an actor got fired, the resume and headshot of every out-of-work actor in the southeast who thought he fit the part landed in the director's email inbox within ninety minutes. How could this man not know his colleague was buried yesterday?

"Um, I'm sorry to be the one to tell you this, but he's dead, he died," Spriz said gently.

The sequence of emotions that played silently across the director's face was almost comical. He started to laugh, in disbelief. Then he stopped himself, and all his skin collapsed into a full-face frown. He shook his head a little, a questioning look on his face. Then his eyes caught fire, and his face burned with anger. He closed his eyes, inhaled deeply, and forced a calm, concerned expression onto his features. "How?" he finally asked. "Was he sick?"

"There was an accident," Spriz said. "Part of a set fell and hit his head, and he died on the way to the hospital. The funeral was yesterday."

"I'd heard there was an accident down there, and that some

actors were hurt. But I didn't know anybody died. And I had no idea it was Brandon. Poor man." His face was still ticking through different emotions. He could not decide how he wanted to feel. In the end, he felt almost nothing. "Poor old bastard. No disrespect, but I hope he's kinder in the afterlife. A mean man. Mean man! But I'm sorry he's dead. Poor bastard." A realization snapped the director out of his half-hearted attempt at grief. "He had a role booked here later in the season. I'm gonna have to audition some more Joe Kellers." MSC had picked *All My Sons* for its February show. Wishart had been cast as the family patriarch.

"How well did you know him?" Tommy asked.

"I directed him. Nine—no, ten shows over the years. He was great, one of the best I ever worked with. But I didn't 'know' him. Nobody did. Nobody wanted to."

"Nobody?" Spriz asked, a little desperately. "Mister…?"

"Stevenson, Ed Stevenson, I'm the AD here." He took her hand in a handshake, softly, and held it a beat too long. "Eddy." *Ten seconds after he hears a colleague died, he's on the make,* Spriz thought. *God I hate directors.*

It made her cringe internally, every time. She gave out no signals. She did not flirt, or know how to. She wore no makeup (she didn't own any), and she ended most days covered in dust and glue. "Doing her hair" meant washing it every morning with Prell shampoo and running a brush through it, still wet, on the way to the car. She'd bother to make a ponytail only when she needed to keep her hair out of a messy project. The rest of the time her hair hung loose about her shoulders, and thanks to her poor posture, it nearly hid her whole face when she was viewed from the side. And still she needed to fend off passes from jerks.

Something about a cast party made matters worse. When men consumed alcohol, they acquired the power to see through her invisibility cloak.

Short men were an ongoing problem. She found them no less attractive than tall ones, nor more so. But half of them seemed to want to show off their virility by grafting an Amazonian princess onto their arm—apparently being tall and thin makes you a trophy of some kind, like an eight-point buck—and the other half treated her with passive-aggressive hostility, as though their insecurity were her fault.

Once Tommy had embarrassed her in a well meant effort to disarm a tiny actor who was bird-dogging her at a cast party Conrad had forced her to attend. "Sorry sailor," Tommy told the little man as he held a hand aloft, bent down at the wrist: "You must be THIS TALL to go on this ride." The actor blushed and slunk away. Spriz was worried Tommy had crippled the poor man until she noticed the squirt a half-hour later with his arm around an actress who stood at least five-ten in flats—a decent consolation prize.

One reason she had liked Brandon was that he'd never made a pass at her, though he was reputed to take impotent swings at anything in a skirt. She supposed she could just as easily choose to be insulted, to assume he found her unattractive. But she didn't believe that. He respected her, and somehow he was not intimidated by her height despite his otherwise conspicuous vanity.

And his well-earned reputation for wanton cruelty notwithstanding, he'd never made comment on her size, not even a friendly joke or backhanded compliment.

She had fended off male attention so consistently that some people in the theatre community assumed she was gay. Spriz wasn't sure about that herself. She didn't know, and really, she didn't care. Romance held little appeal for her, with any gender, and sex held even less. Mostly she didn't think about it. She wasn't lonely.

She wasn't a virgin, either. A boy in high school had liked her, and she appreciated his kindness, so she let him. Afterward, the only emotion she felt was confusion. She could not understand what all the fuss was about.

She snuffed Eddy's candle by getting straight to business. "Eddy, we have his things, his effects, in my car. Nobody has claimed them. I can't just… give them to the Salvation Army. We came up looking for someone who was close to him, someone who should have his things."

Eddy shook his head. "There's no one like that in Monticello, Spitz, I'm sorry, I wish I could help you. He did his job, he kept to himself, except when he wanted to be a nuisance. Everyone avoided him. I'm afraid you're just going to have to give his stuff away. Or keep it. Is it worth anything? Maybe you could give it to the Actors Fund."

"Sorry, Eddy, it's *Spriz*," she corrected, gently. "Rhymes with showbiz."

"*Spriz*, sorry," Eddy apologized. "It's a weird name."

"I know. There's no one? Maybe someone who knows more about him than you?"

"Feel free to ask my actors. I think a few worked with him on other shows. But don't get your hopes up. I never saw him get chummy with anybody. He was always alone unless he was on stage. And keep it down, please, we're about to start blocking."

The freshly nicotine-buzzed actors were skipping back inside as Joan yelled "WE'RE BACK!" Eddy called out to Joan to get the actors who were in Scene One on stage for blocking. Joan yelled, "ACTORS ON STAGE FOR TOP-OF-SHOW." As he climbed to the stage, one actor whispered, too loudly, "We *heard*."

"Gotta work, Timmy, Spiz." Eddy said. "Good luck to both of you. I really hope you find somebody."

As the actors took the stage, Spriz and Tommy walked to the back of the house. They leaned on the seatbacks of the last row, facing away from the stage.

"What now?" Tommy asked quietly.

Spriz glanced over her shoulder at the stage. Eddy was arranging the actors in some sort of opening street-scene tableau. She turned back to Tommy. "Looks like everybody's in the top-of-show. We may have to wait for another smoke break to talk to anybody else. Maybe we should start with the stage manager."

"Should we bother?" Tommy asked. "You heard Eddy. The man had no friends here at the theatre. You wanna check the rest of the town, that's a shitload of doors to knock on."

"I know, Tommy, I know. Lemme think a sec."

As the director dictated the actors' blocking to them, telling them roughly where to walk on stage and when, the actors who had lines in the scene said them flatly, just to keep track of where they were in the script. The old hall amplified and enhanced the actors' softest utterances the way a fine old cello body takes a scratch on a string and swells it into Mozart.

Tommy heard a line he thought he recognized. He turned his ear toward the stage to better hear the next two lines, then turned back and giggled quietly. "*Women Beware Women*," he said.

"Beware of who?" Spriz asked. Tommy had a degree in Theatre. Spriz's training was all on-the-job and her own curious reading. He knew a lot about history and literature she didn't. But he never acted like she was less than a peer. And more often than not, she held her own.

"*Women Beware Women*," Tommy repeated. "It's an English tragedy, seventeenth century. Pretty tony stuff for the sticks."

"Public domain," Spriz observed. "No performance rights to pay. Smart move when money is tight. Look at all the actors they're paying."

"What good does it do to save the money if nobody buys a ticket?" Tommy countered. "Better to pay the hundred-bucks-per-performance or whatever and do *Forever Plaid* or *Nunsense*, something people line up for. As I recall, there were no royalties when Conrad did *William Tell*, and last I heard we were *still* making payments on that white elephant."

"Maybe you underestimate the literacy level up here," Spriz whispered. "The university's just down the road. Maybe there's a big audience for Jacobean tragedy here. For all you know, there's an annual Jacobafest in Monticello. People may come here from all over the world just to get their Ben Jonson on."

Tommy sniffed. "Even the Jacobeans hated Jacobean tragedy. That's why nobody writes it anymore."

Spriz had a snappy retort all ready to go, but stopped herself when a line from the stage caught her ear. She knew that voice! She spun around to face the stage. Tommy did likewise.

He'd cut his hair since *Great Expectations*, and was wearing eyeglasses, which Spriz had not seen on him before. She and Tommy hadn't recognized him, slumped in the seats with the rest of the cast when they first came in. But there he was on the Monticello Opera House Stage, small as life: Lanford, GaliRep's ex-Pip and the little man who had happened to be standing next to Brandon Wishart when all the lights went out.

As soon as Spriz saw him, a tiny flame flickered in her mind. Something had been bugging her, nagging quietly at her every time Tommy started deconstructing the accident. She hadn't really noticed the little light. Until just now.

Ninety minutes later, Joan yelled, "EVERYBODY TAKE TEN," and the cast shuffled out of the theatre and onto the bright sidewalk to smoke.

As Lanford was raising his lighter to the cigarette pinched between his youthful lips, someone grabbed his arm and yanked him toward the corner of the building, his unlit cigarette falling to the concrete. When he had come around the corner, the someone spun him. Spriz had him up against the brick wall, and she loomed over the little man like the Grim Reaper.

Two of the other smoking actors came running around the

corner to see what was happening. Standing behind Spriz, Tommy yelled at Lanford, "It's *your* baby! If you don't want my sister to have it, you're going to have to tell her *to her face!*" The actors turned and shuffled away, quietly.

Straightening his glasses, Lanford called past Spriz to Tommy. "I know you! You're from GaliRep!"

"What about *me?*" Spriz asked, coldly.

"Um, no, sorry, who are you?" Lanford asked.

"I'm props at GaliRep," Spriz answered. "We've met. Twice."

"Oh, okay, sorry," Lanford replied, shrugging sheepishly. "What are you doing here? What do you want?" He sounded a little scared, but Spriz wasn't buying it. He was acting. He'd sounded exactly the same when Pip was a little scared.

"You saw us, up on the stage when we got here," Spriz charged. "Why didn't you say hello? I didn't recognize you at first, but I did notice you were slumping down in your seat."

"I wasn't! I didn't know who you were!"

"You knew *him!*" Spriz said, jabbing a thumb over her shoulder at Tommy. "Why were you hiding from us?"

"I wasn't!" Lanford whimpered. "Could you please take a step back? You're scaring me."

Spriz took one step back. "You knew Brandon," Spriz charged.

"Of course I knew Brandon, I was on stage with him!"

"No, you knew him before! You knew him from here!"

Lanford was perfectly still for a moment. Then he clicked his tongue and took a long, lazy shrug, and suddenly he seemed ten years older and a lot less scared. He took off his glasses and tucked them in his shirt pocket behind his smokes. "I did five shows with that motherfucker. He was my father in two of them. We did one at your place, two here, and two more in Palatka. Even rapists don't serve that much hard time." He pulled another cigarette from the pack in his shirt pocket and lit it with the lighter he still had clutched in his smooth little hand.

"How'd you get this gig so fast?" Spriz asked.

Lanford rolled his eyes. "I booked this job six months ago! Eddy knew I'd have to start late because of *Great Expectations*, and he hired me anyway. I'm a quick study. When the show closed early, I realized I could start up here ahead of the plan. I'm getting paid by both GaliRep and Monticello Stage for this week. Pretty sweet." He smiled. He was proud of himself. When he noticed Spriz's expression, he dropped the smile.

"You hated him?" Spriz asked.

Lanford glowered at Spriz, and his voice dropped to a menacing growl: "*Every. Body. Hated. Him.*" He took a long drag, and blew the smoke sideways from the corner of his mouth.

"What happened when the lights went out, Lanford?" Spriz pressed.

Lanford blew more smoke. "I told the cops everything. The lights went out and he pushed me. End of story. Don't ask me why, either, because I don't know. You'll have to ask him."

Spriz stepped in, closer this time. Lanford felt her warm breath on the top of his head. Eye-level with her breasts, which he could not quite make out beneath her t-shirt, he was scared and turned-on at the same time. Suddenly Spriz barked "LOOK AT ME!" and Lanford snapped his face up so quickly that he pinched a nerve in his neck.

"What happened after the lights went out, Lanford?" Then she whispered, "And where's the *hammer*?"

In the "be a blacksmith" scene, Joe Gargery handed Pip a big iron hammer while tearfully begging him to stay and learn the family trade. When the lights went out, Pip had already received it. When Spriz rounded up the props to put them away, she couldn't find the hammer, but the set debris was still all over the stage, surrounded by yellow police tape with the letters CRIME SCENE - DO NOT CROSS. She had assumed the hammer was buried under the set, and expected to find it there after Karl and Sandy finished strike. Yesterday afternoon when she watched Karl's demonstration and saw the stage clear for the first time, she had forgotten to ask if Karl or Sandy had found the hammer. She was mad at herself for that.

Spriz pressed her nose to within a few inches of Lanford's, her eyes probing his. *Yes. There it is. Say it. You want to. Say it!*

Lanford's eyes welled up, and Spriz knew these tears were real. They spilled over onto his cheeks.

"I did it!" he said, his voice cracking. Tommy's heart jumped.

"I did it! Oh my god I did it!" Lanford buried his face in his hands, slid down the brick wall and crumpled at Spriz's feet. She knelt before him, close, keeping the pressure on. Tommy stepped in, right behind Spriz, struggling to process what he thought he had just heard.

Lanford was shaking. "He stole that scene, every night!"

"The *scene?*" Spriz said, incredulous.

"That was *my* scene!" Lanford cried. "But he made it about *him*, the audience never even saw *me*, he had them eating up that hoke he played! I made up my mind to take it back, to take my scene back, so I threw him a curve, I pulled focus. I stepped away from him right in the middle of his fucking monologue, and I turned front and I started to cry, great big tears. Nobody was gonna watch that ham with little Pip crying down-center in a blue special."

Lanford looked up at the sky, and laughed ruefully. "And *then*… And then that greedy son of a bitch steps into me, takes me in this big hug, and pulls me into him, *turning my face away from the audience* while he finishes his speech! Just *his* fucking face to the audience, *mine* buried in his fat fucking chest! I was so mad, I saw stars! I clenched my eyes, trying to pull it together. Next thing I know, he's pushed me off the fucking stage! I open my eyes, and it's pitch dark, and I don't know what the hell he's done, but he's done it—that bitch *pushed me off the stage!*" Lanford's face was turning red. He looked ready to pop.

He settled himself a bit so he could finish. "I had this hammer, see, from the scene, Pip has this big, heavy hammer."

Spriz snapped, "I know about the hammer, Lanford, I made it."

"Oh, right."

"I put it in your hand at rehearsal. I showed you how to hold it. And I just now asked you about it!"

"Okay, *okay!* I had this big hammer in my hand, and all I wanted in the world was to smack the son of a bitch. I was so angry. I wasn't thinking, I was just so angry. I couldn't see him, but I heard the audience behind me, I knew I was facing the stage, and I just started swinging, back and forth."

Lanford waved his hand from side to side, limply, the cigarette between his fingers leaving a crisscross trail of smoke. Then he froze his hand. "I connected, I didn't know with what, but suddenly I realized what I might have done, and I stepped back, and then I felt this whoosh of air in front of me—I think that must have been the flat falling. Then flashlights started popping on, and I could see the actors all standing stage right, so I went over and joined 'em. And prayed like crazy I had hit the flat and not the old man. I prayed like crazy. And I don't pray."

Lanford's voice was growing softer. It was almost a whisper now. "I didn't mean to kill him. I don't know what I meant to do, but I didn't mean to kill him. I just... I was just SO MAD." His voice rose again, and crackled with the strain. "I hated him so much. I hated him so much. I'm sorry. I'm really really sorry."

After a few moments, Spriz asked, "Where's my hammer?"

"Dumpster behind the theatre, in Galilee," Lanford replied softly. *Three days ago*, Spriz thought. Her hammer was in the county landfill by now.

Spriz stood up, and stared down at the little man far below at her feet. He looked up at her. The tears had stopped, and he looked resigned, defeated. The two of them stayed that way for a few moments. Then Lanford asked meekly, "So what happens now?" He laughed a little. It sounded like a line in a play.

Spriz stood there, silent, letting Lanford's question hang. Then she turned away and walked toward the back of the Opera House, where Cher was parked. Tommy followed.

At the corner, she stopped. Lanford was still on the ground, massaging his neck.

"Hey!" she called. "How come you didn't tell anybody here Brandon died?"

"I just got here last night!" Lanford yelled back, his voice hoarse. "I went to the funeral." He inhaled deeply, then dumped all the air out of his body in a great heave. "So far today... I didn't want to think about it."

Spriz turned away and disappeared around the corner. Tommy remained. He started for Lanford, who had gotten to his feet and was having trouble lighting his next smoke—his hands were trembling. Tommy smacked the lighter out of Lanford's hand and got in his face.

Tommy's voice was soft, but made of iron: "I understand hating him because he was mean to you. But hating him because he was *better* than you? Shame on you. *Shame* on you."

He left the little man leaning against the old building.


They drove all the way out of Monticello and halfway back to U.S. Route 27 before either of them spoke. It was Tommy who broke the ice.

"So? Do we call Galilee PD from here, or go home and tell them?"

"Neither," Spriz said listlessly.

"We have to tell somebody, don't we? I mean, it was still kindof an accident, but it's manslaughter or assault or something still, isn't it? What if he skips town?"

"He's not gonna skip town," Spriz said wearily. "He's gonna go about his business like an innocent man and wait to get picked up, and pray for a miracle that nobody ever comes. Besides, he's got a gig. A working actor doesn't walk away from a paying gig. Even in Monticello."

"We don't tell anybody?"

"We need more sleep. Do you remember a motel along here on the way up?"

"Spriz…"

"I'm hungry again. I can't believe I'm already hungry again. I ate like a horse this morning."

"Spriz!"

Spriz sighed. "It's assault maybe, or battery or something. But I think you have to actually kill somebody for it to be manslaughter."

Tommy held his tongue now, knowing Spriz would explain if he was patient.

Spriz exhaled. "I saw Brandon's wound. It was on the top of his head, right where a falling object would have hit him. You saw how Lanford said he swung the hammer: side to side. There's that, and also he was shorter than Brandon. I don't see how he could have hit the top of Brandon's skull at the right angle. And even if he did, that hammer was plastic. I made it myself. It was hard enough, it would have hurt, but it was light. I don't think anybody could have caved in a man's skull with it. All this time, I never gave the silly hammer a second thought, 'cause it's just not a deadly weapon."

"Neither is a canvas flat," Tommy added. "He said he hit something."

"I think he did. I think after Brandon shoved Lanford, Brandon was walking toward the end of the stage himself, and he walked right into Lanford's swing. Lanford probably caught him on the side of the head or on the temple, and knocked him silly. But he didn't kill him. He didn't even break the skin."

Spriz sniffed and hummed, the way Tommy had heard her do when she was mad at herself. "What?' he asked.

"Oh, dammit, that wasn't even the right hammer!" she whined.

"What?"

"It was a stupid doofer! I made it for another show last year and I had it lying around, so I gave it to them for rehearsals. And then the stupid director fell in love with it and said she wanted to use it for the show. I thought it was too light, that it wasn't believable, but she wouldn't listen to me. So I gave the actors a little clinic on how to hold it in a way that made it look heavy. That was all I could do. I almost laughed when he called it heavy. He must not know what heavy means. I don't understand how he could believe he actually killed somebody with it. It was just a hunk of plastic." *Pisses me off when they wanna keep the doofer*, she thought. *Let me do my job.*

"Acting," Tommy said. He smiled.

"Huh?"

"*Acting*, Spriz. To handle the prop right, to make the audience believe it was a heavy iron hammer and not plastic, he had to make himself believe it, right? Isn't that what you taught him to do? So he spends four weeks of rehearsal and five weeks in performance believing that hammer weighed ten pounds, so the audience would believe it. By the time he started swinging, he'd forgotten it was a phony, a doofer, at least as long as he was on stage. Acting made it real."

They drove in silence for a long time, both reflecting, trying to make sense of the past twenty-four hours. Suddenly, Tommy broke into a big smile, and slapped Spriz softly on the forearm.

"You bad girl!" he squealed. "You let that naughty boy go on thinking he killed someone when you know he didn't! You're spanking him!" Tommy was genuinely impressed, but not surprised. He'd learned never to be surprised by Spriz.

Spriz turned to Tommy and smiled slyly. "I'll send him an email when I get around to it."

Tommy laughed a diabolical laugh. "Okay, so much for him. Back to square one. We got nuthin'. Where do we go next? Palatka?"

"Spriz shook her head slowly. "No."

"No, Palatka?"

"No, we're not back to square one. Everything is different now. We know something we didn't know yesterday."

"What do we know?"

"The only reason I ever believed anything hit Brandon's head on stage was that everybody said he was mostly unconscious when they pulled him out. Now we know Lanford hit him in the dark, so that's that. No blood under the flat. Nothing else hit him on stage. So now we know the fatal blow came after he was pulled out from under the flat, and after Lanford made him helpless."

Spriz turned to Tommy, her eyes wet.

"Now we know he was murdered."

# 11

TOMMY TOOK A LONG PAUSE. "So... new quest? We're not looking for an heir anymore, we're looking for a killer?"

Spriz rolled her eyes. "We're still looking for an heir. We're not the Hardy Boys."

"OH!" Tommy cried. "We would make awesome Hardy Boys!"

"Yes we would," Spriz cracked a smile. Tommy always made it better. "But we're not gonna. I know less than nothing about investigating a murder, and you know less than me. And since the scene of the crime is halfway across the state, we're off to a bad start, wouldn't you say, Miss Marple?"

Spriz made a vow: "We have to find an heir. For him. I need to get that done. We'll worry about the murder or whatever when we get back home, where it happened. Any answers are there. First we'll tell Galilee PD what we think. They may know something that blows our silly hunch out of the water."

"You're not curious? You don't have a theory? It doesn't bother you that the GPD maybe blew this thing?"

"It bothers me," Spriz said. "But I have no theory. You said it yourself, but I didn't listen. Lanford said it too. I think Maisy even said it, in a way. Everybody had a motive. And it would be easy to think it has to be someone we know was at the scene—someone in the cast, or on staff, someone who bought a ticket. But the lights were out forever, and the lobby doors were unlocked. Anybody could have come and gone. It could be a crazy waitress he insulted last week, or a schoolmate he teased who's been building up resentment for fifty years. It could be anybody, and they could be in Australia by now with a new face. Not only that, but it all happened in the dark—for all we know the killer was after somebody else, and missed." She chuckled. "Know anybody who wants to kill Lanford?"

"Besides me?" Tommy replied.

She puzzled a moment. "And I still don't see how somebody makes that bridge fall on cue. When you think about it, it's all a really bad way to kill somebody. Was the bridge just a coincidence? If it's a murder, how can the bridge be a coincidence? The whole crime depends on it. I don't see how it works."

"It worked perfectly," Tommy said. "The man is dead and buried and the county's ruled it an accident. And the only people who suspect it was a murder are us, and you and me can't get ourselves from Galilee to Monticello without screwing up somehow every twenty miles. It's fucking genius."

"Aw, I thought we were doing pretty good," Spriz said, pretending to pout, a skill she'd never mastered. "So what's *your* theory?"

"Everybody had a motive."

"Yes," Spriz agreed. "Yes they did. So… we stay on target, *sí*? No Hardy Boys, at least not until we get home? After Palatka."

Tommy pouted, expertly. "No Hardy Boys."

They continued in silence until they turned east on U.S. 27, toward Palatka.

Out of nowhere, Tommy cried, "I call Frank!"

"Like fun!" Spriz replied. "I'm older, I'm Frank. You're Joe. You are such a total Joe. You were born to be Joe."

"Fine," Tommy said. "We'll both be Frank. When we get home. After Palatka."

Spriz laughed. This is how people cope, she thought. *We're coping here.*

She was exhausted. She wanted to stop and sleep, just for a few hours. But Tommy pointed out that if they drove straight to Palatka, with a half-hour stop for lunch, they could still get there before 4 p.m., in time to talk to both the staff at Palatka Playworks and actors in rehearsal. If they stopped to nap, they'd land in Palatka after the workday was over. It was Friday, some staff and actors would surely be there that night for a performance. But Spriz and Tommy would never want to risk disrupting a show night, even assuming they wouldn't be run out of town for trying. If they got there past 5 p.m., they'd wind up having to kill a night in Palatka and try again in the morning. And there was no telling whom they might find at the theatre on a Saturday, but typically most of the regular staff would take the day off.

"So?" Spriz asked Tommy. "What's your hurry? You got a date? Whatcha got against Palatka? We can stay until Monday if we have to. See the sights. What's *in* Palatka?"

"Absofuckinglutely nothing," Tommy replied. "But I'm curious now. I wanna know what the deal was with this guy, and I'm tired of not knowing. I didn't care before, but now I do, and it's your fault, so let's get it done. Besides, if we get lucky in Palatka by tonight, it's only three hours home from there—we can sleep in our own beds."

Spriz had to admit, her own bed, with her fat kitty purring behind her knees, sounded wonderful, especially with no reason on Earth to get up the next morning. She could sleep all day if the actor roommates kept their grab-assing and giggling down to a dull roar.

"I'll drive for awhile," Tommy offered, even knowing the

futility of the gesture.

Spriz just gave him a look. Nobody drove Cher but Spriz. Nobody changed Cher's oil but Spriz. Nobody did the belts, the plugs, the coolant, brake fluid, steering fluid, air filter, hoses, gaskets, headlights or brake pads but Spriz.

Except for the things that required a lift or expensive tools—tires, exhaust, pulling the engine—Spriz had done all the maintenance on Cher since she bought the little truck. Her Daddy taught her how, and taught her that the only way to really know your car was fixed right was to do it yourself.

Daddy had been raised a Catholic, but Jeep was his true faith. He knew all the little tricks Jeep people learn, such as replacing the little rubber crankcase ventilator grommet and clogged straw coming out of the valve cover when the exhaust started smoking, or using heavyweight diesel engine oil in place of the factory weight, a trick that had been known to keep the 4.0-litre six-cylinders grumbling along past half-a-million miles, or so Daddy claimed.

They got large coffees at a Sunoco, and pushed on.

They went back south through Perry—"Nope, just as bad in the afternoon," Tommy observed—and then turned onto State Route 20 eastbound, a more-or-less straight shot to Palatka by way of crossing the Suwannee River, skirting the southern edge of Ichetucknee Springs State Park, and bushwhacking right through the bullseye of Gainesville, home to the University of Florida and a bigger population than that of Galilee, Perry, Monticello and Palatka combined—times three.

Spriz was fighting not only exhaustion, but also a crisis of faith. Perry had been a total bust. Their brief time in Monticello had uncovered clues, but not any pertaining to their chief purpose. They were no closer to a proper recipient for Brandon Wishart's belongings than they had been exactly twenty-four hours ago when they discovered the receipts that launched them on this fool's errand, and they were approaching their third and final stop.

What made her think the people at Palatka Playworks would have any better information than Eddy had offered? Was it reasonable to think the man might have a blood relative or bosom companion in Palatka when he had been so resolutely solitary everywhere else?

She knew she could have stayed in Monticello longer, asked around some more, but her shyness had gotten the better of her. She had used Lanford as an easy excuse to flip her hair and stomp away so she could avoid having to approach more complete strangers with an awkward question, and she was mad at herself for it. In Palatka, she'd have to be braver and more persistent, or there wasn't much point in going.

As they came into the outskirts of Gainesville, they saw a green highway sign that read, "PALATKA 50." But that's not what caught their attention. Just above, the same sign said, "STARKE 25."

"Starke." Spriz observed.

"Starke." Tommy echoed.

She looked at him. He looked back. She looked at the road.

Another STARKE sign appeared shortly after, this one with an arrow indicating a left turn at the next intersection. Palatka was straight ahead.

She looked at Tommy. He looked back. He raised an eyebrow.

"It's stupid," she said. "We gotta do Palatka tonight. You said!"

Tommy nodded, meaningfully.

Spriz sputtered, "There's no theatre in Starke!"

"Well, if you wanna get technical about it, there's no theatre in Perry either, and we've been there twice today."

"You said Palatka closes at five!"

Tommy exploded: "Screw Palatka! This is Kismet! This is The Universe talking! I'm twenty-five! You're left-handed! The *signs* are honest-to-motherloving *signs!*"

The intersection was fifty feet ahead. Spriz was paralyzed.

Tommy bellowed, "TURN!"

From the right lane, Spriz pulled a hard left, cutting off a blue pickup and evoking an unoriginal gesture from the pickup's driver.

When the din of honking car horns had faded behind them and Spriz had gathered her full and complete wits, she thought for a moment, and then said quietly to Tommy, "You're twenty-seven."

Tommy smiled, but kept his eyes fixed on his phone, where he was Googling the name of the restaurant he remembered seeing on the bulk of Brandon Wishart's Starke receipts. "Just didn't enjoy watchin' you sit on the fence. Live a little, Spaz. I got a good feeling about Starke."

# 12

STARKE WAS A SHITHOLE. Or so it seemed to Tommy. "Seriously Spriz, turn around. I changed my mind."

He was nervous. He wanted a cigarette for the first time since they'd left. Spriz let him have it in the car, with the windows down. Cher had been a smoker's car before she became Spriz's, and the odor had never completely abated. One more cigarette wasn't going to make a difference.

Spriz found Starke unremarkable, not much different from any other inland Florida city of just under six-thousand residents: regular Florida folk going about their business, having families, living their lives. So what if they had no professional theatre? They had backyard barbeques, and Little League. They attended church on Sunday, and volunteered for the bake sale on Saturday. They had evening conversations with neighbors on the porch. She wasn't sure life in Starke was not preferable to life in artsy, intellectual, neurotic, occasionally pretentious Galilee. Nothing rubbed Spriz the wrong way harder than snobbery.

She knew Tommy had a different dog in the fight. Rural southern towns were not exactly known for their gay-friendliness. And statistically, the less performing arts culture one saw, the less likely a place was to be welcoming to outsiders who fell beyond the local approved range for sexual preference, religion, ethnicity and political leanings. Art was a marker for acceptance of diversity.

Just knowing Perry and Monticello supported local professional theatres was enough to satisfy Tommy that he was probably safe there—where there was theatre, there were other gay people who must have found the town tolerable. Spriz didn't judge him for his worry now, it was well earned. But although she would ever be Tommy's loyal wingman and fierce protector, she was also determined not to assume the residents of Starke to be knuckle-dragging bigots unless she saw evidence of that with her own eyes.

As they drove through town toward the restaurant on the north side, they kept looking around for high fences topped with razor wire or other indicators of the State Prison, until Tommy Googled a little and learned that the prison was actually a dozen miles up a road to the northwest, in Raiford.

"So how come they always say Starke on the news?" Spriz wondered aloud.

"When you have nothing," Tommy suggested, "even pretending you have a prison is good PR."

Bisecting Starke on its run from Sarasota all the way to Delaware, U.S. Route 301 was another major passage to the north that had been demoted by the Interstate. Cher traced 301 through Starke's most commercial blocks, which featured not only fast-food places and auto parts stores, but also the high school, the county courthouse, and finally Reese's Real Southern Bar-b-Cue, a tasty-looking place that had been recommended to Spriz and Tommy by the repeat business of a late friend.

They took a small table near the front door and got menus.

Spriz had trouble focusing on the entrées instead of studying the wonderful junk on the walls: rusty old toys, tools, farm equipment and vintage product packaging.

They had a real Royal Crown Cola bottle crate, and a pre-war tricycle. Unlike the lacquered reproductions dotting the walls and ceilings in some chain restaurants, the décor in Reese's featured authentic junk that had to have been pulled out of abandoned fields and ancient barns and attics—Spriz could tell the difference. She kept repeating "Oh boy!" as her eyes wandered along the walls from relic to relic.

She and Tommy argued about who should have to take the first turn asking total strangers if they knew the old man who died in a freak Dickens accident on the opposite side of the state. Finding no compromise to settle the argument, they played rock-paper-scissors, which Spriz lost, three out of three. Tommy must have learned Spriz's tells, she thought, whatever they might be. Evelyn always won.

An attractive middle-aged woman named Karen came to take their drink order. She had a winning smile and a honeyed drawl, which Tommy's experienced ear judged as authentic, but cranked up an extra notch for the barbeque crowd. After ordering a Diet Dr. Pepper, Tommy stared soft daggers at Spriz while she was ordering her lemonade, willing her to pop the question to Karen. She wimped out.

Minutes later, Karen returned with the drinks, and took their food order. While Spriz was asking for pulled pork and corn on the cob, Tommy was softly kicking her leg under the table.

Karen drawled, "Anythin' else ah kin gitcha?"

Spriz started, "Well, actually, we wanted to ask…" She trailed off.

"What kin ah bring y'all?" Karen pressed. Tommy kicked Spriz's shin, too hard.

Spriz noticed the poster on the wall across from their table. "The karaoke… Is that tonight?"

Tommy rolled his eyes.

"You bet, sweetheart, it starts in about an hour. Y'all come sing for us, now, I'll be the one clappin'!" She sashayed away.

Tommy gave Spriz The Look.

"I know, I know," Spriz said. "I'll ask when our food comes."

Ten minutes later the food was delivered by a burly man from the kitchen. Spriz sent him off unsolicited. "I like Karen" was her excuse. Tommy reminded her she was running out of chances.

When Karen came to clear their plates, they both confessed that they were too stuffed for dessert, and Spriz sent her off for the check. Tommy banged his head against the empty table.

The instant Karen returned, Tommy spoke: "Karen, this is gonna sound really weird." Spriz smiled, and kicked him under the table.

"Ow! Sorry. Um, Karen, this is going to sound weird, but we have a friend, an older man, very handsome, who used to come to town here only once a year, for about a week, and then he ate here every single day, sometimes twice. Would you remember him? Do you know who we mean? A man who was here every day for just a week? His name was Brandon."

Karen's practiced smile fell. She looked away, frowned, and ran her tongue over her top teeth. With little trace of her prior southern belle, she bellowed "CA-ROL!" She dropped the check on their table, and walked to her next party. Tommy could see that her smile had returned for other customers, and he assumed her accent had made a similar recovery.

In a few moments, an old woman appeared at the table. She was plump, but she still had her curves, and her white hair was done up in soft permanent curls. She was wearing reading glasses, and a simple country dress, in soft blue with white lace. A white plastic nametag reading CAROL was pinned to her dress. It was yellowing. She needed a new one.

Spriz and Tommy both stared at her face. They turned to

one another, and with their eyes alone confirmed that they were thinking the same thing. As Tommy started extending his upturned palm to Spriz, she was already digging her keys from her jeans pocket. She dropped the keys in Tommy's ready hand, and he excused himself and bolted out the restaurant door.

After watching Tommy take off, the woman said, "I'm sorry, I believe Karen called me your table. Is everything okay, dear? Is your friend alright?" Her voice was high, thin and tender. Spriz figured she was their fixer, the one they called on to placate unhappy customers. Who could stay mad at this sweet old woman?"

"Oh, he'll be right back," Spriz said. "He does that. Can I ask you a question?"

The old woman was a little taken aback, but she hid it well. "Why, of course you can, sweetheart!" Yep. Fixer.

"Well, we were just telling Karen about a friend of ours, and she called you. Maybe you know him? He's an older man, in his early seventies, handsome, and once a year he eats here every day for about a week. His name is Brandon.

Carol's face broke into a smile Spriz wanted to stuff in her pocket and steal from the restaurant, along with the rusty tricycle she coveted. Carol had all her own teeth, and they were lovely.

"You're friends of Brandon, how sweet! How fun that he's made friends with such nice, young people! Where y'all from?"

"We're from Galilee ma'am."

"Oh pish, call me Carol, I'm way too old for ma'am." Carol pulled a chair and sat. "What's your name, sweetheart?"

"I'm Spr—Suzanne, ma'am, Carol. I'm Suzanne and my friend outside is Tommy, and we came up here all the way from Galilee. Do you know it?"

"Well now, I've never been, but I hear it's the prettiest little place! How do y'all know Brandon? He was last here not five months ago, you know."

Tommy had just returned, and as he slid into the booth he

slipped something into Spriz's hand, under the table. She looked down at it, then pulled it up above the tabletop.

"Carol, is this you?" Spriz asked, showing Carol the old Polaroid of the pretty woman. Carol paused a moment, and Spriz and Tommy held their breath. Then she erupted in a hearty, cackling laugh that made Spriz and Tommy laugh along with her.

"Oh my lord, oh yes, this is me. My gosh… Wish I still had that dress, I loved that dress. Wish I still had the figure to put in it, too!" She laughed some more, and took the photo from Spriz in her chubby fingers.

"This is me… I don't know how long ago, but it was at a… a party at a friend's house. Martha Jakes, that was her name, Martha. My Lord. Her Marvin passed on, you know, and she moved up north to live with her daughter. My my…" She stared at the photo, lost in the past. "Look at me… I was a waitress here then, right here, can you believe it? Now I work the register, there's a stool I can use between customers. Can't be on my feet so much anymore. My, look at me in that dress…"

"Did Brandon take that picture?" Spriz asked.

Carol's face clouded over. She looked offended. "Brandon? Why would you think *he* took it? That's silly!" Then she softened. She smiled apologetically. "No, my husband took this at the party. Andy, my husband. He had one of those silly cameras. I lost him fourteen years ago this Christmas. He didn't take care of himself, you know." She had started to look sad, but then she looked confused, and troubled.

She pinched the photo tightly between her fingers. "I *lost* this. I had this picture for *years*, years on my dresser, just laying against my jewelry box, and one day I noticed… It was gone. I had Andy pull the bureau away from the wall so I could look behind it. It was gone. Never found it… Thought I might have thrown it away by accident, or maybe the children…" She stared down at the picture. Then she put it gently on the table, face up. "How… How did you come to have it? Where did you find it?"

"Carol," Spriz said quietly, "I have some news that may be hard to hear."

Matter-of-factly, Carol said, "Brandon's dead."

No one said anything for a moment. Carol started to cry, silently. She grabbed a napkin from the dispenser on the table and dabbed her eyes. Tommy asked, "How did you know?"

Still crying, Carol smiled her ageless smile and shrugged a little. "At my age, people tell you they have bad news, that's always what it is. And it has to be Brandon, unless y'all are friends with somebody else I know."

"No ma'am, Carol," Spriz said. "He died. I'm sorry."

"It's not your fault sweetie," Carol reassured. "But how... How did you get my picture?"

Spriz wasn't sure what to say. "His things, his satchel... He left behind a satchel of his things, his clothes and things, and the picture... was inside."

Carol lay back in her chair, and all the air left her body. Then she inhaled, and pulled herself up smartly. She blotted a tear with the napkin.

"He took it," she said quietly, nodding to herself. "He took it off my dresser. In my bedroom..." She looked into Spriz's eyes, then Tommy's. She was ashamed. She was hoping they wouldn't judge her harshly for her sins.

"He told you about me? Before he died?"

"No, no," Spriz said. "We found your picture after he died."

"But then, why are you here? How did you find me? My name's not on that thing." She picked the picture up and turned it over to check the back for writing.

"We didn't know you were here, Carol," Tommy explained. "We came here because he kept receipts, for taxes I guess, and he had a whole bunch from this restaurant. We came here because we knew he came here a lot. When we saw you, both of us recognized you from your picture."

Carol blushed. "You can tell that's me? I don't look like that anymore."

"Yes, you do," Spriz said. "We both think you do. How else would we know?" Carol beamed. Then she looked sad.

"What did he die of, sweetie?"

"Something heavy hit his head." Spriz hoped she would not have to get into the details.

"Oh my lord, he was hurt? Oh my. Men my age have heart attacks and strokes, they don't get *hurt*. Poor man. Poor sweet man…"

She started to weep softly. Karen came over, put a hand on Carol's shoulder, and glared at Spriz. "What's the matter? What did you say to her?"

Carol waved a hand. "Now Karen, these are good people. They came to bring me some sad news. Brandon is dead, honey."

Much like Eddy had, Karen contorted her face through a few different emotions, unable to settle on just one. In the end, she said only, "Sorry," squeezed Carol's shoulder, and returned to work.

Carol chuckled softly as she dried her eyes. "Karen didn't much care for Brandon. He told her she was fat once. He didn't mean anything by it. I don't know why some people take things so much to heart. So… Y'all are goin' around everyplace Brandon ever went? Is this some kind of, some way of memorializing him or something?"

Spriz looked at Tommy. Tommy looked back, and nodded. He excused himself again. "I'll be right back."

The removal of the male presence from the table loosened Carol's tongue. She reached across the table and took Spriz's bony hands in hers.

"Please understand, I *loved* my husband," she said. Spriz nodded.

"I loved my husband. But Andy and I… We were very young when we married. I was seventeen. That wasn't so unusual then, not around here, not like now, lord, I don't know sometimes what these kids are waiting for. Are you two married?"

Spriz suppressed a laugh. "No, Carol. We're just friends. He's not my boyfriend or anything."

Carol nodded softly. "I loved my husband. But Brandon was everything Andy wasn't. He was *educated*. He knew poetry, and Shakespeare. Did you know he was an *actor* once?"

"Yes ma'am. Carol."

"He knew about so many things I'd never heard of, and I couldn't get enough. When we were younger, he'd come to town and for a few days and we would… meet. Meet places. You understand?" Spriz nodded. "That all stopped after three years, I told him I was a married woman, and that was that. I was so ashamed. But he still came, every year, and then he just *talked* with me after that. Just talk, lovely talk! And he *listened*, too! Oh, to have a sweet, smart man actually *listen* to you, to care what you have to say! I loved my Andy, but I think the last words that man ever heard me say were 'I do.'"

Spriz asked, "What happened with Brandon after Andy… after you lost your husband?"

"Oh, I never told Brandon! I didn't want what we had to change. I didn't want him having… expectations of me, just because I was alone again." She looked at her finger. "Still wear my ring, right up 'til today. It was perfect, just the way it was. I spent half of every year looking forward to seeing him, and the other half remembering him." She winced. "And it's vain and it's silly, I know, but I was afraid if I told him Andy was gone, he might want to… be together, and I'm not the girl I was at 39, I wanted him to remember me like I was then. So I never told him. Now I wonder… I wonder now what he would have done if I'd told him. Too late…"

Tommy came back in, and he gently placed the satchel and the tackle box on the bare tablecloth behind the Polaroid.

"Carol," Tommy said carefully, "Brandon died in Galilee,

where we came from. He's buried there, in the county cemetery, if you ever want to visit him."

"Alright dear, thank you," Carol said, looking confused. "What's all this?"

"Carol," Spriz said softly, "We were really just acquaintances of Brandon's. We didn't know him well. We didn't really know anything about him. No one in Galilee was close to him, and no one came to claim his things, his bag and his actor makeup—which is a very cherished, very personal thing, an actor's makeup, if you didn't know. We don't know who his family is, or where they are, or where his close friends might be. We went on this trip to find them. We went on this trip to find someone who loved Brandon, so we could tell them we were sorry he was dead and bequeath his things to someone who deserves them. We've only found one person who deserves to be his heir. That's you."

Carol stared at Spriz in disbelief, stricken. Then she said simply, "No."

"Please?" Spriz said.

Carol looked at the satchel, with horror. "It's Andy's house!" she cried. Then she whispered, "I… I betrayed him. I betrayed my husband. I can't bring another man's… I can't bring another man's… *things* into Andy's house! I can't! I couldn't! Why did you bring this to me? Why! *Why did you bring this to me?*" She was weeping.

Spriz quickly rose from her chair and took Carol in her long arms, and rocked her softly. She leaned down and whispered in Carol's ear, "We're sorry. I'm sorry. It's alright." Spriz freed one arm from the embrace and slid the Polaroid off the table and out of sight, into her back pocket. Following Spriz's lead, Tommy quietly grabbed Brandon's bag and box off the table, took them to the truck, and stayed there. When Carol looked up from Spriz's embrace, the table was bare, except for the check.

Spriz read the check upside down, quickly calculated a twenty-five-percent apology tip for Karen, and pulled three bills from her jeans pocket. She put the bills on top of the check, and anchored the pile with the table's bottle of Smokey & Sweet sauce.

Carol had begun to collect herself, and was apologizing. "You're such nice young people. I'm sorry I made a scene. I hope… I hope you can understand. I hope you find someone to take his things." She took a step back, and eyed Spriz up and down. "My lord but you're a tall little girl now, aren't you?"

"Did he ever say anything?" Spriz asked. "Did he ever say anything about where his people are, where he was born? Or maybe an old Army buddy, or something? Anything?"

Carol thought for a moment. "Let me think now… He may have said he had a brother, I'm not sure… There was a family name, I think, or a name he always used when he talked about his family, which wasn't a lot… Hoover? Was that it? It might have been Hooper, but I think it was Hoover, he used to talk about the Hoover side of the family. Maybe they were his mama's family?"

"Did he say where they were?"

"I'm sorry sweetheart, he didn't. Oh! Wait a minute!"

"Yes?"

"There was a man… A man he said he acted with. He was very proud of having acted with him, he said the man had been in some big movies, but I can't remember what they were. But I never heard him speak with such admiration about anybody else. What was his name… Bill, I know that. Bill…"

Spriz felt a vein in her neck throb.

"It was Bill… Sayer! Sayer, it was Bill Sayer!" She beamed. "I remember because I told him I liked Leo Sayer the singer, and he said he knew a Sayer. It was Leo Sayer! No, it was Bill Sayer! Bill!"

"Did he say where Bill Sayer lived?"

"Oh… Oh dear, I don't know. I'm sorry. I don't think he did."

Spriz hugged Carol. "Don't worry about it," she said. "It

was really great meeting you. I know why you were special to Brandon. You know, your picture was the only one he had, the only one we found anyway." Carol smiled her priceless smile.

"Here," Spriz said, offering Carol the Polaroid. "This was never his. This is yours." Carol took the picture, and clutched it to her heart.

As Spriz turned to go, Carol touched her shoulder. Spriz turned back, and Carol said, "Dear, don't wait forever. You don't want to be alone when you're my age. If your friend out there isn't the one, find him. *Find him!*" Spriz smiled, turned and headed out the door.

"And Suzanne!" Spriz stopped. "You really don't need to go anywhere at all, or talk to anybody at all, if what you're looking for is someone who loved him, someone who has earned his love in return. You know that, don't you?"


Spriz had her fingers on Cher's door handle when she heard a holler from the restaurant door, back across the parking lot. Carol was standing in the doorway, waving her hand and yelling.

"PALATKA! I REMEMBERED! BILL SAYER IS IN PALATKA!"

# 13

"DID SHE JUST YELL 'PALATKA' AT YOU?" Tommy asked as Spriz climbed into the driver's seat.

"Yes. Yes she did."

"Why?"

Spriz closed her door. "Well, apparently there may be a guy named Bill Sayer in this world who happens to be someone Brandon Wishart actually admired. And if that's not implausible enough for ya, it's possible that, of all the places this guy could be, the most likely is Palatka, Putnam County, Florida, which just happens to be where we were going anyway. How's that for a kick in the pants, Tommyface?"

Tommy smiled like he'd won the Lotto. "Well let's get there, Frank!" He buckled his seat belt.

"Just hold your horses there, li'l Joe." Spriz turned in her seat to face Tommy. Tommy eyed her suspiciously.

Spriz laid down the law. "Palatka is more than an hour away. By the time we get there, it will be too late to go bothering strangers tonight. There is no earthly reason for us to go now. That said, it is far too early to go to bed, and inside that barbeque joint, right there, at this very minute, there's *karaoke* about to happen.

Spriz raised her index finger. "Tonight, we shall find a comfy motel room with cable, and we shall watch *Friends* reruns until we fall asleep, and we shall sleep the sleep of the dead until the maid kicks us out, and only *then* shall we go to Palatka. But before all that happens, *you* are going to go through that door and sing these fine people a song. Because they deserve it. And so do you."

The karaoke track book at Reese's Real Southern Bar-B-Cue apparently hadn't been updated in decades. Spriz teased Tommy by telling him she was looking for songs for him to sing like "I Will Survive" and anything from Queen. She knew what she was doing. The teasing relaxed him.

"Yes, by all means," Tommy said. "Please make me sing a song in the key of gay."

Suddenly he said "four one eight!" and slapped the book shut, looked at Spriz and smiled.

"What?" Spriz asked.

"Not tellin'," Tommy replied.

When it was Tommy's turn, he climbed onto the tiny stage to polite but restrained applause from the sixty or so patrons, and a spotlight hit him dead in the eyes, blinding him for a moment.

After a tinkly piano intro, standing in a purple t-shirt, a blue corduroy sportcoat, tight jeans and wine-colored sneakers, Tommy pulled the mic from its stand, held it against his chest, and sang down into it in a deep, seductive voice, a darker sound than Spriz had ever heard him make.

*Take the ribbon from your hair...*
*Shake it loose, and let it fall...*

The room fell silent but for Tommy's aching pleas, until a

WHOOOP! from the back (Carol) broke the spell and briefly sent excited giggles fluttering around the darkened room.

*Help me make it through the night…*

By the time Tommy slipped the mic back into its stand, most women in attendance, and a few men who found themselves a little unsettled and confused by the experience, would have been very happy to help Tommy make it through that night.

To catcalls and loud applause, Tommy stepped down from the stage, his handsome smile spread wide across his satisfied face. Karen put two fingers between her teeth and sent a shrill whistle Tommy's way.

He hugged Spriz, and was about to make his way to the bar when Carol grabbed him in a big bear hug. He caught the gentle scent on her neck: gardenia.

"That was just the sweetest thing I ever *heard!*" Carol gushed. "I'll tell you what, sweet thing, I don't know why Suzy won't have you, but if she don't want you child, you're *mine!*" She kissed him on the cheek and cackled infectiously.

Tommy would never know why he said it. He was happy, he was having fun, he liked this woman, he was beginning to like everyone in the room. He didn't want to start trouble, he didn't want to make anyone uncomfortable. Maybe it was a test. Maybe he wasn't sure what these people were capable of detecting, and needed to know exactly who they thought they were cheering for. He didn't know, and he never would. All he knew was that his very next words to Carol were clear, firm and involuntary:

"I like men."

To his astonishment, there was no hesitation from Carol. No awkward pause, no puzzlement, no discomfort, no searching for the correct thing to say. She responded instantaneously and without reserve, as one can do only when speaking from the heart: "As pretty as you are child, I imagine you can have your pick! You just hold out for the best one, he'll come along! You are a just a *prize*, sweetheart!" She kissed him again. He hugged her tight.

They stayed to close Reese's. Tommy sang three more songs—including "I Will Survive," the highlight of the evening—and Spriz had another plate of pulled pork while getting Vernon, the owner, to tell her the story of each and every precious, rusty hunk of junk he had hung on his walls, all of which he had collected himself.

After midnight, they found a motel with cable, and watched the last late-nite *Friends* rerun on Nickelodeon. Before they both drifted off to sleep, Tommy had outlined a plan for the two of them to move to Starke and give those fine folks their own small professional theatre. He wouldn't follow through. But he wasn't joking.

Right after they turned in their key just ahead of the 11 a.m. checkout time, Spriz noticed an object in Cher's wayback she had not been able to see the night before, in the dark: Someone had put a rusty tricycle back there.


Like Galilee, Palatka is an arts oasis with a checkered past.

Just across the St. John's River from Palatka proper, East Palatka was once the site of Rollestown, one of the many failed attempts to use Florida as a pedestal on which to construct a utopian society. Disney's Stepford-suburb near Orlando, Celebration, descends directly from Rollestown, which was cooked up in 1767 by Denys Rolle, English philanthropist-cum-lunatic.

Rolle peopled his humanitarian plantation with the finest sort he could scrape out of the London gutters, street punks, deadbeats and hookers whose character he was certain could be redeemed through inhuman toil on a sweltering, malarial Florida plantation. To this core population of miscreants he added a few hundred white indentured servants who soon tired of clearing scrub in the oppressive heat and scattered into the virgin frontier, necessitating their replacement, in this utopian experiment, with African slaves.

After the Spanish came back in 1783, Rolle packed up his utopia and his slaves and hightailed it to the Bahamas, where he spent the remaining thirteen years of his life writing the British Crown to demand reimbursement for the losses he suffered as a result of his own colossal fuckup in East Palatka.

About the only other remarkable historical event in or near Palatka was the 1976 founding of the Florida School of the Arts within St. Johns River State College. FloArts makes a paradox of Palatka, disrupting the old lumber town of ten-thousand workaday Floridians with the Bohemian influence of actors, dancers and painters. The place today is much like a cinnamon bun, a slab of hearty if predictably bland bread sprinkled with nuts.

As they entered the Palatka city limits, Tommy was still Googling. He had tried "Bill Sayer, Palatka," "William Sayer, Palatka," "Will Sayer, Palatka," "Guillame Sayer, Palatka," "Bill or William Cayer, Palatka," "Bill or William Psayer, Palatka," and every imaginable variation of the name with "Florida" in place of "Palatka." He and Spriz were in Palatka at last, but had no idea where to go in Palatka.

They settled into a booth at a Waffle House for lunch, picking over French toast, bacon and their options.

"Maybe we're going about this bass-ackwards," Spriz said, unconsciously borrowing a favorite phrase from her Daddy. "Maybe we should go back to the mortician's in Galilee and see if they'll tell us who those old people were at the funeral."

Tommy chuckled, and shook his head. "No, I eavesdropped on their conversations while we were all smoking in the parking lot. Trust me, they don't want his stuff. If they'd found him miraculously resurrected when they got to town, they'd have buried him anyways."

"Obituaries, for Bill Sayer?" Spriz suggested. "Keep us from wasting our time?" She was running out of will. She wanted to go home.

The whole quest was stupid. Brandon Wishart didn't care what became of his belongings, or he'd have signed a will. Why did she care? She'd been wondering that the whole trip. This morning, clearheaded after a good night's rest, she was beginning to see the answer, and she didn't like it.

He had died alone. She feared she would. She'd wanted to believe that Wishart was not really alone, but merely temporarily separated from his loved ones, as she was. She wanted to believe that bonds survive not only distance, but even death, all for her own silly, selfish reasons. She was also aware that she'd engineered herself a cheap excuse to flip her hair and run away from Galilee right when things were getting tense. She was mad at herself for being a sap and a coward.

"If he had a newspaper obit under Bill Sayer," Tommy said, "it would have popped in one of my searches by now. Either Carol remembered the name wrong, or he's not in Palatka, or he's underground. And if he's not in Palatka, there's a million Bill Sayers everywhere else. You wanna start in California and go west-to-east, or go to Maine? I hear Maine's pretty. We could ride a moose."

Spriz sighed. "We could try Palatka Playworks like we planned, and see if they know where he is. We know Brandon worked there."

"It's Saturday, nobody's gonna be there until the show call tonight. But you just know everybody hated him like everywhere else he worked." Tommy clicked his tongue. "I dunno, maybe around six we can…"

He stopped himself short. "Wait, why would *they* know anything? Is this guy an *actor*?"

"Yeah, did I not say that before?"

"NO you didn't say that!"

"Well, okay, but who else but actors did Brandon know?"

"He knew Carol! He knew YOU!"

"Point taken. Permit me to start over, then. Bill Sayer is an actor who worked with Brandon and who was also in the movies, Carol says. My guess is he's Brandon's age, or older."

"Thank you," Tommy said, mock-curtly. "Anything else you're keeping from me?"

"He wears an eye patch and has a distinguishing tattoo on his neck that says 'Born this Way.'"

Tommy started typing furiously on his phone.

"What are you doing" Spriz asked.

"Internet Movie Database," Tommy replied. "If he was in the movies, he'll be there. *Voila mes enfants!*" He got up and came around to Spriz's side of the booth to show her the list of thirty-seven credits under "Bill Sayer" on IMDB.com.

"There's no bio," Tommy observed, "so it's hard to tell exactly how old he might be. But his oldest credit is '68—he's gotta be past sixty. Oh, and he's definitely Florida.

"How ya know?" Spriz asked.

"Look at these credits in the '90s... *Superboy, Keenan & Kel... From the Earth to the Moon...* This stuff was all filmed here, mostly in or near Orlando." Tommy scrolled down through the credits, noting all the movies and TV shows he knew were shot in the Sunshine State.

"Yeah, he was a local film and TV actor, bit parts, character stuff. Orlando used to be a big film and TV town before you showed up. Lots of actors moved down from New York and other places to cash in. They bought houses. Then it all moved to Canada and everybody got screwed. Some people liked it here and stayed anyway, but the work never really came back."

It's a little-known fact that Florida was the original epicenter of American film production, before Hollywood, shortly after the turn of the century.

Like California, it offered the bright days that were essential before effective studio lighting was invented, cheap land, and varied landscapes and architecture that could easily stand in for the Old West, or the Ottoman Empire, or the Hibernian coast.

But unlike California, Florida was easily accessible from New York by steamship and rail when getting to California was still something of an expedition. And New York was where most of the American entertainment culture, actors, writers and production capital then resided. D.W. Griffith, director of the seminal *Birth of a Nation*, made three feature films in Florida.

The first major film studio opened in Jacksonville two years before the first one in California. Some three hundred silent films were made in Jax. By the arrival of talkies, Jacksonville had ceded the industry to Tinseltown for complex reasons involving Great War wage inflation, racial strife and government shenanigans.

The Florida film industry lay largely dormant until the 1990s, when the state made a last-ditch effort to reclaim a slice of the pie, this time through studios near the theme parks in booming Orlando. The selling point for "Hollywood East" was that it was a more affordable place to shoot than Hollywood proper.

But offering no incentive other than cheapness, Florida soon started losing business to even-cheaper Toronto and Vancouver, and for the second time in a century, the Florida film biz fizzled.

"The credits stop after '99," Tommy said. "He might have retired then, or switched to the stage after the TV stuff went north."

"If he was a stage actor too," Spriz wondered, "why isn't he coming up in searches, in reviews and cast lists the way Brandon did?"

"That's an excellent question." Tommy quickly Googled something, then pressed a link on his screen. Spriz could hear the faint ring tone at the other end of the call coming from Tommy's iPhone.

"Yes," Tommy said into the phone, "Kami Carroll, please. Yes, tell her this is Galilee Repertory Theatre." Spriz had no idea Tommy could do a Conrad impression. It was spot-on.

"What are you doing?" Spriz asked, alarmed. As a propsmistress, she'd never had any dealings with the union, which only represented actors and stage managers. But what she'd heard about it made her nervous.

A child of the rustbelt, Spriz believed in unions, but from her perspective the actors union often seemed more concerned with its own well-being than with its members'. Conrad treated actors well regardless of their union affiliation, and yet he always seemed a little older and balder on days he was dealing with Kami Carroll.

A magnificently put-together lady with a religiously yoga-toned body and an expensively Botox-toned face, Kami Carroll was stinking rich. Actors new to Florida made the mistake of assuming that presiding over the local union office must be a lucrative gig, although it was anything but. Kami's designer suits and frequent cruises were heavily subsidized by a generous lifetime alimony settlement from her second husband, a theme park mogul.

She ran the local because she loved the theatre, and because she believed actors required her fierce protection from "predatory" producers, which in her view included even the little, cash-impaired SPTs toward whom Kami's reflexive combativeness was neither always warranted nor always in the best interests of her members.

Though dedicated to the union in principle, Kami treated the job as something of a hobby. Everyone in the Florida theatre community recognized Kami's trademark '67 Mercedes convertible, and many noticed it parked outside Orlando's swankier day spas and boutique clothiers far more often than it was at the union office.

Tommy put his thumb over the mic on his phone. "Relax, Spriz, it's Saturday. They answer the phone in case an actor needs something, but Kami Carroll is on the golf course, I promise." He quickly resumed his amazing Conrad impersonation. "Oh, okay, well, with whom am I speaking? Ah, Greg, of course I remember you, when was the last time you auditioned for us? Well that's too long, we have some things coming up next season you'd be perfect for, why don't you email me your resume again and I'll take a fresh look at it?"

Tommy winked at Spriz. "Say, Greg, I'm trying to find an actor and it's a fuckin' pickle, you know what I'm sayin'? Looks like he sent us his film resume by mistake, and I want to check out his stage credits but I think his stage name might be different. Do you know of an actor who uses the name Bill Sayer on film but a different name on stage? Of course I'll wait while you look it up, I'm grateful for the... Uh-huh? Uh-huh? That's with a Z and a Y? All righty there Greg, you have a good day now, thanks, and don't forget that resume now, y'hear? Okay then." Tommy pressed the End button.

"Well?" Spriz asked.

"Joseph Zayres."

"Never heard of him."

"Let's see if Mister Internet has heard of him," Tommy said as he started Googling again. "Different stage and film names... This guy was Bill Sayer in the movies, and Joe Zayres on stage."

There's overlap, but actors in most U.S. markets tend to be principally film/TV actors—"on camera" actors—or principally stage actors. This schism is abetted by the fact that there are separate unions for each population, though many actors belong to both unions even if they work almost exclusively in one medium or the other.

Actors choose a favorite medium for many reasons: Some are simply more comfortable in front of a camera than before an audience, or vice-versa. Some know they perform better in one place than the other. Some prefer the culture in one over that of the other—and the cultures are indeed different. And some lean one way because there's more money to be made there, in whatever region in which they've hung out their shingle.

But more often than not, the actor doesn't choose the medium, the medium chooses the actor. People tend to have more success in one than the other, and eventually marry the medium that loves them best.

Some actors do attempt a balance of both stage and on-camera work, but doing so is notoriously difficult. Committing to a play means making oneself unavailable for on-camera auditions and gigs for weeks at a time. On-camera actors who try that often find themselves on the wrong end of a spanking from their agents. Missing a play rehearsal to squeeze in a commercial audition will evoke similar violence from one's stage manager. Some on-camera actors split the difference by doing union on-camera work during the day and non-union stage work, which usually rehearses only at night.

Actors designate their professional names through their unions, and because there are two unions (there were three, until the TV and movie unions merged), an actor can have one name for stage work, and another for on-camera work.

When joining a union, an actor can't choose a name that's already attached to another actor in that union. Michael J. Fox famously added the "J" to his name because there already was a "Michael Fox" in the union ahead of him. A young comic actor named Michael Douglas became Michael Keaton because there was another Michael Douglas ahead of him, just as Diane Hall ceded her birthname to the actress who claimed it first and became Diane Keaton.

Some actors with ambitions to work in all media have

discovered that their dream name was available in one union, but taken in the other. They were forced either to forgo the favorite name—which might even have been their own birthname—for a different one that was available in both unions, or to use one name on stage, and another on camera.

"Why would anybody have two names?" Spriz asked.

"Dunno, Suzanne." Tommy held his phone screen out to Spriz. "But here's Joe Zayres' Palatka address. Let's go ask him."

# 14

*The dragon-boy was small, and afraid.*
*And he was mean, just like the Dragon.*
*The boy-boy, though younger, was taller*
*and he was brave, and everybody said he was good.*
*So God chose him to rescue the mother*
*and he armed himself with sword and shield*
*and faced the Dragon.*
*He failed.*
*And the dragon wrought terrible fury*
*on the boy-boy, and stole his mind.*
*A warning to anyone who came between*
*the Dragon and the mother.*

THEY COULD NOT SEE THE HOUSE from the street, which was completely shaded by long arms of ancient live oak trees, their gnarled limbs tinseled with Spanish moss. The high fence that circumscribed the bungalow was similarly overgrown with jasmine and volunteer vines. Spriz and Tommy found the tall wooden gate unlocked, and walked the flagstone path through a front yard of weeds two feet tall to the three cement steps leading to the front door.

The house had no doorbell button. Tommy knocked on the

aluminum frame of the outer screen door.

A reedy yell came from inside, far from the door: "Nobody's home! Go away!"

Tommy knocked again. They'd come this far.

"Go away!" The voice had gotten closer. Suddenly the wooden inner door swung open, and an old man was glaring at Spriz and Tommy through the screen. "You deaf?" he barked, weakly. "You are *trespassing!*"

Hunched and fragile now, the man had clearly been very tall and strapping in his youth. He had wisps of silver hair on his freckled scalp. A clear tube ran from the oxygen canister hanging from his right hand, around the back of his neck and over his ears to two nozzles under his nostrils. His head was shaking slightly, from either rage or palsy. His skin was mottled, and hung from his cheeks and throat in great folds. His rheumy eyes were the color of a cold fog.

"Mister Zayres," Tommy began.

Zayres interrupted: "Let me save you kids some time. I have no money, so there's nothing you can sell me. And I don't love *Jeeesus*, so I don't want to hear the Good News! You got anything else? No? Good!" He slammed the door.

Tommy yelled, "Bill Sayer! You're Bill Sayer, the film actor!"

The door opened again, slowly.

"You're Bill Sayer," Tommy continued. "You were on HBO, and Nickelodeon. You were in a movie with Donald Sutherland. Was he nice? I've heard he's not nice."

Zayres worked his jaw back and forth. "Who are you?" he asked, suspicious.

Spriz replied, "We're friends of Brandon Wishart."

"Yeah?" Zayres replied. "Really. How's ol' Wish these days?"

"He's dead," Spriz replied sharply. The old man's temper had infected her.

"GOOD!" Zayres snapped, and shut the door again.

Tommy knocked, harder this time.

"Don't bother," Spriz said. "We already learned all we needed to know here." She turned and started down the path to the gate. Tommy followed. Behind them, they heard the door creak open.

"I already know he's dead, he died Tuesday," the old man called out, calmer than before. "That all you came to say?"

"I don't know," Spriz called back. "That depends on you."

"Come in," the old man said airily as he shuffled back into the house, leaving the door open behind him.

Spriz and Tommy entered into a dollhouse-perfect living room that did not look like it had changed in any way since the 1970s, right down to the Philco console television, the shag carpet and the yellowed lace doilies under the Hummel figurines atop the TV's simulated wood cabinet. Also on a doily was the perfect beige Bell telephone perched on a tiny table near the front door; Spriz had three just like it in her stores. Spriz noticed family photos framed on the mantle above the brick fireplace. There had been a wife and mother here once, and children, four of them. Grandchildren too.

The lights were off and the windows open, dim light filtering through yellowed lace curtains that breathed in and out gently with the negligible breeze. Spriz didn't see any registers in the ceiling; this house had never had air conditioning installed. There was a faint odor blending notes of spoiled food, urine, liniment and furniture polish.

They made their way through a similarly tidy time-capsule of a dining room. More framed photos lined a mahogany sideboard.

From the dining room they came to a disheveled kitchen with a black & white checkered floor, its iron sink packed with dirty dishes, the countertop strewn with empty frozen entrée cartons. Tommy whispered in Spriz's ear, "This guy has a third name—Miss Havisham!"

Through the back of the kitchen, they entered a small room

that had been tacked onto the house long after it was built. They had to step down six inches into it. At a glance they knew that this was where the sick old man spent all of his time except when he was using the kitchen they had just passed through, or the bathroom that they hoped not to see.

The narrow room was oriented around a worn-out leather recliner that had a crushed pillow on it and a sheet crumpled into the crack between the seat and armrest. Spriz suspected the man spent both his days and nights in that chair, and bet that if she ventured into the bedrooms she would find them tidily frozen in time. A crop of pharmacy bottles sprouted from a side table next to the recliner, and on the floor next to the table sat a phalanx of oxygen canisters, like bowling pins. One of the two small, sliding windows was plugged with an air conditioner.

A small LCD television rested on a plywood stand a few feet in front of the recliner. No doubt some generous soul had brought the TV here out of pity after 2009, when analog broadcasts ceased and the man's old Zenith or Philco portable was rendered mute.

Zayres was seated in the recliner, eyes closed, skin pale and clammy, inhaling oxygen deeply through his nose. He had overexerted himself going to the door to rail impotently at trespassers. Spriz and Tommy gingerly relocated piles of clothes and newspapers out of small chairs and onto the floor, and sat. They waited for the man to recover.

When he finally opened his eyes and looked at Spriz, she said, curtly, "Thank you for asking us in. How did you know Brandon was dead?"

The old man started to chuckle, but the chuckle lapsed into a cough. "He invited me to his funeral," he wheezed. "Wasn't that just so awfully special of him? I declined his gracious invitation. Maybe I'll go next time." He hacked. Spriz noticed the palsy continuing.

She also noticed the ball chain that looped around his neck and disappeared under his shirt. A ball chain isn't jewelry, Spriz knew. The man probably had an emergency call button so he could summon paramedics if he fell and broke a hip. A little button to do the job of the wife who had probably died—and whose decorating and housekeeping had been so effectively embalmed here—and of the middle-aged children who, for some reason, had abandoned their ailing father.

"So," the old man asked with a cruel smile twisted on his face, "Do they know who killed him?"

Spriz and Tommy were knocked back by the question. After a few tense seconds, Spriz said simply, "It was an accident."

The old man laughed, and again the laugh devolved into a coughing fit. When he had caught his breath he said, "A *flat*? A man is killed by a falling stage flat? Don't make me laugh. Ol' Wish finally pissed off the wrong person. Looks like whoever did it got away. There's justice for ya. I'm surprised he lasted this long. I know people who've wanted to see him dead for fifty years."

"Like who?" Tommy asked.

"Take your pick."

The man regarded Tommy. "How do you know about Bill Sayer?" he asked.

"Another friend of Brandon's told my friend Spriz—that's Spriz, I'm Tommy, Hi—she told Spriz about an actor Brandon admired named Bill Sayer, who lived in Palatka. I looked up your credits on the Internet. We couldn't find an address for a Bill Sayer in Palatka so we called the stage union and asked if Bill Sayer had another name."

"Damn union's not supposed to give that information to just anybody," Zayres said.

"I sounded important on the phone. I'm an actor too."

"They give you my address?"

"No sir, I found that on the Internet."

The man looked alarmed. "My street address is on the *Internet*? How did they get it? I don't use the damned thing!" He inhaled through his nose to calm himself, and then puzzled a moment. "So what are you two twits up to? Wish hire you to write his posthumous life story? *Memoirs of the World's Greatest Actor?*"

His use of language was simple and straightforward, but his diction was perfect, and his accent had touches of the refined mid-Atlantic sound favored by actors when playing well-educated Americans. Age and infirmity had taken the punch out of his voicebox, but his strained song still carried the bright resonance that comes from serious training and long experience.

Tommy started, "We were looking for someone—" but Spriz cut him off.

"We're looking for people he owed money to," Spriz said. She wanted to know what this man's deal was, but she had no intention of gracing him with Brandon's things. His bile disqualified him. "He left some cash behind and, well, he made so many people unhappy, we figured the least we could do was settle his debts if we could, not for him, but for them. Did he owe you?"

"That's the dumbest thing I ever heard," the old man said. "You kids need a better hobby. I recommend fucking. That's what I'd be doing right now if I were you. Why don't you go find a back seat someplace and leave me alone."

"How did you know him?" Spriz pressed.

"Oh…" the old man started before pausing, not sure he really wanted to get into it. "Wish and I go way back, way back. We were roommates at the academy in the late fifties. That's the American Academy of Dramatic Arts, the good one, in New York. Wish started early, I came late. We were in the same class but I was six years older. Wish followed me around like a puppy the whole two years. After graduation we shared apartments for awhile. Could never afford to live alone, neither could Wish."

"So you were friends?" Spriz asked. She'd noticed he had yet to use the word, or any synonym for it.

"You think his *friends* are your best bet for people he owed money to? You're barking up the wrong tree, young lady. I never heard about him owing money to anybody. You're wasting your time. And mine. He didn't have any friends."

"Not even you?"

Zayres shrugged. "What's a friend? We were companions, I guess you could say, roommates. I didn't like the bastard more than anybody else, but I didn't mind him, his vitriol rolled off my back. It worked for what it was, another broke actor to share the rent. I found his company convenient. Is that a friendship? You tell me."

"When did you fall out?"

"Who says we did?"

"Why not go to his funeral then?"

"Look at me, young lady. I don't get around too well."

Spriz wasn't buying. "You hated him. Or you were mad at him. I saw it the first time I said his name to you."

The man shrugged again. "Other people," he said.

"Other people?"

The old man's face grew pensive, then sad. His voice softened. "I met Alice. Another person."

"Alice was your wife?"

Zayres nodded. "When it was just Wish and me, somehow I never noticed how... *vicious* he was. Then I started seeing Alice, after Wish and I decided we'd try our luck down here, when the work in New York starting drying up and neither of us had the balls to face L.A. Alice never complained, but I could see it in her face. He said things to her. He hurt her feelings. I never really understood why everybody hated the man so much until I saw him through her eyes."

Zayres cleared his throat. "We had it out, him and me. I told him he had to be nice to my girl, or I'd make sure he never got near her. He acted like he didn't understand either option. So I decked him, and I walked away. Never saw him again. Kept up with his whereabouts through the grapevine, you know.

Always thought one day I would hear some good woman reformed him, or they gave him a pill that put him right, and then I'd ring him up." Regret was peeking through Zayres' practiced hardheartedness.

"The thing is… The thing people don't understand is, I'm not sure Wish knew what he was doing. I know that sounds strange, but I honestly don't think he believed he was hurting anybody. He wasn't mean—I mean, he *was* mean, but he had a screw loose or something, he was missing a gear, I think. I think he was too far gone before they invented Asperger's, but I've wondered if he had that. He made everybody hate him. Who does that on purpose? Who enjoys being hated? The man made no sense."

"He never married?" Spriz asked.

"Never got close. Would *you* give that man a second date?"

Spriz almost asked the man if he'd heard about Carol, then thought better of it. They all sat quietly for a moment.

"How'd you wind up with two names?" Tommy asked.

"Oh, hell, well, I couldn't use my own name. I joined the screen union first and took Bill Sayer. I just liked the way it sounded, I have no idea where it came from. Ten years later I come to the stage union, and can you believe it, there's already a Bill Sayer doing dinner theatre in Illinois. I tried Bill Zayer, but that was taken too. Then Bill Zayres, but he was on Broadway doing *Pippin*. I wasn't getting anywhere screwing around with the last name, so I tried Joe, my father's name, and finally rolled a winner."

"What's your real name?" Tommy asked.

"None of your damn business. You wouldn't believe me."

Tommy smiled. "Try me." He was expecting to hear a Jewish name, or maybe an Armenian one, or one that was hard to spell. Or a girlie name; a man whose real first name was Marion had become a star after taking the screen name John Wayne.

Zayres sighed. "Cagney. My name is James Cagney. My

father was Joe Cagney, and my mother, rest her soul, named me after her favorite movie star. And wouldn't you know it, when I started working, that fat little mick was retired, but still belonged to both unions? The man was just selfish. I had as much right to my name as he had, and he wasn't using it anymore! Not his fault I guess. Goddamned unions. Goddamned cheaters."

"Cheaters?" Tommy asked, involuntarily.

"Yes, cheaters! Cheaters and snakes, all of 'em! You see how I live here, I have nothing, all because the stage union stole my pension!" Zayres coughed so hard he gagged.

"How'd they do that?" Spriz asked, challenging the old man. She'd known his type before. Someone else was always to blame for all his misfortunes.

"Almost thirty years I pay in, and they paid me back for more n' ten years after I hung it up, and then nothing! Zippo! The checks stop coming. So I called the local, and she tells me the fund's broken—she actually said 'the fund's broken' because of the recession—and she says I'm gonna get my money, don't you worry, but it's tied up for now because none of the kids who are still active are paying in, there's no work. Apparently they spent all the money I sent them, and my pension is supposed to be paid by the current members, except they're not working, so I get screwed! I'll get my money she tells me, sure thing. It's going on *two years* now, and not a penny! Cheaters! They know I'm not gonna last long enough to make 'em pay, and then it's all…" He turned the crank on his oxygen. He'd gotten worked up, and needed a hit to come down.

Tommy shook his head. He spoke carefully to the red-faced old man. "Mister Zayres, that doesn't sound right. The fund's not 'broken.' I know about other actors who are living off their pensions plus Social Security, friends who used to work with us at GaliRep."

"Maybe it's time to call the union again," Spriz suggested. "Maybe the national office in New York this time." Maybe the national office would explain that he had already received every dollar to which he was entitled, Spriz thought, and tell the sour old coot to quit bitching. A lot of people worked their whole lives and got no pension at the end. She would.

"Sounds like somebody made a mistake," Tommy said. "You deserve your pension."

"Deserve?" the old man wheezed. "Did I deserve to wind up like this, suckin' factory air out of a steel balloon? Did Wish deserve what he got? Deserve and fifty cents'll get you a cup of coffee. Or used to."

"We'll let you be now," Spriz said, starting to stand. "We appreciate the time. We just… We have some things of his, nothing much, that should go to his family. You don't know where they could be, do you?"

The old man chuffed out a wet cough, then turned his eyes toward the ceiling and thought carefully. He inhaled deeply through his nostrils. "Wish had a brother somewhere, if he's still alive. Seems he said."

Spriz suppressed a little yelp. Tommy smiled.

"Where?" Spriz asked.

"How should I know? Twenty years ago he was in a nursing home. Where was that? Indiana, or someplace."

Tommy looked at Spriz just in time to see that her heart had missed a beat. She looked as though she'd been slapped on the cheek. Her face was burning.

"Where now…? Fishers, I think. Wish put him in a nursing home in Fishers, Indiana, his people are from there, or nearby, he used to say. The brother's in a wheelchair, but that's not why he's there. He wasn't right." Zayres tapped his skull with a withered fingertip. "Brain injury or something, Wish said, I don't really remember. Anyway he's probably six feet under."

Zayres noticed Spriz's expression. "What's your problem?"

"I'm… I'm not feeling well, Mr. Sayers, Zayre, Zayres," Spriz sputtered. "We have to go now." She started out, then turned abruptly.

"Do you have a will? Do your kids know what to do with you and all your things when you die?"

"Yes, I have a will," the old man responded sourly. "I'm grateful for your concern about my affairs. You'll be happy to know I expect the will to be read very soon. They'll all finally visit for that!"

"Bye." Spriz walked quickly through the empty house and out the door.

"Goodbye sir," Tommy said. "I'll see if any of your movies are on Netflix—that's on the Internet, they show old movies on the Internet. I'd like to see your work."

"Sure kid. Don't blink. Oh, and kid?"

"Yeah?"

"Donald Sutherland was a prick."


Back in Cher, still parked in the shade fronting Zayres' house, Spriz was gripping the steering wheel at ten and two and resting her forehead on twelve, the hard plastic cool against her hot skin.

"Hoosiers," she said softly. "Not Hoovers, not Hoopers. *Hoosiers.* I shoulda known." She leaned back in her seat and smudged a tear away."

"Hoopers?" Tommy asked.

"Nothing," Spriz replied. "Something Carol told me. It doesn't matter. I'm not going back."

"Nobody's asking you to go back," Tommy said reassuringly. "And since you decided to spaz out before we got the brother's first name, I'm not sure we have enough to go on, anyway." He was trying to kid her. It wasn't working.

"I can't go back. How can I go back without seeing him? I don't want to see him."

"Nobody's saying you should go back, Spriz. We've done more than anybody had a right to expect already, and Indiana is a bridge too far. But it's a big state. Would you have to see him just because you crossed the state line? Is he anywhere near Fishers?"

"It doesn't matter. I *won't* see him! I can't. I can't go. How can I go to Indiana and not see my father?"

"Would they even let us in, where he is?"

"They'd probably arrest me the minute I set foot in the state anyways."

"From what you've told me, it doesn't sound like you broke any laws. And it's been what, six years? You think your picture's up in the post office? It's not like you've been living under an alias. You've been filing your taxes. You voted, you have a driver's license. If anybody wanted you, they'd have come for you by now."

"I can't go back."

"You're a big girl, Spriz, you can do anything you want." Tommy had recited this aphorism to her many times. This time he added, "Including not going back."

Spriz turned to Tommy, her eyes shining, imploring. "Home! I want to go home! Now!"

"Take us home, Sprizzle Stick," Tommy said softly as he pointed two fingers straight ahead. "Right now."

Spriz turned the key, and pulled off toward Florida Route 20 West.

Neither of them spoke all the way to Gainesville. The car was silent but for the grind of Cher's six crude cylinders and the rumble of her tires. Along the way, Spriz decided she'd had enough of the Florida back roads. When they came to Interstate 75 just past Gainesville, she'd take it. On a Saturday, unless there was a pileup somewhere along the way, I-75 South would be the quickest way home.

And Spriz desperately wanted to be home. She wanted to take a very long, very hot shower, and then crawl into her bed with her ungrateful cat for a minimum of 24 non-stop hours. When she finally woke up, her memory would have reshuffled the events of the last three days into an order that made sense, so she could put them away. It was time to worry about other things, such as how long she could afford to be out of work, and whether anyone in Galilee might want to entice an experienced ex-waitress out of retirement for a few months.

Then there was the little matter of telling the Galilee police her reasons for suspecting that Wishart had been murdered. Since Starke, she'd been mostly successful at pushing that thought out of her mind.

She'd done her best for Brandon, and if she'd failed, she'd still done a damn sight more than anyone else had. There was nothing left to do.

Indiana? Indiana was probably another dry hole anyway. If they'd gone, they'd have discovered that his brother died years ago, or moved, to God knows where. Or worse, they'd find him and he'd tell them he had no interest in his brother's death or his brother's belongings.

If they went to Indiana, they'd either hit another dead end or ricochet onto another goose chase, and she was in the mood for neither. What next? South Dakota? Saskatchewan? She swore she'd never go back to Indiana, and she meant it. She was not going to Indiana.

As proof, she continued on Route 20 underneath the I-75 overpass, and then turned left onto the southbound onramp toward home. Tommy exhaled softly, torqued his body toward his window and started a nap.


Three miles later, Spriz woke Tommy up when she snapped, "Aw, goddammit to HELL!" and veered alarmingly into the far left lane, then into the narrow breakdown lane by the grassy median, where she stopped.

She threw Cher into four-wheel drive, stomped on the pedal and turned hard to the left. She careened down the steeply banked, v-shaped median, which contained no barrier other than a deep, muddy gully at its bottom.

She plowed hard across the ditch at an angle, splashing mud all the way up to Cher's windshield and completely coating Tommy's window, and bounced back up the far side of the median into the opposite breakdown lane, where she stopped.

She shifted Cher into two-wheel drive, yanked the lever that sprayed fluid onto the windshield and flapped the wipers a few times, and then stomped on the pedal again, leaving a smoky skidmark in the breakdown lane before pulling into the passing lane of I-75 North.

His heart pounding, Tommy looked down at his palms, which were bleeding a little. He had balled his fists so tightly that his fingernails had dug little grooves.

# 15

THE TEMP NEEDLE was leaning hard to the right and Spriz had just noticed a whiff of steam, so she pulled over into the breakdown lane and popped the hood. They were on I-65 just inside the Kentucky state line, an hour past Nashville, whose neon interior they had traversed at around midnight.

"Six years I drive around Florida in million-degree heat without a problem," she muttered to Tommy as they examined the engine by flashlight. "I drive north in October, she bursts into flames." Cher's upper radiator hose had sprung a pinhole, and she'd been stealthily spraying antifreeze on her engine since upper Georgia.

From her kit in the wayback, Spriz pulled the special tape she used to wrap failing hoses. It wasn't a permanent fix, but it would probably hold until they got home and she could order a new hose online. She could always get a new hose at an auto-parts store in the morning, but she hated those places.

For one thing, no matter how clearly she demonstrated her mastery of all things Jeep, the men at the parts counter treated her as though she could not tell a muffler from a lug nut. For another, she found parts stores unforgivably overpriced, especially for items like hoses. Simple rubber tubes that probably cost ten cents to manufacture and would fetch no more than a buck if sold as dog toys or plumbing, hoses routinely cost thirty dollars or more at parts stores. She'd sooner starve on the side of the road. She'd wrap this one up good and tight, and order a new hose online for five bucks from home. Assuming they ever got home. She was beginning to have her doubts.

Even after she had patched up the hose, they were stranded until they could top off the radiator. They waited no more than twenty minutes on the dark highway before a kindly young Kentucky State Police trooper gave them a gallon of 50/50 antifreeze from his trunk. Spriz barely understood him, so thick and lazy was his drawl. She had forgotten that driving north out of Florida, one enters the South.

At Tommy's insistence, they checked into the next motel they saw.

By late morning, they had crossed the Indiana state line. Southern Indiana is hilly and wooded, and not altogether topographically dissimilar from northern Florida. Tommy was disappointed to see little farmland for the first few miles after they crossed into the state. In part to distract Spriz, he asked where the cornfields were.

"Common misconception," Spriz explained. "Indiana's a manufacturing state. Welcome to the rustbelt. You'll probably see some farmland coming up in a bit, once the state starts leveling off. But if it's endless fields of corn and beans you want, Iowa's that way." She jabbed a thumb north-westward.

She'd been keeping up a good front, cracking jokes while carefully moderating her breathing, doing her best to stave off the anxiety attack she'd known was coming. She tried to stay focused on her quarry, Brandon's brother, and to push all other thoughts out of her mind.

But other thoughts and terrors intruded, and as Cher pressed deeper into Indiana, Spriz started to itch all over, and to sweat. She cranked up the A/C despite a mild October day. Then she noticed her vision was getting blurry. She pulled over into the breakdown lane, and mumbled "Drive, please," as she got out of the car to go around to the passenger side. Tommy made her repeat herself before he got out.

He had trouble getting the driver's seat to move forward to where he could reach the pedals, and more trouble adjusting the mirrors. The seat and mirrors were stiff, having been in the same position for nearly ten years.

In the passenger seat, riding north on I-65 toward Indianapolis and Fishers beyond, Spriz could not hold back the tide of recollections. In her mind and heart she kept reliving that desperate night six years ago when she had run as fast and as far from this place as she could…

… She had no clothes with her but those she wore. On her meandering way south, she had stopped outside of Nashville to pawn the few pieces of jewelry her mother had left her, for gas money.

Like a sailor on a rough sea, she kept tacking: When on the Interstate to gain distance as quickly as possible, she worried she was too easy to track in her gaudy purple truck, and she slipped off to the back roads. On the back roads, she feared she was too isolated, too vulnerable if caught, and gravitated back to the crowded highway.

She finally settled on a strategy of travelling two hours at a time on the Interstate, then taking a back road crossways until it connected to a different Interstate, then traveling another two hours on the next one. By nightfall she was confident that she had traced such a crisscross-crazy route that no one could know where she was unless they had LoJacked her car—which she knew was a possibility, though before she left she had checked all the usual places a bug might hide in.

From experience, she knew she always had about thirty miles left after the little low-gas warning light began to glow. It had popped on thirty-nine miles back. She was running on fumes. She didn't want to stop, but her cash was gone, and she had nothing left to sell except the truck itself. She breathed deeply, calming herself. There was safety in darkness now, just as there had been nineteen hours ago when she'd silently slipped out of the compound, her heart hammering.

By now she'd put more than a thousand miles between herself and her troubles, as the crow flies. She turned into the next parking lot she saw. Her little truck sputtered and died as she was pulling into a spot. She shifted into neutral and let the Jeep coast the final few feet unpowered.

She knew she was in Florida, but had no earthly idea exactly where in Florida she was. She'd left the Interstate and its helpful green signs hours ago. She had never been anywhere outside of Indiana before, except Chicago as an infant, or so she had been told. And after everything she had witnessed in the past six months, she no longer believed anything her father had told her.

She had pawned her wristwatch back in Nashville, and knew the clock in her Jeep's radio to be untrustworthy and also set an hour early, as the southwestern corner of Indiana intruded into the Central time zone. But the sun had set hours ago. She guessed the time was past nine, perhaps later.

She noticed that the parking lot was nearly full, and wondered what sort of business operated in the adjacent building that could so thoroughly populate a parking lot at this time of night. The hour was too late for peak traffic in retail or a restaurant, but too early for a club. She guessed it had to be a downtown movie house.

Downtowns had police patrols. She couldn't sit in the car all night—she would be noticed, and there would be questions. And she'd been in the car for nearly a full day. More than a thousand miles, crisscross, like an insect evading a boot. It was a warm Florida evening. She could risk getting out to take a walk while she tried to figure out what to do next. She was hungry. And thirsty. And sleepy.

She stepped out of her little truck and stretched her long, skinny limbs. She started down the block, her long legs loping along, her practiced inconspicuousness dialed up to its highest setting.

As she came around the corner, she was startled by bright lights pouring from tall storefront windows. Inside the building she'd misidentified as a cinema, a big party was underway on the other side of the glass. Some people were in formalwear, and most were in dressy evening clothes.

*Florida people are fancier than I'd heard*, she thought.

The partygoers were chatting excitedly and milling about great long tables covered by white linens that glowed against the blood-red carpet. Some tables were loaded with bottles and champagne flutes, others with pastries and hors d'oeuvres.

She'd get kicked out for sure. But they probably wouldn't call the police, and she was pretty sure she could fill her mouth plus her pockets before anyone noticed her.

She quickly gathered her loose hair into a ponytail and secured it with a blue rubber band from her jeans pocket. She stiffened her spine and pulled the heavy chrome handle on the tall glass door. She strode inside like she belonged, her t-shirt and jeans be damned—though luckily she was not the only person there so attired. She noticed several young people at the party wearing black t-shirts and black jeans or chinos—even their shoes were black. *Goths*, she suspected.

The quickest way to draw attention in a situation like this was to look like you were trying to avoid it, she knew. Strut around like you own the place, and nobody looks at you twice. But she also knew the trick would fail eventually, and the clock was running. She headed straight for the table holding the most calories.

Four tiny pigs in blankets went down as quickly as she

could consume them without looking like a stray hound who'd sniffed out an unguarded picnic. She stuffed six more piggies in her jeans pockets. She had some baby carrots, and some celery sticks, and some white and yellow cheese cubes, and she downed half a can of Diet Coke in one gulp. She was starting to feel much better. She was now prepared to be ejected, anytime now would be fine.

But no one seemed concerned by her presence, or even interested in her. Many of the partygoers thronged around a very tall, bald man with a barrel chest. He was wearing a tuxedo and smiling broadly as he clasped hands and patted shoulders. He must be charismatic, she thought.

As she deftly stuffed her ninth little piggy into her mouth, all the lights in the room flashed off, then on again, three times. She was briefly afraid the power was failing. But then the volume of the chatter in the room surged, and everyone started walking in the same direction, away from the tables. If she didn't move, she would soon be alone, and sticking out like a lone buffalo on an empty prairie. She would have to make her way out the door, or join the crowd wherever they were going, and she had to do one or the other right now.

There was food here, and surely a bathroom, which she would need eventually. And it would seem she had been accepted by this tribe, at least for now. She slipped into the stream of people.

The crowd funneled through a set of double doors into a cavernous room, with high banks of seats. On the floor in front of the seats was a rather phony-looking approximation of a *fin de siècle* English drawing room. She'd seen others like it in books. As she entered, she noticed a small padded chair just inside the doors with a basket on it containing a pile of the little pamphlets. Some of the others were carrying the pamphlets in their hands. She did as the Romans did, and grabbed one as she passed.

The river of patrons splashed in all directions as they went for their seats. Two of the young Goths passed her, but instead of heading to seats, they disappeared behind the tall black curtains on the far side of the room. She was about to take an empty seat on the aisle a few rows up when she noticed a few patrons comparing the numbers on their ticket stubs to little brass plates on the tops of the seatbacks. *Shit.* Reserved seats, like at the minor-league baseball games Daddy used to drag her to.

She put her back against the side wall along the stairs and nonchalantly studied the Victorian scenery on the stage below while waiting to see if a seat might be empty for her after everyone with a ticket had sat. She felt as though she were playing the Guinness world-record game of musical chairs.

As the flow into the room thinned and the crowd settled, she noticed two empty rows at the back of one bank of seats. She made her way up the side stairs to those rows, but again leaned casually on the wall, waiting until everyone else had been seated. She flipped through the program she had picked up. The play was *The Importance of Being Earnest*, and the theatre was some place called GaliRep. A leaflet inserted in the program informed her that tonight was opening night.

She had never seen a play before, except for little school plays, but she had read many, including this one. She knew from the drawing room set that Act III was about to begin. Act I took place in an apartment, and Act II in a garden. At last, she had her bearings. She had crashed the opening night gala during intermission, and was about to see the final act of the play. Without a ticket. After stealing a pound of hors d'oeuvres and a Diet Coke.

Soon soft orchestral music came through hidden speakers all around, and the lights over the seats slowly dimmed away to black. The rows near her remained empty. She grabbed a seat near the center of the back row. Then she stood up again so she could extract the wieners from her pockets without destroying them. She sat again, put her precious piggies on a paper napkin in her lap, and settled in to watch a play. It had been a long day. Why the hell not?

Warm morning light rose on the set below her, and goose bumps rose on her forearms. Under the lights, the set looked real—more real than real. It was breathtakingly beautiful, like a full-color dream. Two women were on stage in glorious costumes, all bustles and bows and bright colors. They were chatting in a very arch way. They were funny.

She loved the actors, but she already knew the story, and she kept getting distracted by the tech. Where was the sound of those chirping birds coming from that made it sound so real, so natural? Which of the lighting instruments over her head and along the sides of the stage were projecting that perfect, golden hue onto the set? Where did they get that amazing jeweled *lamp*, o-my-god! How had they made the floor look like oak planks? She had just walked across it, she knew it was painted plywood. What was making the light outside the window look like it was filtered through leaves and branches?

She was inside the world's most mesmerizing windup toy, and she wanted to marvel at it. But also, being mechanically minded, she wanted to unscrew its bottom, spread its parts out on a benchtop and figure out how it worked.

And she wanted never to go back outside. She wanted to stay forever, and wear a bustle and drink tea and trade *bon mots* and gossip with Cecily and Gwendolen in the warm morning light, birds tweeting merrily outside the window…

"Miss? Miss?" She heard a deep voice, and felt a large, powerful paw on her shoulder. She opened her eyes, and saw the blurry silhouette of a huge man looming over her. She pulled herself up quickly onto her bottom and scooted away from him. Where was she?

She was on the floor, in front of the row of seats from which she had enjoyed most of Act III before a full stomach, exhaustion and a darkened room conspired to put her to sleep.

She recognized the man. How was that possible? Everyone she knew was a thousand miles away. Was she dreaming? She started to panic—had someone from Indiana come for her? She was relieved when she realized he was the man from the party, the big man who had been wearing a tuxedo. He had changed into slacks and a polo shirt, a tattoo of the Florida State University Seminoles mascot inked into the skin of his muscular right forearm.

As she pulled herself up into a seat, she saw that the theatre was empty, except for the two of them. The lights were on over the seats, and the stage area was dark but for a single bright bulb topping a tall pole. She apologized, groggily.

"That's okay," the big man said, taking a seat beside her. "Although my audience falling asleep hardly bodes well for the run."

"What time is it?" she asked.

"Eleven or so," the man replied. "The play ended a half-hour ago. I wouldn't even have known you were here except I was in the dressing rooms making sure the lights were off, and on my way back out across the stage, I heard snoring."

"Sorry," she said, blushing.

"It wasn't loud," the man said, smiling. "But I don't like climbing up here. I've got a trick knee."

"I'm really sorry. I was up all night last night. I didn't mean to fall asleep. It was *wonderful.* I really loved it. I wish I had seen the first two acts." *OOPS.*

"You didn't have a ticket, did you?" the man asked. His tone was not accusing. He had a kind face.

"No. I'm sorry."

"Don't worry about it," he said, with a wave of his hand. "As it is, we give away lots of free tickets to opening. We 'paper the house' to get word-of-mouth going, to sell the rest of the run. Half the people here tonight didn't pay. One more comp won't hurt us. Just promise to tell your friends you liked it, okay? What's your name?"

"Suzanne," she said too quickly. That was dumb. She shouldn't have used her real name. Too late. So far she had run out of gas, fallen asleep in a crowded public place, and given out her real name to the first person who asked. She was starting to suspect she sucked at being a fugitive.

"I'm Conrad, Suzanne, I run this place," the man said, offering his hand. Suzanne shook it firmly, and smiled back. "So, what was *wonderful* about our little play?"

"*Everything!*" Suzanne gushed. "It was just so… pretty! And the actors were funny, and the costumes were gorgeous! I've never seen anything so magical before."

Conrad almost blushed. Most of the people who gave him compliments worked hard at sounding erudite rather than elated. This Suzanne was refreshing.

"There were some things that confused me though," she said, and then she regretted saying it. One does not critique the first real play one ever sees, especially a play one did not pay to see, especially a play one saw less than one-third of.

"Well, it's nineteenth-century English culture," Conrad said pleasantly. "Even I don't always understand all of it, and I directed it."

"Oh, yeah, that must be it," she said, relieved. Then she got mad at herself. She wasn't stupid. She wasn't going to play stupid. "No, it wasn't that, I understood the play perfectly. Your actors are good and loud. It was the furniture."

"The furniture?" Conrad chuckled.

"Well, yeah." She pointed down at the drawing room set, lit dimly by the glow of the single bulb on a pole. "That wicker chair is gorgeous, and the red velvet pad makes it look fancy enough to go in the drawing room, but this is what, 1895 in Northern England, right? They weren't so much with the wicker, especially not in the drawing room, but you could have used it for the garden scene in Act II. And the wood floor is amazing—it looks like real planks even though I know it's just paint, right?—but these people wouldn't have let it show, they'd have covered every inch of it with fancy carpet. And that sideboard looks good there, but that's really a dining room piece, not a drawing room piece."

Conrad couldn't believe his ears. The set had looked perfect to him before. Now he wanted to set fire to it and watch it burn. "Anything else?"

"Well, I wasn't gonna say anything, but Merriman, the butler? He kept bringing things in on a pewter tray. These people wouldn't feed a dog off pewter, only silver would do. You can polish up a steel tray to make it look just like silver, you know, I've done it."

"How do you know all this?" Conrad asked, still not sure whether he was insulted or impressed.

"Oh, my Da—my father used to have a pawn shop, more of a junk shop, really, but we had lots of antiques, and he had lots of books in the back about how to tell when and where a chair or a table was made, or how to spot a fake. I pretty much grew up in back, that's where I went every day after school, and those books had cool pictures and a lot of history and stuff in them. When I got older my Da—my father, my Daddy, I call him Daddy, it's a thing, I'm adopted—he taught me more about furniture and décor, especially how to fix stuff and restore it so it looks like new. He took in a lot of busted-up antiques on the cheap, and him and me polished them up and sold them for five times what he paid." She was surprised at how freely she was talking to this man. It wasn't like her, and it wasn't smart. But for some reason she trusted him instantly. And she hadn't seen a really kind face for so long.

"Your father taught you all that?"

"Well, yeah," Suzanne said sheepishly. "But I mean, that's stupid, I just notice stuff like that, I'm sure nobody else cared. The play was really really great."

Conrad regarded Suzanne for a moment. "Are you free during the day?"

"I guess. Why?"

"We have internships starting week after next. All the spots are taken already, but I have an idea for a new one, just for you. You interested?"

"What's it pay?"

Conrad laughed. "Not a god-damned penny, it's an internship. But you'll learn a lot and you'll have fun, and you'll be a part of this theatre, and down the road you can turn that into a paying job, maybe here, maybe someplace else."

"Thanks. I'll think about it."

"Fair enough. Come back when you're ready. It was nice meeting you, Suzanne. I need to lock up now." With a wry smile, he added, "I'll relay your concerns to the propsmaster."

When they both stood up, Conrad was briefly surprised by Suzanne's height, but to his credit all he had to say on the subject was, "Oh!"

Suzanne used the ladies' room before Conrad locked up, and then she and he parted ways on the sidewalk in front of GaliRep. She walked for several blocks in the opposite direction from him until she was sure he was long gone, then she doubled back to her Jeep. She'd have to risk spending the night in the back seat. In the morning bright and early, she'd see if anyplace within walking distance needed a waitress. If she got a job right away and it left her enough spare time, she might look into that intern thing. That place was cool.

She still didn't know the name of the little city she had reached at the end of her rope, or whether she would like it. But that didn't matter now. This town would have to do, until she put some cash together. For now, here was home, wherever here was. In a few weeks, she'd move on, maybe further south to Miami. Miami sounded like the sort of place a girl could disappear, if she needed to.

The propsmaster at GaliRep predated Conrad's time as AD, and was overpaid, incompetent, insubordinate, and protected by an angel on the board. Two months from now, Conrad would go to the board with a proposal to save the company a bundle by firing that lazy bastard and letting the new props intern who was such a fast learner do the job unpaid. Even the propsmaster's protector could not refuse such a sweet enhancement to GaliRep's bottom line.

Suzanne did all the props for almost a full season, unpaid, while also waiting tables. Sometimes she spent upwards of 60 hours at the theatre on a week when she also waitressed for 30 hours or more. Conrad couldn't have been happier—until the day Maisy marched into his office and gave him hell for exploiting that poor girl and demanded that he put her on staff like the previous propsmaster, even if he had to pay her slave wages. Maisy picked her battles, and so almost always won the ones she picked.

Spriz would never learn about that encounter, and never know how much she owed Maisy. But she knew what she owed Conrad. She'd known all along that he was exploiting her, and she never cared. On a night when she feared her life was over, he offered her a new one, a better one. She owed him everything.

# 16

GASPING FOR BREATH, the old man lay prostrate and alone on the checkered linoleum of his kitchen floor.

The clear tubes trailing from his oxygen canister were nearly at the front door, a good thirty feet away. He had not enough wind left even to crawl or drag his body beyond the kitchen and along the old pine planking. His field of vision was beginning to narrow. For many months he had known he would die soon. He had not expected to die like this.

He craned his head just high enough to see through the kitchen doorway to an old framed photo of his Alice. It was up on the sideboard in her parlor, which he had faithfully kept just the way she liked it for every day of the thirty-eight years she had been gone. He would see her again, only moments from now. When his focus drifted to pictures of the kids, he remembered their gift, a gift he vaguely recalled having received ungratefully.

With great effort, he tugged at the ball chain around his neck until a pendant the size of a hopscotch stone popped out of his shirt collar. He turned the pendant in his hand and pressed a big button with his thumb as hard as he could, though he well knew it was already too late.

From the speaker in the base unit up on the countertop, he heard a woman's voice ask if he was all right. He lifted his head an inch toward the box, and with all the breath he could gather, he wheezed, "The bitch… she killed me! She killed me!" He dropped his head to the cool, dirty linoleum.

As he heard the woman's reassuring voice report that an ambulance was on the way and then ask him what he had meant, James Robert Cagney, 79, also known as Bill Sayer, also known as Joe Zayres, father of five, let loose his closing line, a death rattle.

# 17

A BEDROOM for nearby Indianapolis, little Fishers had its own public library, which held a copy of its local white pages, in which they found no listing for any Wishart at any address. Tommy had already confirmed as much on his iPhone before they arrived, but Spriz believed in libraries.

The nap Spriz had taken in the passenger seat for the last two hours of their journey had worked like a medically induced coma, enabling her to sleep through the worst of her anxiety and leaving her not only refreshed, but determined. The hell with the white pages. She had an idea.

Spriz approached the desk and asked the librarian, "How would we find the addresses of all the nursing homes in Fishers?" The young librarian blinked twice at Spriz, said not a word, and picked up a tiny yellow pencil to scribble something on a tiny scrap of paper. She handed the paper over the desk to Spriz, and finally said, "That's the only one, in Fishers. It's just up the road. If you want more choices than that, you'll have to go to Indianapolis."

"This will do fine, ma'am," Spriz replied, and she smiled. The librarian was the first real Hoosier she'd spoken to in six years. She seemed familiar. More reserved than a Floridian, straight to the point, but pleasant. She didn't realize until this moment: She had missed these people. Some of them.

"Wishart, sir, W-I-S-H-A-R-T." Spriz spelled the name for the desk clerk at the home.

"First name?" the tiny man asked with a curt smile. *Damn.*

Quickly, Tommy said, "Poppy. His name is Poppy, that's what we've always called him, everybody called him Poppy. He's our great uncle. Our cousins say he's here."

"That's a nickname," the man said sourly. "You don't know your great uncle's first name?"

"No," Spriz replied. "For Pete's sake, do you know *your* great uncle's first name?" She'd forced herself back to Indiana, and she was not going to be thwarted now by a clerk who was taking his job too seriously.

"Yes, I do, young lady." *Damn.* Time to tack.

"Do you have more than one Wishart here?" Spriz asked.

"No." *Aha! He's here!* Spriz thought. The nasty little man was just testing their qualifications.

"Then what difference does it make?" Spriz argued impatiently. "The man here named Wishart is our Poppy and we want to see him, please. He's our great uncle. He'll be happy to see us. Our cousins say he's lonely. They say somebody interferes when visitors come to see him."

The little man arched an eyebrow at Spriz. She stared him down. Somehow in that moment, they reached an unspoken accord. The man's expression softened. "Have you seen him here before?" the man asked. He was no longer resistant, but his tone said that although he had decided to go along, they had best not think him their fool.

"No," Tommy replied, honestly.

"Then it's been a very long time. He's been here for twenty-two years. Forgive me, but I'm sure you were children when he arrived, and I doubt he would recognize you now. I'm sorry to tell you, he probably wouldn't recognize you if you'd seen him yesterday. As I said, he's been here a very long time. Johnny will take you to him." The little man called to an orderly. "Please take these two to Mister Wishart's room."

As they turned to follow Johnny, the desk man said, "Please keep your visit brief. Sam tires easily. Johnny will collect you in fifteen minutes."

Spriz prayed the fifteen minutes would be worth the thousand miles.

As Johnny led them in, he rapped twice on the open door and called out loudly, "You got visitors, Sam!"

Sam Wishart's cozy room was tidy and smelled faintly of disinfectant and soup. Besides a rolling tray table for meals in his room, he had only a bed, a nightstand, two small armchairs, and a bureau, all antiques that had probably arrived with him twenty-two years ago.

A half-dozen framed photos decorated the top of the bureau, the velvet-covered backs and stands of the old frames reflected in the mirror. On the nightstand stood a water glass and an old digital clock, the kind where the numbers make a little *clack* as they flip over. No books or magazines anywhere… Spriz guessed that Sam didn't read, or couldn't. She also noticed that the hi-gloss wall paint was the same pale green as theatrical glow tape, and wondered whether the room glowed in the dark.

The overhead fluorescents and his bedside lamp were off, but the soft autumn light from the big window was enough, perfect for an afternoon nap.

Sam was seated in a wheelchair at the window, facing away from the door. He'd been woken up by Johnny's knock, and took a moment to come-to before slowly turning his wheelchair around.

"Visitors?" Sam asked in a rasp, incredulous.

"Poppy!" Tommy squealed. He hopped over to the old man, bent and embraced him about the shoulders. Sam smiled broadly and patted Tommy on the back. Spriz turned and saw that the orderly had gone. She quietly closed Sam's door and took one of the armchairs as Tommy released the old man and sat in the other.

"Kids!" the old man exclaimed hoarsely, still smiling. He waved his shaggy head from side to side. "I don't believe it! How did you find me?" He was indeed very happy to see whomever he thought they were.

"Hi Sam," Spriz said, smiling back. "It's good to see you."

He was unlike his brother in almost every aspect. By the creases and liver spots on his face and hands, he looked much older than Brandon, but knowing how well the actor had concealed his age, Spriz was disinclined to presume too many years separated the two. Though hidden by baggy trousers, his legs were visibly skeletal, atrophied for decades. But the length of his narrow torso, now hunched over, revealed that he had once been tall and rangy, where his brother had been stocky and muscular before turning to flab.

Sam had a thick mane of silver hair, where his brother had been bald. He was open and gregarious where Brandon had been pinched and officious. His wrinkles traced the path of a lifetime of grinning, where his brother's face bore downturned marks carved by his withering scowl.

But Sam's eyes, his grey-blue eyes, deep-set and wide apart, were Brandon's, as much in color as in shape. There was no mistaking the DNA in those eyes, even magnified as they were by his Coke-bottle eyeglasses. Their tortoiseshell frame was from the '70s, Spriz guessed, or perhaps even earlier, she wasn't sure. Eyewear was more Maisy's domain.

"My goodness me!" Sam said, looking Spriz up and down. "You're all grown! My god but you're your mother, through n' through. I bet people tell ya that a lot, huh?" Spriz was growing uncomfortable with exploiting the man's confusion, convenient though it was.

"Sam, Mr. Wishart, my name is Suzanne, and this is Tommy. We're friends of your brother."

The old man puzzled a moment. He started to smile, then his face fell, and his papery lips started to tremble. He wheeled backward a full step. His grey-blue eyes watered, and his mouth twisted into a frown, almost a child's frown. "Bran is dead," he muttered. "Bran died."

Tommy looked at Spriz. "Next of kin," he said sadly. Brandon must have left the funeral home instructions to notify Sam.

"Are you dead?" the old man asked honestly. "Your friend is dead. Dead friends, dead friends…" He drifted, dropping his face to his chest. Spriz and Tommy exchanged glances. They didn't know what to say. Suddenly Sam lifted his face again and smiled broadly, residual tears on his bony cheeks but his eyes dry. "Kids!" he exclaimed. "I don't believe it! My goodness me. Little Laurie, tall as a tree!"

"Yes Sam, Brandon died," Spriz said. "I'm very sorry. When did you last see him?"

"My god but you're your mother, through n' through!" Sam replied. "She's dead too, course. Ever' body's dead now, I guess. Shame."

Tommy spoke slowly. "Sam, did Brandon visit you, or write to you?"

"Shrimp!" Sam cackled at Tommy. "You too, baby Charlie, Bran is a shrimp like you. Tell him alla time, he gets so *mad*, I laugh! Bran's dead, did you know?" He was still smiling.

Joe Zayres had warned them that the man "wasn't right" and mentioned a brain injury. By Sam's dementia, Spriz was tempted to diagnose Alzheimer's, but she reminded herself that Sam had required the care this place provided long before he became a senior citizen.

She had been laboring not to stare at Sam's head, to avoid offending him, but took a good look now.

Spriz had noticed that something was wrong with the man's skull. Even under the silver mane, she could still see that it was... lumpy, asymmetrical. There was a broad place on the side of his head that was flat. A birth defect? A tumor? Spriz couldn't help recalling the bloody divot in Sam's brother's skull. No, something had hit this man, a long time ago, something hard and heavy. So hard and heavy it might have killed him, but he had survived.

Something—or someone—had hit Sam Wishart so hard in the head that he had not been able to think straight, or move his legs, ever since.

Brandon? She didn't want to think him capable of it, but maybe. That might explain a few things. Zayres said Brandon had put Sam here. Did that mean Brandon was Sam's attacker, or his caretaker? Or both?

She didn't want to be rude, but she'd come a long way and her fifteen minutes were ticking. "How'd you hurt your head, Sam?"

To her surprise, he understood her question without elaboration, and chuckled and rubbed his scalp, tousling his silver mane. "Oh, this old thing? That was the Dragon, li'l Laurie. Got bit." He winked at her.

"The dragon?" Spriz asked?

"Oh c'mon, cousin Bran ne'er told you 'bout the Dragon?" Sam asked, offended and suddenly lucid.

"Sure he did!" Tommy interjected. "Brandon talked about the dragon. But he said you were the expert. Brandon told us to ask you about the dragon."

"Dragon hurt us, Charlie. But don't be scared, he's gone now."

"What happened to him?" Spriz asked.

"Bran's dead. Thought you knew."

"No, not Brandon," Spriz said. "The dragon, Sam, what happened to the dragon? Why did he bite you?"

"Brandon happened, li'l Laurie. My big brother is a hero,

sure you know. Slew the Dragon!" *Good god,* Spriz thought. *Brandon was the older brother!* Sam was a little brother, grown old too soon in this place for old people.

"Bran don't like to tell the tale, so I tells it. Used to tell me stories he made up when I was a baby. Later made 'em up together and we acted 'em out to mom. But this one's mine, Bran lit out. Starts a long time ago."

Sam craned his face closer to Spriz, and with his fingertips he beckoned her and Tommy to come in closer, as if he were about to share a secret. He smiled slyly.

The story poured out of Sam like old wine from a barrel, and word-perfect. He had trouble putting together new sentences, but this story had been imprinted on his engrams, long ago, and he knew it by heart. Maybe his mom had helped him get it right.

"A long time ago, a Dragon had stolen a family not his own," he whispered ominously. "A mother and two boys. The Dragon kept them in his rocky, steamy lair. Where no one could hear them cry. They cried in pain. They cried in fear. They cried for rescue from the Dragon!"

His rusty voice rose and smoothed out as he pulled himself up tall in his wheelchair. Sam had some of the actor in him, like his brother. "The Dragon raised the two boys in his own image. One boy became a *dragon.*" He growled the word as he raised his arms like wings. "The other remained a boy." He dropped his arms, and then touched his fingers to his chest and smiled gently. "The mother remained a mother, with a mother's burden. The mother wept beneath the Dragon's claw." He sniffed, and his old eyes began to glisten.

"The dragon-boy was small, and afraid. And he was *mean,* just like the Dragon. The boy-boy, though younger, was taller, and he was brave, and everybody said he was *good.* So God chose him to rescue the mother, and he armed himself with sword and shield and faced the Dragon." Sam paused, his mouth turning down again into his child's frown. "He failed. He failed, and the dragon wrought terrible fury on the boy-boy and stole his mind. A warning to anyone who came between the Dragon and the mother."

Sam paused and puzzled for just a moment, and then found his place. "Now the Dragon was afraid the mother would try to escape. So one day, he went to steal her mind, too. The boy-boy wanted to protect her, but he couldn't. He couldn't stand up anymore."

Sam's frown flipped up into a fierce, toothy smile. "But because he was part dragon, the dragon-boy had magic in his blood! He stepped between the Dragon and the mother. The Dragon reared back on his hind legs and spread his wings, and took in a big, big breath. He was about to burn the dragon-boy to a cinder."

He raised himself up in his chair again. "The little dragon-boy cast a spell, and grew himself. He threw back his shoulders, and they grew. He puffed up his chest, and it grew. He stretched his body taller, taller, taller! He stuck out his chin so the Dragon would see that he was not afraid! He grew and grew until he was as big as the dragon, then bigger! The dragon-boy took in a big, big breath, and he let forth the loudest, deepest roar ever heard in the kingdom. People heard it for miles and miles around. They thought the world was ending." He looked carefully into Tommy's eyes, then Spriz's, making sure they had understood him.

"When the Dragon heard the dragon-boy's terrible roar, he shrank. He shriveled. His wings collapsed into skinny little arms. The fire in his lungs went out, with a tiny puff of smoke—poof!—until he was just a man, a mean little man, scared to death of the dragon-boy. The little man ran away, never to return. He was never a dragon again." He slowed his last few words as though about to say, "The End," but then he played the surprise coda.

"The grateful mother went to kiss the dragon-boy—but it was too late. Because he wasn't worthy, God had cursed him.

He was all dragon now. There was no boy left. And his curse was that no one could touch him without getting hurt. So he flew away from the mother and brother, out into the world, then into people's dreams, where he could breathe his terrible fire and roar his terrible roars, which he loved to do."

He closed his eyes, and recited his last few lines as though praying: "The new dragon's mother and brother forgave him for becoming a dragon, because only they knew why he had done it. They went on, together, and lived happily ever after. They knew, one day, the new dragon would do something to please God, and God would let him be a boy again, and he would come home." Sam held the moment in suspense, then added softly, "The End." He gave a small, dignified bow from the waist. Tommy clapped a little.

"A family not his own," Spriz said to Tommy. "Sam, the man, the dragon, he wasn't your father? What happened to your real father?"

Sam shrugged. "Dunno." He yawned.

The light in the little green room had grown dim as the October afternoon was running out, and Spriz and Tommy both jumped a little at the sound of Johnny's voice. "Time to go, y'all. Sam needs his rest."

Spriz turned to Johnny, and spoke a little too sharply. "He seems okay t' me!" Johnny smiled sheepishly at Spriz, then nodded toward Sam. When Spriz turned back, Sam had dropped his chin to his chest. The old boy-boy snored softly. Spriz put a hand on his arm. Then she and Tommy got up to go.

"We'll come again, Sam," she whispered before heading to the door. She meant it.

As she passed Sam's bureau, Spriz stopped. An old photo had caught her eye, and she picked it up. A mother and two boys, standing on a wooden porch against a front door. One boy was tall and lanky, standing casually with one hip thrust to his left and smiling broadly. The other was shorter, and handsomer, with a broad chest and eyes that burned. He seemed to be daring the camera to knock the chip off his shoulder. Spriz wondered who was taking the picture.

Between the teenage boys stood a mother. She was smiling shyly, but her eyes were sad. She was bone-thin and had long, stringy hair spilling about her shoulders. She was much taller than her teenaged sons. By the relative height of the doorway behind the mother, Spriz could tell that she was nearly six feet tall, maybe taller. A lump formed in Spriz's throat. *Brandon Wishart, you weren't all dragon. You were a sentimental fool.*

# 18

OUTSIDE SAM'S ROOM, Johnny turned in the opposite direction from the lobby.

"Where we goin' ta?" Spriz asked. Tommy looked at her curiously.

"S'posed to take you to see Ms. Curtain," Johnny replied dutifully.

As they followed behind Johnny, Tommy said quietly to Spriz, "You talk different here."

"What?"

"Since we got here, your accent is different. You sound like them. And I never heard you say 'Fer Pete's sake' before today, ever."

Spriz smiled and said, "Well 'scuse me fer livin'!"

"See? Quit!"

Johnny led them around three corners, past dozens of little patient rooms, until they arrived at a cramped office with the name A CURTAIN on the open door. Exactly as he had done at Sam's door, Johnny rapped twice and called out loudly, "You got visitors, Miz Curtain!"

He departed as a round, sixtyish woman with glasses stood

up from behind the desk and motioned for Tommy and Spriz to take the two chairs facing her desk. "I'm Amanda Curtain, VP of finance here. Please, have a seat." Spriz realized being a vice president wasn't as glamorous as she'd always imagined.

Amanda waded in cautiously. "Please first understand that I know you are not in any way responsible parties for Mr. Wishart. You're a great niece and nephew, I take it? But you're the first family visitors he's had in many years. I was hoping you could assist me in addressing the problem of his outstanding balance."

"His bill isn't being paid?" Spriz asked.

"Well, much of his bill is covered by state and local funds. We're quite good about filing all the necessary paperwork to ensure that our guests receive all the benefits they are entitled to, Social Security, disability and so on. But as you know, this is a private facility, and government sources cannot cover the total cost. Since Mr. Wishart's arrival, the remainder has been paid by his brother, a Mr. Brandon Wishart. Those payments have stopped, we don't understand why, and the account is seventeen months past due. And I understand now that the brother has… passed on? Mr. Wishart, Sam, has his mail read aloud to him. I'm sorry for your loss."

"Thanks," Spriz said, and Tommy nodded. "But he died just the other day, not yet a week ago, even. The bill is seventeen months past due?"

"Just the part paid by his brother, but yes. We've been mailing letters to Brandon Wishart at all of the addresses we have on file, all places where he was employed, apparently, and he has never responded. We've been writing to him for well over a year, and nothing, and now…. We have no other relatives on file, no one else we can speak to about someone taking over his affairs. We know Sam had no wife or children. His mother had been his sole caretaker until she passed away, and then he came here. Can you suggest anyone at all whom we might contact? Is it possible he had any other siblings?"

Spriz and Tommy sat silently for a moment. Spriz finally said, "I can't think of anyone off the top of my head, no, but we'll ask around the family and see if we can get someone to contact you. What happens if his bill isn't paid?"

"This is difficult," Amanda responded carefully. "Sam is an old friend to everyone here, and we've been looking into other resources of course, charities and such, in hopes of making up the shortfall. But we are answerable to a parent corporation. We cannot simply carry him. We might be able to write off the past-due balance, but if someone doesn't step up for his monthly care going forward, if we can't find another source of revenue, I'm afraid he'll have to move to one of the state facilities. They're perfectly adequate, he would be well looked after. But he won't get the same level of care there, and we're worried about how he may react. He doesn't like change. This is his home."

Spriz reached into her pocket and produced a roll of bills in a rubber band. "Here's two hundred and sixty-five dollars cash. Please apply it to the past-due balance. How long do we have?"

"Another month. Two, perhaps. But I'm afraid two hundred and sixty-five dollars does little to—"

"Just take it, please," Spriz said. "It's Sam's. His brother left it to him. I'd like a receipt."

As Spriz was about to climb into the driver's seat, she noticed that Tommy wasn't getting in, and she looked back to see him standing at the rear hatch. She walked behind the little truck. "What?" she asked innocently.

Tommy turned his eyes to Cher's rear window, and to the brown leather satchel in her wayback, behind the rusty tricycle. "You know what."

"What's he gonna do with it, Tommy? He won't know or care what it is. Johnny'll stash it in a closet, and when Sam passes on they'll give it to Goodwill." With her index finger, she started lazily drawing a cartoon dragon in the dried gully-grime on Cher's rear window. "Might as well just give it to Goodwill ourselves as leave it with Sam."

"Yes, we might as well," Tommy replied, frustrated. "The trail ends here, Spriz. There's nobody else to give it to. Can't we get that stuff out of the car so we know we're really done and we can really go home? I mean, I could use a little closure about now, couldn't you?" If Spriz missed her chance to leave Brandon's belongings here, Tommy feared, she'd never let it go, she'd nag at herself over what to do with the bag 'til kingdom come, and drive Tommy quietly mad.

"We're going home, I swear, straight home. The quest is closed, unreachable star reached, blah blah blah. But I'm not leaving his things here. I'm taking the fastest road out of Indiana and that bag is coming with me. I know what to do with it now, and pinky-promise I swear on my cat it requires no more road trips." She extended her left pinky, which Tommy playfully grabbed with his own.

"Just out of curiosity, what are you gonna do with it?"

"Del Close, Tom-boy. Del Close. Came to me while I was thinking about Sam's skull." Tommy nodded his assent.

"Now you gonna get in the damn car," Spriz snapped, "or are you and Sam gonna pick out curtains together?" With a flourish, she finished drawing the flames coming out of her dragon's mouth, admired her work for a moment, and then returned to her seat, fully prepared to drive away without Tommy if he didn't get his ass in the car this time. He did.


From Fishers, the road south toward Florida was not the fastest way out of the Hoosier State. So Spriz made a beeline east at Cher's top flatland speed of 69 MPH and entered Ohio only eighty minutes later, heaving a great, long sigh as she crossed the state line. She'd survived. She was proud of herself. Maybe she could cross Indiana off the short list of things that frightened her.

She hung a right at Dayton, and just past Cincinnati she reacquired I-75, the way home.

Halfway through Kentucky, Spriz heard Tommy inhale, and she braced herself. She knew she'd been sharp with him back at the home, and she figured Tommy had been silently working up a good emotional retaliation for a few hundred miles. He was about to bitch about her, and in a moment she'd have to make up her mind whether to bitch back or make nice, a choice that would depend on how much whatever Tommy said next pissed her off.

To her surprise, Tommy hadn't been fuming about Spriz all this time. His mind was on something else.

"Why stop paying Sam's bill?"

Spriz rolled her eyes. *God save me, the Hardy Boys are back.*

"I mean, why, Spriz? Nothing changed. He pays for twenty years and then suddenly stops? Doesn't seem like they had any contact, Sam can't have done anything to piss Brandon off. The man worked about the same number of gigs year-in, year out. He didn't suddenly buy a house or a car, nothing on his end changed. I mean, he made pretty much the same money every year, I saw his tax returns. Oh—wait!"

"Wait what?"

"His tax returns!" Tommy awkwardly clambered between the front bucket seats to get to the back seat. Spriz kept her hand on the gearshift to prevent Tommy from accidentally kicking them into Park.

His knees on the back seat, Tommy leaned into the wayback and unzipped the satchel. He extracted the oaktag accordion folder containing Brandon's papers. He turned and sat, propped the folder in the seat behind Spriz, pulled out Brandon's tax papers, and began flipping through the returns and attached statements.

"What are you looking for?" Spriz asked as she wrenched the stiff rearview mirror into position to see what Tommy was doing.

"There was a thing in his taxes, statements about… Yeah, here, dependent care deduction. Brandon claimed a dependent care deduction every year for the money he spent on Sam." He quickly flipped through the pages. "Every year for the five years here, including last year and the year before. Same amount every year. Spriz, he still took the full deduction even after he stopped paying the home!"

Spriz was confused. "He cheated on his taxes? He stops paying Sam's rent but takes the deduction anyway? That lawyer, Ryan Mountain, he said Brandon had tried to cheat before."

"Yeah, you told me he also said Brandon made so little money that cheating got him nothing. And if he made the same money but stopped helping Sam, he'd have plenty of extra cash, so why risk it all by cheating on his taxes? They check this stuff, you know, the nursing homes have to file statements about what they get, and the IRS compares it to what people claim. My mom makes the same claim for my grandpa and she gets a statement from the home every year, and what she puts on her tax return has to match what's on the statement. He'd never get away with it. I guess maybe he wouldn't know that."

"He'd know it by now!" Spriz interjected. "Tax-filing time was what, six months ago? If he filed a bogus return six months ago—wait, or even a year and half ago—wouldn't they already be all over him, garnishing his wages or whatever they do?" She thought for a moment. "Ryan Mountain would have known. Ryan went over his taxes, he would've stopped Brandon from doing something so stupid."

"He didn't stop him," Tommy said from the back seat, shrugging. "Spriz, it's right here. And the lawyer signed where it says 'Preparer.'"

"What if he sent the money, but somebody at the home is stealing it?" She thought about the difficult little clerk at the front desk.

"Maybe," Tommy replied. "But they'd get caught. I can't

see a way to do this that doesn't lead to an investigation that's gonna catch somebody, whether it's Brandon or somebody at the home. And it's not really that much money. I mean, it's a lot of money to you and me, but is it enough to go to jail over?"

"Brandon was getting old. Old people forget things. Could he have just forgotten to pay Sam's bill?"

"The home was sending him letters, everywhere he worked. And the statement for his taxes is still gonna show him that he didn't pay. Besides, didn't you say he had no bank account? He couldn't write a check, he had to be paying Sam's bill by direct debit from his paychecks. The theatres he worked at were sending the money on his behalf, they had to be. This is so weird."

"He coulda cashed his check and mailed a money order," Spriz countered.

"Occam's Razor!" Tommy declared.

"Okay, okay, please don't Occam's Razor me," Spriz replied. "Do me a favor, call that lady and give me your phone?" Over her shoulder, she handed Tommy Amanda Curtain's business card from her pocket.

"Her name is Amanda!" Tommy snapped. "God, Spriz, you met her to-*day*!"

"Whatever, just dial."


Amanda told Spriz she'd heard Brandon had used various means over the years to pay Sam's bill, including mailed money orders. But for the four years she'd been holding the purse strings, and she believed for at least a few years before that, Brandon had simply made his pension benefits payable directly to Sam's account, by electronic deposit.

The amount paid was about forty dollars more every month than was due, so the home transferred the overage to a separate, personal spending account in Sam's name, which Sam had never touched. From time to time they had reminded Sam that he had a little money, and asked if he wanted help shopping for anything or to go on a trip, but he was never interested.

Now Sam's personal account was empty. The home had scavenged it, with Sam's permission, to cover the first four months of nonpayment from Brandon. Sam's room and board were seventeen months past-due, but the payments from Brandon's pension had actually stopped twenty-one months ago.

Tommy was puzzled after Spriz finished filling in Amanda's side of the conversation. "Pension benefits? He wasn't retired yet."

"I thought the same thing," Spriz said. "But she seemed to know what she was talking about. Soon as we get home, we need to talk to Ryan Mountain again, and see if we can get anybody at the union to gab about the pension. Maybe by finding out what happened to Brandon's money we can figure out a way get Sam's bill paid from now on."

Tommy chuckled. "When exactly did you adopt Sam Wishart?"

"Couple hours ago," Spriz replied. "Inherited him from his mom."

Seconds later, streams of thick steam came billowing through the gaps around Cher's hood.

# 19

BY FLASHLIGHT in the breakdown lane on I-75 South, Spriz confirmed that the same radiator hose had sprung another leak, a gusher this time. As she wrapped more tape around the new bad spot, she said, "This hose has had it. We'll be lucky to make it home."

"Why is it always Kentucky?" Tommy asked.

"We need antifreeze, or water at least," Spriz said as she closed the hood. "I think the last exit had a truck stop. Can't be more than two or three miles. Not too cold out here, be nice to stretch our legs. We've been in the car for… how long?"

"I don't know anymore," Tommy replied. "Is it still October?"

Spriz carried the flashlight as they backtracked to the last exit, less to light their way under the nearly full moon than to make themselves more visible in the breakdown lane lest some idiot run them down pulling off to take a leak. Tommy carried along the empty jug from the antifreeze the nice trooper had given them the previous time they had broken down in Kentucky. If they couldn't score some coolant at the exit, they could probably still find a way to fill the jug with water.

"Twenty-one months is pretty close to two years," Spriz said as she kicked an RC Cola can out of their path.

"Yeah? So?"

"So you and me know another guy who says he started having trouble with his actors' union pension about two years ago. What do Brandon Wishart and Joe Zayres have in common besides belonging to the stage actors union?"

"They're old," Tommy replied. "They know each other, or they used to. Nobody likes them." He thought for a moment, then said quietly, "One is dead, the other will be pretty soon, I think."

"Lotsa theatres closing in Florida," Spriz mused. "Who loses out when the theatres close?"

"Us!" Tommy replied. "Actors, crew, everybody. Our friends. The audience."

"Who else? Who only makes money when producers pay actors? Who besides the actors goes broke when actors aren't getting paychecks, the ones that have their dues deducted automatically?"

"The *union*? What are you thinking?"

"Dunno yet," Spriz answered. "But think about this: Which is more likely, that Brandon suddenly out of nowhere decided to abandon his brother after twenty years for no reason, or that the union somehow fouled up his pension and he never found out about it so he could make them fix it?"

"He *did* find out about it, Spriz. The letters from the home. And I'm still not convinced the money was ever really coming from a pension. The man was still working!"

"I know, I know. I still find it easier to imagine the union screwing up than Brandon screwing Sam over. Soon as we talk to Ryan Mountain I wanna talk to Kami Carroll, too."

"Good luck with that," Tommy said. A warning.


The lights at the last exit turned out to be a roadside tavern, not a truck stop, and the only antifreeze in sight was in the window of the mom & pop gas station across the street, which closed early on Sundays.

The night had not seemed cold at first, but by the time they reached the crowded tavern, Spriz's teeth were chattering. She took a stool at the bar to warm up while Tommy and the jug went in search of a spigot. The Kentucky bartender asked Spriz what she'd have.

"You got hot cocoa?" she asked as she stood her flashlight on the bar, lens down.

The bartender didn't bat an eye. "Instant."

"Make it a double."

As the bartender turned away, Spriz sensed the empty stool next to hers acquiring an occupant. Then she caught his odor, a vapor of gasoline, sweat, cigarettes and whisky. Her chilly body felt the heat radiating from his, but the sensation was not comforting. The tiny hairs on the back of Spriz's neck stood up. She swiveled her stool to turn her back to him, and tried go invisible. *Please don't. Please please don't.*

"Well if you ain't a tall drink o' water," the man said. Spriz thought *how original.* She ignored him.

"Aw, c'mon, don't do me like that, sweetheart. Just bein' friendly. Buy ya a drink? C'mon."

Spriz ignored him. *Please stop.*

With his steel toe, the man slowly turned Spriz's swivel seat to where her body was facing his. She looked up. He was bigger than she'd have guessed from his high voice. His hair was long and dirty, some of it in back clutched in a queue by a brown rubber band. He wore a hunting vest over a baseball shirt, tight jeans and greasy workboots. He slurred his words. He'd been there awhile.

"One drink, pretty girl? Just one? I don't bite." His lips curled into a crooked smile. "Lessen you want me to."

Spriz ignored him. *Please stop.*

"Aw, c'mon. You'd like me once you got know me. Just

one li'l drink? Pretty please? Whattaya like to drink, sweetheart?
What's yer name?"

The bartender dropped a fat mug of cocoa in front of Spriz
and wandered back away without stopping for payment or to
ask if she wanted to start a tab. Apparently Swiss Miss was on
the house.

Spriz picked up the heavy mug, said "Excuse me" as
blithely as she could manage, and swiveled her seat away from
the man. She scanned the crowded tavern for another empty
seat.

"HOT CHOCLIT?" the man roared, loud enough that
other patrons heard him over the jukebox and turned to look.
"Hot choclit with a spurt o' whip cream on top!" He leaned
over as though peering down into the mug, and bust out
laughing. "Oh no, baby—look like you lost your cherry!" He
cackled at his joke, then lowered his voice and took a shot at
tenderness. "Aw sweetheart, yer *cold*, lemme warm you up
some."

Reaching with his hand this time, he swiveled Spriz's seat
his way, causing Spriz to slosh cocoa on the bar. A trickle of hot
cocoa ran off the lip of the bar and scalded Spriz's thigh
through her jeans. She quickly put down the mug and picked up
a napkin to blot her burning leg. The man slid forward in his
seat, closing the gap between himself and the pretty girl.

"*Stop!*" she commanded. The man smiled. He moved his
hand from the swiveling seat to Spriz's hip. Spriz batted his
hand away, jumped to her feet, grabbed her steel flashlight in
her left hand, cocked her arm, and took aim.

"*DAVID?*" A squeal came from behind Spriz.

"David!" Tommy chided as he inserted himself cozily
between Spriz and the man. Spriz checked her swing and let her
arm drop, the flashlight at her side.

"So who's Miss Skin and Bones?" Tommy asked the man
loudly while looking Spriz up and down. "Hmmm?"

Tommy turned, bringing his face close to the man's, and

whispered to him, looking deep into the man's bloodshot eyes. "One night, that's it? No call, no reply to my messages? That night *meant* something to me, David! I know it meant something to you, too! I could feel it!"

Other patrons couldn't hear what Tommy was saying, but they were watching. From the corner of his eye, the man saw them watching. He looked as though he could not decide whether to scream, run away or throw up. He settled for mumbling, "I don't know you, man," turning away and hunching over the bar. He pulled a smoke from his shirt pocket and lit up.

Tommy grabbed Spriz's arm. "His loss." With his free hand, he picked up the jug of water from where he had set it on the floor; he had filled it in the men's room. As he pulled Spriz toward the door, he said, "Let me tell you what you just missed, girlfriend."

Tommy knew Spriz would need some quiet time to settle, so he indulged in a cigarette and waited patiently for her to speak first as they made the cold walk back to the little truck.

Finally Spriz said softly, "You always tell me I'm a big girl. I didn't need rescuing."

"Who says I was rescuing *you?*" Tommy chuckled. "But since you're such a big girl, here." He held out the jug to her. "My arm hurts." Spriz traded Tommy the flashlight for the jug.

"You okay?" Tommy asked gently.

Spriz sighed. "Cocoa burned my leg, and now I gotta walk around with this big sticky stain on my jeans." She sighed again. "I really wanted that cocoa."

Spriz saw her long shadow suddenly leap up in front of her, and felt a bright light burning behind them. They turned and saw high halogen headlights bearing down on them from a vehicle running in the breakdown lane.

Tommy and Spriz turned together and sprinted up the lane

away from the lights. After three steps Spriz dropped the jug.

They knew they couldn't outrun a motor vehicle, but neither could see an alternative to running up the breakdown lane. To the left, cars and trucks were flying by at eighty miles per hour. To the right was a wide steel guardrail, and beyond it, blackness.

As the headlights gained on them, they could see nothing between the rail and the treeline. That likely meant a steep embankment down to a deep gully with God-knows-what at its bottom. Tommy tried to shine the flashlight into the gully as they ran, but in the bobbing beam they still couldn't see what lay past the rail.

The headlights were coming close, the growl of an engine growing louder. In a moment they would have to choose between leaping over the rail into the black gulley or running out in front of a semi on I-75 and counting on a miracle. They were out of breath. Tommy was falling behind.

When it was not more than fifty feet behind them, the vehicle halted. Spriz and Tommy ran a few more steps, then stumbled to a stop. They couldn't have run much farther anyway.

The engine was humming and the headlights were still glaring, but Spriz's eyes had adjusted enough for her to see that it was a pickup truck that had been following them. The passenger-side door swung open, and Spriz saw the silhouette of a small man step out, with some sort of short, thick rod in his hand.

From the driver's side stepped the man from the bar. Spriz knew him from the outline of his vest and the queue of hair atop his silhouette. The men came together at the front of the pickup, then began walking slowly toward Spriz and Tommy. Neither man spoke. Spriz then noticed that both men were carrying clubs of some sort. The short stick with a knob on the end she marked for a tire iron, the other one may have been a prybar, she guessed.

Spriz grabbed Tommy's shoulder and pulled him beside her. She squared her body to face the men, and stood tall. "Stand up!" she told Tommy, who straightened up and drew back his shoulders.

Her face toward the oncoming men, Spriz whispered, "Try to push them into the road. We can't take them, but maybe the traffic can."

From behind them, Spriz and Tommy heard the crackle of tires on gravel as a bright light suddenly drew up on the two men, making them clearly visible. The men stopped in their tracks. Spriz looked at their faces, and was surprised to see their expressions registering not homicidal rage, but fear.

Spriz and Tommy quickly turned their heads to find out what was making all the light behind them, and saw the bright beams of another vehicle coming to a stop in the breakdown lane, facing opposite the pickup. It must have made a hairy turn somewhere to get into the breakdown lane, because it was pointed against the flow of traffic. Spriz turned back toward the men just in time to see them climb into the pickup and peel onto the highway, gravel spraying from their rear wheels. Out his window, the driver flipped them the bird as the truck sped away.

"What *is* it with pickup truck guys and the finger?" Tommy said breathlessly.

Spriz turned again to see a trooper walking purposefully toward her and Tommy from the other vehicle, a Kentucky State Police patrol car. She lost her balance and started to fall— Tommy caught her by the elbow. She felt dizzy, she tasted metal on her tongue, and she realized she was sweating, despite the chilly air.

She had never been in a fight, not a real one. Now she'd almost had two in the last half-hour, including a barfight and a roadside brawl. Her Daddy had taught her to avoid fights. "Let 'em call you a coward," he'd told her. "If you ain't hurt, and you ain't hurt nobody else, it's a good day."

The tall, stout trooper approached Spriz with that iron authority unique to veteran highway patrolmen. "Susan Prissy?"

"That's me," Spriz replied. *Whatever.*

"Ma'am, I have instructions to take you and anybody who's with you to the state line."

"Wait!" Tommy interjected. "Did you see those two guys who just drove off?"

"Yessir."

"They were after us!"

"They injure you?" the trooper asked flatly. Spriz and Tommy shook their heads.

"They drive off with somethin' belongs to you?"

"No," Spriz said firmly.

"Then I got no interest in them tonight," the trooper concluded.

Spriz's heart was settling down. Time to put the rednecks behind them and deal with whatever fresh hell this was about to be.

The trooper started over: "I have instructions to take you both to the state line. There we will be met by Tennessee authorities who will continue to escort you to  the Georgia line. Georgia will hand you over to the Florida Highway Patrol at the Florida line."

Tommy was more frightened now than he had been thirty seconds ago when he was about to have his brains beaten in. "WHY?" he asked. A young trooper had now exited the patrol car and was coming up behind the older one.

"Sir, I'm not authorized to answer questions. I'm here as a courtesy to the Florida Highway Patrol. My instructions are to get you two to Tennessee. They'll tell you in Florida what they want with you, I imagine."

Spriz asked, "Are we under arrest?"

The older trooper huffed, looked down, and shook his head. He really did not want to have a conversation about this. "Ma'am, no ma'am, you are not under arrest at this time."

"Then we can go?" Tommy asked.

"Sir, ma'am, my instructions are to ask you to come voluntarily. Should you refuse, my instructions are to arrest you. Now, it's your business, but if it was me, I'd volunteer."

Spriz started to ask, "What about my—"

"We know about your car, that's how we found you. Officer Robey here will follow us in your car—come take her keys, Billy—and other officers will pass it along, state to state." Spriz pushed down the anxiety she was starting to feel at the idea of multiple strangers driving Cher. She knew it was the least of her problems right now.

She handed her keys to the young trooper. "You'll have to put water in the reservoir before you can drive her. I dropped a gallon jug by the guardrail a little ways up the road." She pointed north with her thumb.

The young trooper sighed and looked up at the older one. The older trooper said, "You heard the young lady, Billy, run get her water and then we'll all go back and get her truck." Trooper Robey glumly drew a flashlight from its belt holster and trudged north.

The veteran officer held out an open hand to Tommy. "We'll stow that torch in Miss Prissy's car, son."

As Tommy surrendered the flashlight, Spriz asked, "Can you at least say where we're going once we get to Florida?"

"No ma'am, I can't."

"Well then," Spriz said casually, "we unvolunteer. Arrest us."

The trooper scowled.

Tommy chimed in, "Yes, and please read my rights to me very slowly. I'm not very bright. I may insist on having some things explained to me a few times before I'll confirm that I understand them. Should we find somewhere to sit down?"

The trooper looked away for a moment to the traffic zipping past them, and then to the moon beyond. *Always on a full moon*, he thought. *That's when I get 'em.*

He turned back to Spriz and said softly, "Florida HP is gonna deliver you into the custody of the city police in someplace called Palatka for questioning, and that's everything I know, Scout's honor. But I didn't tell ya that, y'hear?" He winked at Tommy.

Through the long relay in the dark back seats of four different police cars, Tommy made little jokes now and then to break the tension, but Spriz said not a word.

*Six years*, she thought, over and over. *Six years in a hot basement in Florida and I was safe. But I had to go to Indiana. I had to go, and now they've got me. I'll never see Galilee again.*

Only when they had almost reached their destination did Spriz think to borrow Tommy's phone and leave a message for the only lawyer she knew.

# 20

Spriz was disappointed by the tiny interview room. There was no trick mirror on the wall through which cops could spy on a suspect. No video cameras, at least none that she could see. No chrome ring on the small table or any of the chairs for cuffing dangerous suspects to the furniture. The fluorescent lights overhead did not flicker or buzz ominously. The little room was comfortably air-conditioned and carpeted, and painted a pleasant peach. It was about as intimidating as a treehouse, and a good deal less depressing than the GaliRep conference room. For not the first time, Spriz realized *Law & Order* had lied to her.

The appealing design of the Palatka PD's interview room was only the latest surreal touch in a whole night of surreal events. Spriz was exhausted, confused, and depressed, and too tired to be scared. For six years, she'd known a night like this was coming. *Let it come.*

Tommy was right: she'd broken no law. But she'd been told so many times that it wouldn't matter whether you'd broken a law. If the government saw you as a threat, they could lock you up for as long as they wanted to. They had ways.

They had vague charges like "conspiracy," and "sedition" which enabled them to put you away simply for knowing the wrong people, or for being in the wrong place at the wrong time or—worst of all—for refusing to tell them what they wanted to know. Homeland Security and the FBI had broad, secret powers to deal with threats—real or imagined—however they saw fit. Rub them wrong, and it wouldn't matter whether you'd so much as jaywalked. They'd label you an "unlawful combatant" or a "material witness" and stick you in a hole. There would be no trial. You'd just disappear.

Spriz had been in the wrong place. She had known the wrong people. The government would charge her with something—anything—to compel her cooperation. Not getting it, they would throw away the key. Of that she had been assured, again and again. Such was the inevitable fate of those foolish enough to leave, they told her.

Someone had seen her and recognized her, or more likely, her car. They had people everywhere. Somebody had seen her, and had made a call, and now here she was. Six years in a basement. She should have stayed there. And now she'd dragged Tommy into it. She was so *stupid*.

Her new life was over. The end of her old life was about to begin.


Spriz sat alone in the little room, uncuffed, for a half-hour, and despite the severity of her predicament, or perhaps because of it, she was getting more sleepy by the minute. Just as she was considering laying down in a corner to catch forty winks, Detective Vicky Farrell came through the door and introduced herself.

Petite, buff and barely older than Spriz, the detective greeted Spriz with an air of professionalism and unassailable confidence. Spriz recognized the type: She was a young black woman who had risen into the upper echelon of a man's profession in a good ol' boys' southern city. She no doubt had to be very, very good and very, very tough, and she carried herself in a practiced way that said, "Underestimate me at your peril." She wore pressed professional slacks and a white button-down, turned up at the cuffs.

"So, Ms. Prizzi," she said as she took a seat on the other side of the table from Spriz, flipped open a manila folder and began leafing through some papers, "would you mind telling me why you fled the state?"

"Where's Tommy?"

"Mr. Gustafson is fine. You can see him shortly. Now why'd you flee?"

"Flee?" Spriz replied, innocently.

"All right. Leave. Why did you leave Florida, Ms. Prizzi?"

Daddy's voice whispered in Spriz's ear. "When all else fails, give the truth a try. You can always go back to lyin' if the truth don't work."

Spriz said, "We were visiting the brother of a friend who died."

"In Kentucky?"

"No, he died in Galilee."

Farrell made a curt smile. "My apologies for not being more precise. I meant to ask whether the man you were visiting was in Kentucky."

"Indiana. We were back in Kentucky on our way home. Hence my objection to 'flee'."

The detective seemed confused. "You were on your way back?"

"The Kentucky police picked us up on I-75 South. That's Florida-bound. They didn't tell you?"

The detective was silent for a moment while she looked at her papers. "You could have doubled back. You don't exactly follow straight lines." She flipped to a page in her folder. "We retraced your steps until you fled—sorry, left—left the state.

Let's see here… Up to Perry and Monticello, *back* to Perry, over to Gainesville, to Starke, Palatka, then Gainesville *again*, all in two days, and then we find your tire tracks making an illegal U-turn across a grass median in the middle of I-75. You wanna tell me what that was about?"

"Had my head in the clouds and I took the wrong exit," Spriz shrugged. "I guess I knew I wasn't supposed to make that turn, but without any snow one gets so few chances to four-wheel it in Florida. You want the fine by cash or check?"

Farrell looked at her papers again. Spriz could tell by the stillness of the detective's eyes that she wasn't actually reading, but playing for time. Finally Farrell asked, "What's your relationship to James Cagney?"

The detective had changed the subject. Score one for Spriz. "Who?"

"James Cagney. Of Palatka."

"Oh!" Spriz remembered. "Um, no, I don't have a relationship to James Cagney. I only met him yesterday, or the day before… What day is it today?"

"It is very early Monday morning."

"Day before yesterday, then, Saturday. But I met him under a different name, Joseph Zayres." Spriz wondered what the old man could possibly have to do with this. Perhaps the detective was just warming up, or setting Spriz up to get snared by a contradiction in her timeline. Or could it be that Joe Zayres was the one who turned her in? *Is the world that small?* Stranger things had happened. Today, in fact.

"Yes, we know about that name. Any idea what he's hiding from?"

"Hiding?"

"In my experience, a man with three names is hiding from something, usually something not good."

"Three names?" Spriz had forgotten one.

"He has an expired license in the name James Cagney, his phone and other utilities are under Joseph Zayres, and he gets checks in the mail made out to Bill Sayer. An honest man doesn't live like that."

Spriz suppressed a smile. "That's true. He's an actor. His real name is James Cagney, his stage name is Joseph Zayres and his screen name is Bill Sayer. It happens. The checks are probably small residuals for TV shows Bill Sayer was on."

Farrell cleared a little catch in her throat. "Well now," she said plainly, covering a note of embarrassment in her voice, "I guess that explains that."

Spriz saw the opening, and grabbed it. "Happy to satisfy your curiosity. Now it's really late and I'm really tired, so why don't you tell me why I'm here."

"James Cagney is why you're here, Suzanne."

"Yes? *And?*"

"And he's dead."

The detective's words rocked Spriz's soul. *This can't be a coincidence. It can't be!* Then the aftershock hit: *This isn't about Daddy.*

"Dead?" Spriz asked.

"Yes. We have reason to believe he was murdered. And we have reason to believe a woman killed him."

"How'd he die?" Spriz asked.

"You tell me," Farrell replied.

"You think *I* know?"

"A neighbor saw your car parked in front of his house Saturday, mid-day. She says you came out of Mr. Cagney's house alone, followed a minute later by a man we assume was Mr. Gustafson. You and he talked in the car for a few minutes, and then drove away. The neighbor says she saw you clearly and you were upset, crying. And now Mr. Cagney is dead."

Spriz's head was spinning. She was feeling bad for the old man, still adjusting to being off the hook for Indiana and in big trouble for something she'd never imagined, and involuntarily calculating how Joe Zayres' death clinched her hunch that Brandon was murdered. "Tell me how he died. Please?"

Detective Farrell looked hard at Spriz for few moments, then said, "Okay. Somebody moved his oxygen out of reach. He was found two rooms away from it, and obviously couldn't get to it in time, we're not sure why yet. But the coroner confirms the C.O.D. as asphyxia."

"How do you know it wasn't an accident?" Spriz asked.

Farrell smiled a detective's I-know-something-you-don't-know smile. "Because the old man called for help, and he told an operator, and I quote, 'She killed me.' And because there are a lot of fingerprints on the oxygen canister. Some are his, some belong to a home health aide who visits, and two sets belong to workers in the place that fills the canisters. There's one set unaccounted for. Little fingertips, probably a woman's."

"She got him upset," Spriz said softly, sadly, almost to herself. "He needs his oxygen when he gets upset. She must have gotten him all worked up and then separated him from his tank."

The detective leaned back in her chair and eyed Spriz suspiciously. "But you don't really know him, you say?"

Spriz sat still, silent.

Farrell placed her palms flat on the table and looked into Spriz's eyes. "I can't compel your prints unless I arrest you, and I'm not quite ready to do that, not yet. But if you volunteer your prints, we can eliminate you right now. What do you say?"

Spriz smelled a rat. "What if I wiped off my prints? What if I wore gloves? What if I never touched the canister, but instead maneuvered Joe away from it? How does you having my prints eliminate me?"

The detective sighed. "It doesn't," she said, deflated. "But you were there, and fully capable of moving that canister or moving him. That's opportunity and means. Plus, you fled the state immediately after. I'm derelict if I don't check you out for motive."

"Go crazy," Spriz said. "Have a ball figuring out my motive for murdering a man I only met two days ago for half an hour—who was frankly about a week away from dying anyway, rest in peace—and then hanging out in front of his house for awhile afterward before 'fleeing,' and *then* coming all the way back to Florida to get caught instead of staying four states away, where I supposedly fled to. And while you're working on that, think about this: An old friend of Joe Zayres—sorry, James Cagney—was also … this is Monday? … was also murdered last Tuesday, a week ago tomorrow, just a few hours' drive from here, in Galilee."

Farrell was interested. "Who?"

Spriz read Farrell the Cliff's Notes, from the flat falling on Brandon to learning that Lanford had clubbed him on the side of the head—though she revealed neither Lanford's name nor the name of the city where they found him. She wasn't sure how much she'd say if the detective pressed for details.

"He can't have been killed by the flat, and he can't have been killed by the hammer," Spriz concluded. "That leaves murder. It's the only explanation. And now another old actor, one who knew Brandon, winds up dead under similarly mysterious circumstances only a few days later? We have a serial killer in Central Florida, Detective Farrell, and he hates actors. Or she." Spriz waited for a response from the detective, who took a good ten seconds before speaking.

"You do realize that if what you're telling me is true, the prime suspect in both murders would have to be the person who knew both men and was in both cities at the time of the murder? Namely you." She took a breath. She changed tack.

"It's worth looking at, Ms. Prizzi, but it's thin. I'm not one to assume coincidence, but that's what this looks like to me. Not that it matters, but just FYI it's not a serial killer until there's at least three bodies. As for proving Mr. Wishart was murdered, you've got no means, and no real motive, and about a hundred people in the dark with opportunity. And even though they're wrong all the time on TV, in real life medical examiners and coroners aren't actually stupid. They are almost always right. If yours says it was an accident, I'd put all my chips on accident and let it ride. But none of that gets us to the heart of the matter of the moment: Cagney is dead, a woman did it, and you were the last one to see him."

"Fine," Spriz said pleasantly. "I was there. That's all you have. You don't even have a guess about motive, and no proof I did it. If you did, I'd be under arrest. You don't even know that I was the last person to be there. I'm just the last person who was there at a moment when the neighbor happened to look out the window, yes?"

The detective looked straight at Spriz. She shifted in her chair.

"*Yes?*" Spriz saw something in the detective's face. "Yes! There was someone else, wasn't there?"

Farrell's manner changed subtly. She dropped her Bad Cop affect, and began talking to Spriz like an equal, a partner.

"Did you see a vintage sports car near Cagney's? Small, with a narrow wheelbase?"

"You're saying there was someone else."

"Nobody saw another car. But…"

"But?"

"There are tire tracks overlapping yours where you parked. An unusual size, a size that shows up mostly on older coupes, foreign."

Spriz folded her arms. Another car. They had nothing. Why was she here? "No. I didn't see another car pull into the space after us, I didn't see a little foreign sports coupe in the area. Can we go?"

Farrell inhaled, and almost asked Spriz another question. But she stopped herself. She stood up. She looked down and shook her head a little as she gathered her papers into the folder. Then she said simply, "Wait here," and turned to go.

As Spriz watched Farrell walk the three steps to the door, she noticed fleetingly how nicely the detective's slacks cupped her firm derrière. She looked away and chalked the feeling up to exhaustion.

Just before opening the door, Farrell turned to Spriz. "I'm sorry about all this. It was not my decision."

"Make it up to me," Spriz said impatiently. "Tell me where Tommy is."

The detective answered apologetically. "He's fine, really, I promise. He's talking to Sergeant McGill, who's just trying to get some background. It's standard procedure, it's nothing."

Spriz saw a hint of a smile sneak onto the detective's lips. "What?" she asked.

"Oh, I saw the sergeant getting coffee right before I came in here. I don't think he enjoys talking to your friend." She opened the door.

"A 1967 Mercedes 250SL convertible!"

The detective stopped.

Spriz said, "The tire tracks. Could they be a 1967 Mercedes 250SL convertible?"

"I don't know," Farrell replied. "Did you *see* a 1967 Mercedes 250SL convertible?"

"No." It was the truth.

The detective closed the door and locked it behind her.

Spriz sat there, more confused than ever. They knew she didn't do it. They'd known all along. Why was she even questioned? Why drag her all the way from Kentucky for nothing? Why lock the door if she wasn't under arrest?

She worried about Tommy.


The ancient sergeant furrowed his brow above his spectacles. "All right then, let's try talking about something else. What were you doing in Kentucky?" he asked pointedly.

"I was in *Kentucky*?" Tommy replied. He looked surprised.

"Yes. You know you were."

"*Seriously?* Kentucky. No, that doesn't sound like me."

"Of course you were in Kentucky, son. That's where they

picked you up."

"Are you sure about that? I think I'd remember if I was in Kentucky. I really think I would."

The sergeant flipped through the papers in his folder. "It says right here! Kentucky highway patrol picked you up on I-75, north of Corbin. You don't remember that?"

"No! How would I know where I was in relation to Corbum? I wasn't the one driving."

"No! you don't remember being picked up by Kentucky—" He stopped himself, inhaled quickly, and then exhaled slowly, through pursed lips. The sergeant continued calmly, measuring his words. "If Kentucky State Police picked you up, then you were in Kentucky. They're not allowed to pick you up anyplace besides Kentucky, you know."

"Exactly!" Tommy said. "So if they *did* pick me up someplace else, who has more reason to lie, me or them? I'd think a sergeant would be a little more suspicious of what he was told!"

The old sergeant paused. He took a handkerchief from his pants pocket and began cleaning his glasses, which did not need cleaning. "Why'd you flee the state?"

"Which state we talkin' 'bout now?"

"FLORIDA! Why did you flee Florida?"

"Oh, gosh, where should I start? The politics mainly, I think. The humidity. The big bugs, the tourists. Case you hadn't noticed, Florida blows."

The sergeant looked up at Tommy, wounded, and set his eyeglasses on the table. "I was *born* here, son. I grew up here. Florida is my home."

"Oh, me too."

The sergeant restored his glasses to his nose, and returned to his papers. After a moment, without looking up, he said quietly, "A man should have a little more respect for where he comes from."

"Couldn't agree more," Tommy said. "You're the one who

can't stop talking about Kentucky."

Spriz waited in the little interview room, which was looking less and less pleasant the longer she was in there. She wondered if the sun had come up yet.

Though her body was spent, her mind was racing. She was relieved that none of this was about Indiana. She had made it there and safely back to Florida and nobody was the wiser.

She felt bad about Joe Zayres, and how rude she'd been when she left his house. She was certain whoever murdered Joe must have murdered Brandon as well—was it really a woman?—and she was pretty sure the murders were tied up with the pensions, if for no reason other than that the pensions were the only mutual object out of place, besides the bodies.

She had put her head down on the cool, hard table and was very nearly asleep when she heard the door unlock.

"Suzanne?" a man's voice said. She turned her head to face the door, but kept it against the table.

She saw the sideways image of a man in a suit and tie: tall, trim, and very handsome, with gorgeous honey hair trimmed and highlighted by a skilled, no doubt costly stylist. He reminded her of the pile of Ken dolls Daddy once had in the bargain bin.

She lifted her head as the man came into the room. His hands were empty. He carried no folder or notepad. Standing on her side of the table, he offered his hand: "Michael Ames. You can call me Mike." Spriz shook the man's hand. He had a good, friendly grip and his skin was well moisturized.

Mike took a chair next to Spriz, and asked if she was thirsty, or hungry. As he apologized for the hour, he smiled sheepishly at Spriz and ran his fingertips through the perfect sweep of feathered hair above his forehead.

*Oh, my…* Spriz thought. *This boy is goooood.* All her senses went on high alert.

"I hope detective Farrell wasn't too tough on you. These small-town cops—"

"She was perfectly pleasant," Spriz interrupted. "We swapped recipes. So you're what, Good Cop?"

The bogus shy smile again, followed by the hair sweep. This clown could even blush on cue. "You've got me all wrong Suzanne, you really do, but I understand. You've had a long night and it must be hard to know who to trust. I'm here to help you. I'm with the FBI."

"Really. How pray tell can the FBI help me?" *The FBI. Shit.*

"For starters I can get Roscoe P. Coltrane there off your back. I've seen their case, Suzanne, you've got nothing to worry about. I haven't had a chance yet, but as soon as we're done here I'm gonna go out there and make this whole mess go away. I'm really sorry you got mixed up in it."

"That's awful nice of you, Mike."

"Now, I know you must be tired, so let me get right to it so you can go home. Bet you'd like to be home, huh?"

"Yes."

"I'm working on another case, and I'm really hoping you can help me out by giving me some background."

"Uh-huh."

"You went through, lemme think, Georgia, Kentucky and Indiana?"

"And Tennessee. Can't get from Georgia to Kentucky without Tennessee."

"Yeah, of course, yes, Tennessee. So, what'd you do in Georgia?"

"Nothing. Passed through."

"And Tennessee? Kentucky? Did you make any stops, do anything? See the sights?"

"Gas and fast food, Mike, that's all." *Here it comes.*

"What was in Indiana?"

"The brother of a friend who died last week. We paid our respects, then turned around."

"Where was this brother?"

"A nursing home."

"Where?"

"Fishers. It's North of Indy."

"Yes, I know Fishers. What else?"

"Nothing else. We took a round trip to the nursing home."

"That's it?"

"That's it."

Mike looked down, smiled and rubbed his nose. "Suzanne. C'mon."

Spriz waited.

"I don't think you're being straight with me Suzanne, and there's no need for that. You're not under arrest. You're in no trouble. Look around, there's not even any cameras in here. You're completely safe."

"Coulda fooled me. The door was locked."

"Deputy Dawg locked the door, I can't tell you why. I *un*locked it. It's still unlocked. I am here to help you. But I can't help you if you hold things back from me. Now what else did you do in Indiana?"

"Drove straight north from Kentucky to Fishers. Saw the brother. Drove east to Dayton, then south to Kentucky, where you had the state police pick us up."

Mike raised his palms. "That wasn't me, Suzanne, I swear. That was the Keystone Kops here."

"Uh-huh."

"Why Ohio?"

"Fastest way out of Indiana." She was telling nothing but the truth, but she could tell the truth would not set her free. It wasn't what the FBI man wanted to hear.

"Suzanne." He shrugged, and smiled knowingly. "C'mon. Come on, Suzanne. You want me to believe you went all the way to Indiana for the first time in six years and didn't see your father?"

"I don't know who or where my father is," Spriz said flatly.

"Of course." Mike smiled. "My mistake. You went to Indiana and didn't see your adopted father, Donald Anthony Prizzi?"

"No. I didn't see him."

Mike paused. He looked at the ceiling, then at the floor. He grimaced.

"Of course you did, Suzanne. I know you did. There's nothing to gain by lying to me, because I know you did." Irritation crept into his tone. "Please don't treat me like I'm stupid. I'm not treating you that way, okay? Now what did you and Donald talk about? Where did you meet?"

"Mike, I can't help what you think you know. I didn't see my father. If that's all you wanted to talk about, I'm gonna go find a place to get some sleep, because there's nothing I can tell you. I didn't see him, didn't talk to him. I've had no contact with Don Prizzi for six years. But I think you already know that."

"I know you talked to him yesterday!"

"No you don't! Because I didn't."

Ames took a deep breath, and got up from his chair. He pushed the chair away from the table, then crouched where it had been, facing Spriz. He took Spriz's right hand in both of his soft hands. Spriz thought he looked as though he were about to propose. He spoke gently, almost seductively.

"I don't think he's a bad man, Suzanne. I really don't. I think he's a good man who fell in with a bad crowd. You can help me get him out. We can turn him around, we can save him, together, and then you and him and me, together, we can put some very bad people in jail where they can't hurt anybody ever again. Help me help your father. He's not a bad man. I know it."

He waited for a response from Spriz, or a sign. She gave him neither. She was showing him a steady expression of resolve while willing herself invisible. It wasn't working.

Special Agent Ames sighed heavily, then chuckled. He

released Spriz's hand. He shook his head, and then he ran his fingers through his goddamned hair again. He stared at the floor. Spriz was looking at the top of his head. She could not see his face as he spoke.

"Here's the thing, Suzanne. You can help me, we can get your father out and you can both go home. Together. Safe. Scot-free. Or…" The FBI man got to his feet, and loomed over the seated Spriz, holding the back of her chair with one hand and laying the other on the table in front of her. "Or you can keep playing me like you're doing, and I promise you, you and your Daddy will never see each other or the light of day again."

Spriz held her fear in check. "You can't bluff me. I know the law and I haven't broken it. My lawyer is on his way here."

The special agent laughed. "Oh hell, Suzanne, bring five lawyers for all the good it'll do you. Don't you get it? I've got you already, Suzanne. I've got you already. I've got you on conspiracy, multiple counts, from six years ago, and there's no statute of limitations coming to save you on that. Right this very minute I've got you on harboring a fugitive and obstruction of justice. Hell Suzanne, if I really wanted to, I could pin those two murders on you, easy. *You* could be the actor-hating serial killer!" He laughed again.

*No cameras in here,* Spriz thought. *Suuure…*

Ames stopped laughing. He spoke slowly, seriously, as though he were taking a blood oath: "I've got your Daddy on *treason*, Suzanne. And for that, they're gonna hang him, Suzanne, just like in the westerns. They're gonna hang him by the neck 'til dead if you don't talk to me."

Spriz's confident front was starting to fail her. "I have nothing I can tell you! I didn't see him! I didn't see him! How can I tell you what I don't know?"

"You saw him! I know you did!"

"My hand to God I never saw or spoke to him! Apparently you don't know as much as you think you do, Mike!"

Suddenly furious, the FBI man jerked Spriz's chair, and it

jumped an inch. "Would you like me to tell you just how much I know about you, *Spriz?*" Spriz's heart skipped when she heard her name from his lips.

"Would you like to know the street address of the rectory step you were dropped on at eleven months? The latitude and longitude? Would you like the name and current whereabouts of the woman who dropped you there?"

"Stop it. I didn't see him!"

The man got in Spriz's ear, his voice low, his breath hot. "I know your SAT scores, every grade you ever got. I know Paulie Jenkins was your first kiss. I know Kevin Garland was your first lay. I know your father took you fishing and bow-hunting in the southern Indiana woods—ever ask him why he didn't just adopt a boy instead of making you into one? I know you hate lima beans. I know the day, date and hour you left your father's house and drove to Galilee. I know the title of every book you ever took out of the library, and how long you kept it. I know every movie you've watched online. I know who you voted for, where you buy groceries, the radio station you listen to, who you email, every prescription you've ever taken. I know you treat yourself to a donut every time you buy gas. I know your roommates' names and criminal records. Wanna know which of the men living outside your bedroom door had a rape charge expunged?"

Spriz was almost doubling over. "Stop... please..."

"Shall I tell you when your next period is coming?"

"*Stop...*"

"You think we don't have eyes everywhere? You think we don't have satellites? I know what time you left Galilee Thursday night, I know the feed store where you crashed. I know every song your buddy Tommy sang at the barbeque joint. I know you blew a hose in Kentucky on the way up, I know you ran up I-65 to Indy, I know all about old Sam Wishart and his money troubles."

He straightened up. He reached down with his left hand,

grabbed Spriz by the chin, and yanked her face up. From his right hand, he extended his index finger, and he punctuated his next words by jabbing it at Spriz's face.

"I know *everything*, so don't sit there and tell me you didn't see him! TELL ME WHAT HE SAID, Spriz, or *so help me God!*"

It wasn't the chin-grab that did it. It wasn't anything the special agent had said, or the way he jerked her chair, or his yelling, or his threats.

It was the finger. Jabbing at her, penetrating her personal space. That finger flipped a switch in Spriz.

So quickly that the FBI man never saw it coming, Spriz clamped her strong left hand around the offensive digit and bent it backwards just far enough to paralyze Ames. Instinct took him over, telling his body that if it moved a muscle she might bend the finger a little more, and the pain would be overwhelming.

Without letting go, Spriz slowly stood up. She spoke casually to the man cringing below her.

"You shoulda stuck with the aw-shucks act, Mikey. It mighta worked. I bet it gets you all kinds of tail back at the bureau. But you got impatient, and impolite, so here we are. Now, I don't 'know' all sorts of things like you do, I can only guess, but here's what I think. I think if you had such good eyes on me you'd know I never went anywhere near my father. Since you don't know that, I'm guessing you lost track of me at some point, maybe for an hour, maybe longer. Your satellite lost me in the clouds, or your tail stopped to take a leak and couldn't pick up the trail. Somebody screwed the pooch, and it's on you, and now you have to tell your boss that after making you watch and wait for six whole years I finally went back to Indiana and you have no earthly idea what I did there. Sure sucks to be you right now."

Spriz saw beads of sweat break out on the man's brow and upper lip. She called out, "Detective Farrell! I know you're watching. You better come save this asshole's piano career!" A moment later, the door opened, and Farrell stepped in, slowly. She stayed by the door.

Her eyes fixed on Ames', Spriz said to Farrell, "You got a place I can lie down for a while?"

The detective replied calmly. "Yes I do. Come with me and I'll show you."

Spriz moved her face closer to the FBI man's face. "If we should ever meet again, I recommend you refrain from pointing this thing at me. Because if you do"—she released the finger—"I will snap it clean off and toss it to the drug dogs." She stepped to Farrell, and they exited together, leaving the attractive FBI man exercising his injured hand, flexing it in and out of a fist.

As Farrell conducted Spriz to the couch in her office, Spriz asked, "You saw all of that?"

"Yes," Farrell replied. "I gotta say, I loved the last part." She smiled a pretty smile at Spriz.

# 21

"SPRIZ? SPRIZ, WAKE UP."

When she opened her eyes, Spriz did not at first recognize face of the man who had been gently jostling her shoulder, but she liked it. It was a mature and dignified face, with a good strong nose and gentle eyes. Above the face were marvelous flops of wavy brown hair that seemed incongruously thick over a visage that correctly marked the man as past forty.

As her head cleared, Spriz identified Ryan Mountain, whom she had called hours ago from the back seat of a Florida Highway Patrol car. She remembered having liked his face the other time they'd met, at the meet-and-greet, and even recalled fantasizing that should she ever choose to have a boyfriend, she might select the Ryan Mountain model, only younger and a hundred percent less married.

"What time is it?" she asked as she sat herself up on Detective Farrell's red couch.

"It's a little past nine, Spriz. Sorry to wake you up, but I need to get back. You're all set now, free to go." He handed her an envelope containing her license, cash and keys.

"How'd you spring us?"

"They hadn't checked the decedent's LUDs yet, his phone records, so I made 'em. The neighbor said she knows exactly what time you drove off because her NASCAR race was just starting on TV. There were five calls made from Mr. Cagney's house in the two hours after you left. Most were to business lines so we couldn't get anybody at those numbers right away, it was too early. But one was a residence, and the man at that number said he knew Cagney and swore that he'd heard Cagney's voice at the other end, and that Cagney had sounded upset but nowhere near death. That was more than an hour after you left."

"Thanks," Spriz said wearily. The nap had been insufficient.

"Spriz, I'm not sure you realize how much trouble you were in. You were the prime suspect in a murder!"

"Nah, I wasn't, really."

"That's not what they told me."

"I'm sorry, I should have called you back and told you not to come. I was never a suspect. I think they were just holding me for the FBI."

"Yes, Spriz, speaking of the FBI," Mountain scolded, "the police say they have you on video assaulting a federal officer! You're lucky he's not pressing charges."

"Watch the whole thing. No jury would convict me."

"Spriz, for the love of God, tell me what's going on!"

"Maybe later, it's a long story. It's okay for now. I just want to find Tommy and go home. I'm really grateful that you came. You can bill me."

Mountain smiled. Spriz had no idea that the legal services she'd received in the last few hours would cost her about two-month's gross pay if he billed her, which he would not dream of doing. One of the luxuries of senior partnership was the option to work *pro bono* anytime you bloody well felt like it.

"Sure thing, Spriz." He put a hand on her shoulder.

Spriz felt a warm little tingle at his touch. *God Spriz, you need sleep.*

Mountain said, "But I hope you'll talk to me about the FBI when we get home. Whatever it is, you shouldn't have to face it alone, Spriz. Take my help."

As Spriz opened the door to Farrell's office, she said, "I will, but really, I'm okay. Thanks again." Then she got curious. "Hey, who else did the old man call?"

"Just the actors union. Two calls to the local in Orlando, and one to the national office in New York. Oh, and his bank, but it's closed Saturdays. Why?"

Spriz didn't answer. Mountain thought she looked a little stricken. "Spriz?"

Spriz appeared to shake off whatever she'd been feeling. "Just curious," she said, and she smiled. "Do you know if the man he spoke to was another actor?"

"No, Spriz, I don't. What if he had been?"

Spriz shrugged and smiled. "Nothing. See you back home, Mr. Mountain, Ryan."

"See you back home, Spriz."


As Spriz came out to the squad room, she heard a hubbub off to her left, then raucous laughter. She followed the sound around a corner to see a clutch of a dozen blue uniforms drinking coffee.

Some had come off duty a while ago, but hadn't been able to tear themselves away to go home yet. Others had just come on shift, but hadn't really started working. All of them were packed around a table at which sat three more officers, plus Tommy, holding court.

"So now both these guys are walking towards us in the breakdown lane, and they're honest-to-god Hell's Angels, six-five, three-hundred pounds each, at least. The one on the right has a machete, and the one on the left has a big wad of chain, and he's swinging it in a circle, like this, you know? My friend starts to run and I say wait, don't run—we'll push 'em into traffic!" A chorus of "whoa!" and "no!" and "oh my god!" spun around the master storyteller. Spriz smiled.

"They get right up on us, and the chain guy swings, and I duck, and the chain accidentally takes out machete guy!" The blue circle laughed. "Now machete guy's getting up, and I don't know *what* the fuck we're gonna do now, when all of a sudden there's all this light and noise, and six Kentucky smokies pull right up behind us, one after the other, BANG BANG BANG BANG BANG BANG, full lights and sirens! Those mooks musta wet their leather pants! They were back on their hogs and outtasight like rabbits! Man, it was *beautiful!*" Laughter and claps, all around.

Tommy saw Spriz as she approached the circle. "And that's my ride, boys and girls! Y'all be good now!"

They all said goodbye to their new friend Tom, patted his back, told him to stay safe. Lakeisha, a large officer who on most days directed traffic, gave Tommy a sensational bear hug that lifted him off his feet.

As Tommy approached Spriz, he noticed a look on her face. "What?" he asked innocently.

Spriz rolled her eyes and went looking for the parking lot. Tommy followed.


Among the many advantages of a tall purple Jeep is the rapidity with which one can pick it out in a crowded parking lot.

Minutes after leaving the stationhouse Spriz and Tommy were back on board. Spriz was just about to start the engine when they heard one of the rear doors open.

They both whipped their heads around to see Detective Farrell climb into Cher's back seat and close the door behind her. She had changed out of her slacks and button-down into jeans and a Dead Milkmen t-shirt. She positioned herself in the center of the bench seat, and leaned forward to offer her hand to Tommy.

"Hi Tommy. I'm Vicky."

Spriz raised an eyebrow. "Vicky?"

Vicky turned to Spriz and smiled. "Outside the stationhouse, yeah."

Spriz explained to Tommy that Vicky had been her interrogator. Tommy jumped to the wrong conclusion: "God, leave us alone, we didn't do anything!"

"I know," Vicky said to Tommy. "I really do. I'm sorry."

"Yeah, about that," Spriz said. "You knew we were innocent all along. I could tell. Why'd you bring us in at all?"

"I didn't know before we put out the BOLO," Vicky explained. "I really didn't. I didn't have a case yet, but I thought we had enough to bring you in for questions. After they picked you up in Kentucky, I got the report on the tire tracks, and I knew I had too little to pull you in, I had to do more work first. I went to my captain and told him I was going to call Kentucky and cut you loose. But there was a flag."

"A flag?" Tommy asked.

"It's like an automatic alert system," Vicky explained. "The FBI put electronic flags on Suzanne's records in various databases—DMV, taxes, so on. Anytime anyone in law enforcement looks up Suzanne in those databases, a text alert is automatically sent to her friend with the sore finger."

Tommy looked at Spriz. Spriz said, "Tell ya later."

"The neighbor's description of the car and its driver led me to Suzanne's records, and just by looking at those I unknowingly shot off a flare for Special Agent Douchebag. By the time I went to see my captain, he'd had calls from an FBI section chief and a deputy assistant director. The fibbies wanted to talk to you, Suzanne, but lacked probable cause to hold you. Lame as it was, *I* had probable cause. My captain said, as a courtesy, we were bringing you in, and to make it look good, we were to treat you like any suspect. I hated the whole thing. I got through it by telling myself you *could* have done it, and so as long as I had to interview you anyway, I was going to give it my best shot. I had a hunch the phone records might exonerate you, so I put that little task off until your lawyer showed up. He's cute, by the way."

"It's okay," Spriz said. "I get it, it's okay. My boss makes me do stupid things too. And my friends call me Spriz."

"Thanks," Vicky replied. She smiled. "Spriz?"

"So is that the only reason you're in my back seat?"

"No… You may be interested to know that one of the vehicles that take the tire size that matches the treadmarks we found on top of yours at James Cagney's house is indeed the 1967 250SL. You wanna fill me in, Spriz?"

Tommy looked at Spriz again, and arched an eyebrow. Spriz said, "Later, I promise!"

But Tommy didn't need to hear it. "That's Kami Carroll's car!" he said.

"Who's Kami Carroll?" Vicky asked.

Spriz and Tommy tagged-teamed explaining how they had learned that James Cagney wasn't receiving his actors union pension for mysterious reasons, and how Brandon's pension had stopped paying Sam's nursing home bill at around the same time Cagney's tap went dry.

"Now look," Spriz assured. "I have absolutely no earthly reason to suspect Kami Carroll of anything. Except she has the right kind of car—so do lots of people, I know—and every time we learn something new it points a great big red arrow right at the Florida union office, and she pulls all the strings there."

Tommy added, "And she's an evil bitch."

"Yes, there's that," Spriz agreed. "She is widely believed to be, as Thomas puts it, an evil bitch."

"What's it add up to?" Tommy asked Vicky.

Before Vicky could answer, Spriz broke in. "There's more, Tommy. Ryan told me the last calls Joe Zayres made in his life were to the union, his bank, and a friend, probably an actor. He made these calls right after we were there. Right after we told him he should look into what happened to his pension." Her chocolate eyes were apologizing to Tommy as she watched his. They registered the exact moment he realized what they had done.

"Oh my god, Spriz! We got that man killed. He started asking questions. He started asking questions and they killed him to shut him up!"

"We don't know that," Spriz said sadly. "But maybe."

Spriz turned to Vicky, who nodded. "Maybe."

Tommy thought for a moment, then said quietly, "Do you think Brandon Wishart started asking questions too?"

"These two old guys had something else in common," Vicky said. "They were both alone. That's a bullseye for fraudsters."

"How?" Spriz asked.

"Well, it's hard these days to pull off a scam like this. People have too much information access on the web. They check things out. They compare notes with others. But old people don't use the Internet. Now, old people with family around, they're no good, the kids look stuff up for 'em. But old and alone? If they have a question, they pick up the phone, and as long as you can make sure the call comes to you, you can tell 'em anything you want, and they'll believe it."

"Some old people use the Internet," Tommy said. "My gramma does."

"And those people are easy to identify," Vicky explained. "Any geezer who ever emailed the union office or registered for the website, you weed him out. The rest? You rob 'em blind."

"You think there are more victims of the scam?" Spriz asked.

"I don't really know. We don't even know yet if there *is* a scam. But how much can an actor's pension be? I saw James Cagney's bank statement. Scammers are greedy. They don't take the trouble for chump change. They have to be careful not to hit so many people that they draw attention, but I bet there are lonely, old actors all over Florida who aren't getting their money."

"What do we do?" Tommy asked.

"We play dominoes," Vicky said, and she smiled wickedly.

"Dominoes?" Spriz asked?

"All we have to do is prove there is a scam," Vicky explained, "and that James Cagney was asking questions about it, and that Kami Whoever's tire treads match the photos from the scene. If we can establish just those three facts, the rest of the dominoes fall. We'll have opportunity, means and motive on this Kami person for Cagney's murder. If the pension records show that your friend was a victim of the scam, that's motive in his death and the Galilee PD might reopen."

"So," Spriz asked, "You get a warrant now for the union's records?"

"NO!" Vicky snapped, mock horror on her face. "A labor union? We so much as hint that we want to look at a labor union's books and they'll erect a brick wall made of lawyers. We'll spend a year in court just getting the records, and by then every trace of this flimflam will have been wiped away and Kami will be conveniently retired in a tropical paradise with no extradition treaty. We need to get inside that union office and sneak a peek at just a couple of records. We're not violating the union because the union's not a suspect. That should give us enough to arrest Kami on the murder, which in turn gives us probable cause to grab the records we need on the spot—just for the murder, in principle, but from there it won't be hard to turn them over to the state fraud cops, all before the union can wind its lawyers up."

"Good luck getting inside the union office," Spriz warned. "You won't get past the front door without a union card. I've heard that place is like a private club. We need a union member to get us in. I know some actors who could help. Let me think."

Tommy raised his hand sheepishly, like a kindergartner asking to go potty.

Vicky said, "I know Cagney's financials. I only need a fast

look at the payouts and I think I can connect the dots."

Tommy said quietly, "I'm a union member."

Spriz said, "Is there a way to trick whoever's working the front desk into—" She turned to Tommy. "Yer a *what?*"

"I'm a member," Tommy repeated. "I belong to the actors union. I have a card and everything."

Vicky said to Spriz, "Nice day for a drive to Orlando."

"Yes," Spriz agreed. "Yes it is."

"Stay here," Vicky said as she got out of the car. "I gotta go change again, and see if I can get one of my crime scene guys and my computer forensics guy to come along. You can ride with us, or follow so you won't have to come back for your eggplant here afterward. I know Orlando is sorta on the way home for you."

"We'll ride with you," Spriz said. Vicky closed the door behind her.

Tommy shot Spriz the eyebrow.

"Shut up," she chided. "And how come you never told me you belonged to the actors union?"

"Never came up."

"It's like I don't even know you. You still pay dues?"

"The dues aren't much. And you have no idea how hard it was to get into the union in the first place. You can have my card when you pry it from my cold, dead hands!"

# 22

MEMORANDUM

TO: SAC INDIANAPOLIS
FROM: SA AMES, MICHAEL (100-9765U)
RE: INTERVIEW RPT - SUBJECT PRIZZI SUZANNE
THERESA AKA SPRIZ DOB 11/13/80

BACKGROUND - From 2/6/08 subject resided in
unincorporated Warrick Co. IN on land deeded to PATRIOTS
VIGIL INC. PVI is target suspect in joint Bureau/DHS/ATF
investigation ref: 6278T08. Inter/exter surveillance confirms
subject resided on PVI compound with her father DONALD
ANTHONY PRIZZI DOB 3/17/39 believed to be high in
suspect organization's leadership. Subject discovered missing
from Patriots' Vigil compound in AM on 9/19/08. Subject's
whereabouts unknown until FL voter registration and drivers
license applications 10/08. Subject under general surveillance
pursuant to federal material witness warrant 10/24/08 as is
believed to possess knowledge of suspect organization's
leadership/social structure, supply chain, compound layout,

communications, and weaponry/fortifications. Subject's leverageable relationship to ranking PVI officer categorizes her as High Value (HV).

SUMMARY - Subject remained within FL boundaries until 10/17. Local police BOLO and subsequent records searches alerted Bureau. Satellite track and ground surveillance followed subject through 5.5-hour visit by auto to IN on 10/18 during which no contact with suspect organization was observed or recorded. Subject apprehended by police for questioning on local matter. SA Ames questioned subject while in local custody re: contact with suspect organization. No actionable data retrieved. NOTE: Subject may be surveillance-aware.

RECOMMENDATIONS – 1) Continue current surveillance program, augment with interception/analysis/archival of all personal communications.
2)Append profile with notation: VIOLENT
3) Initiate background check and pre-surveillance plan for associate THOMAS EVELYN GUSTAFSON aka THOMAS Q GUSTAFSON DOB 4/18/87 (SSN 590-65-0575) curr. res. Galilee FL.

Reported 10/20 SA AMES, MICHAEL (100-9765U).
cc Command, Domestic Terrorism Joint Task Force

# 23

KAMI CARROLL ESCORTED TOMMY from the reception area into her private office. She told Greg at the front desk not to disturb them, and closed the door behind her.

"So, Tommy, I don't believe we've met before, have we?"

"No, I don't believe I've had the pleasure." In fact he had. Three times.

Kami motioned Tommy to the small guest chair, and settled into her tall leather chair on the opposite side of her wide maple desk. She glanced at her computer screen. "I looked up your member profile after you called. What's the Q in your union name for? Your real middle name is Evelyn."

"You answered your own question," Tommy joked. "And I couldn't just drop the middle initial because there was a Thomas Gustafson ahead of me, believe it or not."

"Why Q?"

"It's from 'John Q Public.' I'm an everyman."

Kami let out a little laugh Tommy didn't quite buy. "So, you said you had a 'very serious matter' to discuss? A private matter?" She tried to screw a concerned expression onto her Botox-paralyzed features, but wound up looking constipated.

"Well, I don't want to get another actor in trouble. But it's my union too, and I think a man I know is… stealing from the union."

Now Kami really was concerned, "Stealing? Who?"

"I don't wanna bear false witness against a union brother until I'm sure, Kami, you understand."

"Of course. Please tell me what you can."

"Well, he's an old man, well past retirement age, but he still works three or four shows a year, about forty weeks in all."

"Yes?"

"I overheard him telling another actor about his pension income. He seems to be getting his retirement payouts even though he's not retired!"

Kami clicked her tongue and shook her head. "Is that all? You had me worried."

"But he's stealing!"

"No he's not! Once a member is fully vested, he gets his retirement disbursement as soon he reaches retirement age, whether he stops working or not. For heaven's sake Tommy! I'm a busy woman."

"What's retirement age?"

"It depends on the year he was born. How old is he?

Tommy had to think. "Um, seventy-three, I believe."

"Then he's been getting his retirement payments since he was sixty-five. It's simple and it's perfectly legal. We do not require members to stop working. They start getting their pensions once they're of age, as soon as they ask for them."

Kami stood up. She was about to hustle Tommy out the door and call to see if the massage appointment she had canceled was still available.

"Well, that clears that up," Tommy said. "I guess now I know I can trust what he told me about the union."

Kami was concerned again. "What did he tell you?"

"He said some people he knows haven't been getting their pension payments for, like, two years and they don't understand why. Do you know what he's talking about?"

Kami sat. She thought for a moment. She said, "Not getting their pensions? They must be mistaken. You know, pension eligibility is very complicated, and the laws change all the time. I'll wager these members only think they're entitled to a pension."

"Really?" Tommy said. "You said before it was simple."

"I meant that receiving it was simple," Kami corrected. "But there are complex reasons why someone might not be entitled to a pension."

"Like what?"

"It's all on the union's website, on the Retirement page." Kami stood again, and gestured toward the door. "Greg can show you, if you'd like."

"They've got a lawyer."

"A lawyer?"

"Some bigshot, I forget his name. He says he's gonna find all the union members who aren't getting their pensions and work for them for free, file something my friend called a 'class action.' Oh! I remember! The lawyer's name is Mountain, Ryan Mountain!"

Kami sat. She had heard of Ryan Mountain. His name was in the papers. She knew a realtor who was friends with his wife. They belonged to her club. She'd heard they belonged to several.

"This is silly," Kami said, laughing a little. "Everyone who's supposed to get their pension is getting it, I'm sure. Who's your friend?"

"Oh, he's been in the union all his life."

"My, that's good to hear. What's his name?"

"His real name or his union name?"

"Either."

"I'm not sure I should say."

"I think you should."

"I don't know… It feels like I'm betraying a confidence.

No offense."

Kami stood up again, and came around her desk to sit in a guest chair next to Tommy. She lightly brushed three soft fingers capped by expensively painted nails across Tommy's forearm. "Tommy, do you love your union brothers and sisters?"

"Every last one."

"Well, Tommy, they need this union—you do, too, we all do. We all need this organization to look out for us, to keep us from being exploited. When someone spreads lies—and I'm sorry, that's all this is, lies!—when someone spreads lies about this union, that protection is weakened, and we are all in danger. Do you understand?"

"Yes, I do. I really do."

"My job is to protect this union, so it can protect you. Do you understand that?"

"Yes."

"Then tell me your friend's name, so I can look into this and find out what's really happening. I will not tell a soul about you."

"Promise?"

Kami crossed her heart and kissed her fingertips.

"Okay. His name is Brandon Wishart."

Kami's frozen face didn't budge, but her eyes burned. "That isn't funny!" she snapped as she rose, maneuvered back behind her desk and sat. "Brandon Wishart is dead." She glanced at her computer screen. "And I know you know he's dead, because you work at GaliRep!" She leaned back in her chair, and eyed Tommy suspiciously. "What is it that you want here?"

Tommy giggled foolishly. "Did I say 'Brandon Wishart'? Did I really? Oh my stars, Kami, I gotta confess, I'm on Day Three of this colon cleanse, and half the time I don't know what planet I'm on, you know what I'm sayin'? I can't even have more juice until tonight, I am flaking, big time. I didn't mean that, I'm sorry."

"I should hope so."

"My friend's name is Joseph Zayres. He says Hey."

Kami's eyes went wide. She bit her lip. She locked her eyes on Tommy's, searching. Tommy stared back.

Neither spoke for thirty seconds. Finally Kami said slowly, "What do you do at GaliRep, Tommy?"

"I'm a costume shop assistant."

"What are they paying you?"

"Florida minimum wage plus fifty cents." He said it proudly.

Kami smiled. "You know, it's a shame, a beautiful man like you hidden away in a backwater like Galilee. Lots more clubs in a big city like Orlando. More action, more 'friends' to make..."

"Go on," Tommy said.

"Come work for me here. I'll triple your pay."

"Well, that's another thing I was coming to see you about, actually. I think I want to act again."

"A juicy role in any theatre in town, to introduce you to Orlando theatregoers. I can make it happen like that!" She snapped her fingers. "A phone call!"

"How would I rehearse, with my day job here and all?"

"I'm flexible."

Tommy considered for a moment. "Okay, I'm tempted."

"It's yours for the taking. All you have to do is tell me what you think you know, and how you know it."

Tommy stood, put his fingertips on Kami's desk, and leaned over it. "Tell me what you did, and how you did it!"

Kami swatted the air in front of her face. "I did nothing! I don't know what you're talking about!"

"I know you stole from the pension funds! Admit it!"

"I did nothing of the kind! You're… You're trying to entrap me!" She looked Tommy up and down. "You're working with the police! You're wearing a wire!"

"A WIRE?" Tommy raised up and yanked open his shirt,

popping off four buttons and displaying the hairy chest of which he was indecently proud. "I'm not wearing any *stinking wire!*"

Tommy pressed his fists onto the desk, and leaned in closer this time, the tails of his open shirt draping over Kami's blotter and desk clock.

He whispered, "I'm just keeping you occupied," and smiled his winning smile.

Kami exploded out of her office.

"GREG! Turn off your computer NOW!"

She was too late. A young detective was standing at the reception desk, comparing two printed photographs of tire treads, one in each hand. Behind her, a man was looking at what Kami could tell were pension accounts on Greg's computer. Greg was standing by the front door, looking mortified.

"Kami Carroll, you are under arrest," Vicky said as she put down the tire tread photos, lifted a pair of handcuffs from her belt and approached.

"This is all a mistake!" Kami shouted as Vicky snapped on the bracelets and turned her toward the door. "Greg, call my lawyer! Not the union lawyer, *my* lawyer, call Becky! And don't tell them anything!"

As cuffed Kami was about to be perp-walked out the front door of the union office and into the waiting plainclothes car, she heard someone say her name again, and Vicky stopped pushing. Kami looked up to see the long face of a very tall woman she didn't know.

"Brandon Wishart," Spriz said. "How did you do it? I wanna know."

Kami Carroll snarled, "LAW-YER!"

Vicky shoved Kami through the open doorway.

# 24

SPRIZ SLEPT FOR NINETEEN HOURS, non-consecutively. She had finally made it home from Palatka at about 9 p.m., after giving her formal statement and then sharing an iHOP supper with Vicky and Tommy. She slept until early the next morning, when she pushed her fat cat aside and got up to fry and eat an entire half-pound of bacon. Then she returned to bed until late afternoon.

She awoke feeling like a million bucks, fully refreshed for the first time in a week. She took a scalding, steamy shower that was so long, she turned off the water only when it began to run cold. She put on clean, soft clothes.

She saw that her roommates, who were off somewhere, hadn't done dishes the whole time she was gone. She happily hand-washed them, and put them in the rack to dry.

She gave Osric a long petting session in her big chair. He pretty much insisted on it.

She picked up a hefty fantasy novel from the coffee table, and saw that it had a bookmark sticking out from about halfway through the pages. But she couldn't remember having read the first half. If she was going to read it now, she'd have to start over. She put it down.

She fired up Netflix on her laptop, and started to watch *The Hunger Games*, which she had resisted watching thusfar mostly because people kept recommending it to her. By ten minutes in, the dystopian Earth in which the story took place had so completely depressed her that she switched it off.

She looked at the clock: 5:47 p.m.

She looked out the window. It was nearly November, cool and sunny in Florida, with sunset due within the hour. She wanted to go outside but could not think of what she'd do when she got there.

She started a load of laundry.

She picked up the house phone. She'd memorized Vicky's number. Should she call? Better not. She'd just seen Vicky yesterday. She didn't want to be a pest. Vicky had promised to call when there was news. Was it too soon for news? Yes, Vicky hadn't called, and that meant there was no news. Should she call and check? No. Vicky would call. Would she?

She called Tommy.

"Hey," she said.

"Hey."

"Get some sleep?"

"Oh, god yes, it was *wonderful*. I just got up. I'm still in my jammies. I may never take them off. This is *heaven*."

"Yeah, it's pretty sweet. I got up a little while ago. It's good to be home, huh?"

"Yeah, good to be home. Click click click there's no place like it!"

"Yeah," Spriz repeated. "So, um, I was thinking about going in to work."

"Cool," Tommy replied quickly. "Pick me up."

They saw only two other cars in the GaliRep parking lot when they arrived just before dark: Conrad's old Isuzu Trooper and

Maisy's little Honda wagon. Apparently Tommy and Spriz weren't the only GaliRep staff members who didn't understand what "layoff" meant.

As Spriz and Tommy walked around the corner from the parking lot to the side of the building—Spriz carrying the rusty tricycle she couldn't wait to add to her collection—they noticed a fuzzy, black sphere next to the employee entrance. As they approached, the sphere unrolled like an armadillo, lifted its head and revealed itself to be Gina in her Ninja assistant stage manager uniform. Her bicycle was chained to one of the small trees the city had planted in the sidewalk.

"Gina," Spriz asked, "what are you doing here?"

Gina shrugged. She looked like she may have been crying. "I didn't know what else to do. This is where I come on Tuesday nights. But the door's locked and ASMs don't get a key."

"It's safer locked when there's only a few people in the building," Spriz explained. "You could have called Maisy or Conrad to let you in. But they might have sent you home. Didn't you get the email?"

Gina shrugged again. "Yeah I got it. But, I dunno. I felt like I should be here. I mean, it's Tuesday. It's a show night."

Spriz smiled gently at Gina. "Yeah, Gina. You're right. It's a show night." She turned to Tommy. "Show night."

Tommy nodded. "Show night."

Spriz unlocked the door, and three pros marched into the theatre.

When they reached the stage, Gina peeled off up the steps beside the seats. Ana Maria had asked her to sort and file away the gels—the squares of colored plastic put over lights to change their hue—when she got a chance, and now she had one. The gel file was in the control booth, the gels from *Great Expectations* in a daunting polychromatic pile in front of it.

In the hallway outside the dressing rooms, Tommy started to turn towards the costume shop, but Spriz stopped him and asked him to come downstairs first to help her stow away the big dining table on which they had autopsied Brandon Wishart's belongings.

After they hung Spriz's rusty trophy from Starke on a hook over the toy department, Tommy stayed on the side closest to the door while Spriz scooted across the tabletop to the far side and then stood facing Tommy.

"Okay, how do we do this?" Tommy asked.

"We have to flip it first," Spriz replied. "This way." She used her hands to demonstrate a clockwise (to her) flip.

"Are you sure? Didn't we flip it the other way when we put it down?"

"Exactly, so now we have to flip it the opposite way to put it back."

"Yeah, but it doesn't look like it will flip that way. The legs will snag on that shelf."

Spriz looked under the table. Tommy was right.

"Well, I guess we flip it the other way."

"Same problem on the other side, Spriz."

Spriz looked under the table again. Then she stood up and took a step backward, mentally measuring the tabletop. "What if we flip it up from my end?"

"Too tall," Tommy said. "It'll jam against the rafters. Won't fit."

Spriz stared at the table for a moment as if waiting for it to tell them what to do. "Well, Tommy, goddammit, I mean, we got it *here* somehow!"

"Maybe it grew while we were away."

Spriz was considering the best way to saw the damn table in half when the desk phone at the back of the prop room rang.

Tommy had never seen her run for the phone before. He turned his back and sat on the table, to give her the illusion of privacy. On his phone he opened a solitaire game that didn't require a signal.

Spriz yanked the handset free. "Hello?"

"Hi Spriz, it's Detective Vicky."

"Hi Detective Vicky!"

"You weren't home so I tried you at work. Why are you at work? Aren't you fired or something?"

"There's always work to do in a theatre, even if you're fired. What's the word?"

"Well, I've got good news and more good news, and bad news and more bad news. Pick where I start."

"Good news!"

"Good choice. Kami Carroll is going away, and that's a lock. I've got her prints on the oxygen canister, her car at the scene, and records proving she was diverting James Cagney's pension. And both the phone friend and the New York union office confirm Cagney was asking around about his pension the day he died. She's toast."

"Yay you!"

"Yay me, but it gets better: The good good news is that the state has picked up the fraud investigation, with the feds helping out 'cause it involves a union and banks. I'm out of it, but so far they're being nice and letting me peek over their shoulder 'cause I broke the case. The team is pushing my prosecutor to cut Kami a deal on the murder so she'll spill on the fraud, but I can live with that. She'll do hard time regardless, and I did my job."

"Have they found more victims of the pension scam?"

"Hell, yes! Thirty so far, all over the state, all men, including your friend—Brandon Wishart was one of them. I think they're gonna find twice that many, at least. Lonely old actors, every one, most retired, but a handful like your friend, still working while drawing a pension, or trying to, anyway. It's bigger than I thought, and kinda brilliant."

"Brilliant?" Spriz had unconsciously inserted a half-inch blade into her X-Acto handle and was lazily carving a cartoon dragon into her wooden benchtop as she listened.

"Looks like she customized the swindle for each mark, telling different stories to different victims depending on what she thought would work. Cagney's phone friend says she told Cagney the pension fund had been 'broken' by the recession and unemployment. She said the same to some other guys. But some guys who had been drawing their pension for a few years were told they had been paid by mistake, that they were never entitled to a pension, something about not working enough weeks. Kami Carroll told 'em she could keep the union from suing them to get its money back, but only if they didn't make a stink. A few put up a fuss anyway, and whenever that happened Kami just called it a mistake and gave 'em their money, no harm no foul. The whole thing was predicated on the assumption that enough victims would just roll over and take it, and a lot of them did. I guess James Cagney was fussing too loudly for Kami's comfort. He called New York, and apparently that was a no-no."

Vicky started to laugh. "A few guys, she actually blamed it on Obama!"

"Obama?"

"Some of these ol' Florida boys, they watch a lot of FOX. They'll believe the moon is made of cheese if you tell 'em it's the president's fault. Kami told these guys Obamacare wiped out their pensions somehow. They bitched and moaned and called for impeachment, but not a one of 'em ever doubted it was true."

"What did she tell Brandon?"

Vicky paused a beat. "We may never know, Spriz. We got the stories from the other victims. We may never know what your friend was told unless Kami Carroll tells us herself, and so far she ain't talking, she's lawyered up. She may have told him nothing. She may have figured since he never saw the money, he'd never know that it stopped."

"Can't be," Spriz said, shaking her head. "That lady at the home, Amanda Curtain, she was sending letters all over the place. He had to know."

"Yeah, see, I have a theory about that," Vicky said. "But that's the bad bad news. Bad news first. You ready?"

"How ready should I be?"

"I'm nowhere on your friend's death, Spriz."

"Oh," Spriz said softly. She set the knife down on the unfinished dragon carving.

"The scam is only motive if he knew about it and threatened to expose it; otherwise, Kami's better off with him alive. The money stops when he dies. And there's just no proof he knew. He never called the union or the bank to ask about his pension, didn't complain to friends or talk to a lawyer, not as far as the fraud team can tell so far. They're not done looking."

"He didn't have any friends," Spriz said sadly. "Just me, sorta, and a waitress in Starke. But Kami killed Joe Zayres. Doesn't that make it likely she killed Brandon, too?"

"Spriz," Vicky said firmly. "Kami's whereabouts are accounted for, with witnesses and records. She hasn't been anywhere near Galilee, not on the night your friend died, or in the days before. I'm sorry."

"It's okay," Spriz said softly.

"I called Galilee PD and talked to a detective Bauman, Steven Bauman, told him what I thought, but he wouldn't even consider re-opening the investigation. Piece of work, this Bauman. I don't think I succeeded in convincing him I was a real detective."

Spriz huffed. "Well, I mean, it's not like I ever thought she did it with her bare hands! Kami's famous to Florida theatre people. Someone would have noticed her here. But she could have an accomplice, right?"

Detective Farrell's tone took a sharp turn from sympathetic to stern. "Spriz, I want you listen to me very carefully."

"Okay…"

"Kami Carroll's lawyer, Becky, keeps making the same point with the fraud team, and it's a good one."

"What's that?"

"Her client already has more money than she can spend. Why would she risk it?"

"Because she's an evil bitch!"

"Spriz, please listen. The team has been following the money trail. They haven't found all the money yet, not by a longshot. They've found life insurance policies on some of these guys, though. Looks like the pension money was just the beginning—the real jackpot was to come, when the guys started dying off. If the team finds a policy on your friend, that might make motive, and we can try again. But they've found some money, like I said, and the fact is, the trail does not lead to Kami Carroll."

"That can't be!"

"Kami doesn't have it, Spriz. The trail leads to several different funds, well-disguised. The pensions and the life insurance pay to those funds. And from there… from there it leads to two small professional theatres."

"I don't understand…"

Vicky inhaled. "The team isn't there yet, but here's what I think they're gonna find. Kami didn't do it for the money. She did it for the theatres, and the union. Theatres going dark is bad for the union, everybody loses. I think Kami was building a slush fund to keep struggling theatres open until the business turned the corner."

Spriz's head was spinning. "What does… How? How do you know?"

"Well, I don't really. But your friend is the key."

"Brandon?"

"See, the trick with a hustle like this is controlling the flow of information. Pensions send out statements and newsletters, and the government sends out tax statements with pension info on them. You have to prevent the marks from seeing this stuff, or the whole thing gets blown. The old guys who are really retired, they're pretty easy: You just file the right changes of address at the right time, and you can get all the stuff that might tip your marks diverted to you, and you can shred it and send 'em dummy tax statements and other things they'd miss. But guys like your friend who still work, they get all their mail at the theatre, right?"

"Yeah, we have a wall of cubbyholes in the office for mail. The actor names on the cubbies change with every show."

"Yes. Those guys are always filing changes of address at the end of every gig so their mail will follow them to the next one, and their filings would supersede whatever the scammers might have filed. There's no way to stay ahead of it. Eventually, something is going to slip through and reach a theatre where the actor is working."

"So?"

"So then the only way you can make the scam work is to have someone inside the theatre. Someone in a position to skim off any unwanted communications. Someone who could make sure your friend never saw the letters from the home in Indiana. Someone at every theatre where they were sent. And I can't think of a reason the theatres would be helping Kami Carroll divert money into her own Prada purse. It had to be the other way around. She was helping them."

Spriz felt sick. "Vicky?"

"Spriz, I think Kami Carroll had at least one accomplice, maybe more, in each of the theatres that was drawing from the slush fund. Two theatres so far, but they'll find more. And since it's a good bet Amanda Curtain mailed a letter to your friend at GaliRep and he never got it… There could be someone you know who's pretty upset with you right now."

Detective Farrell waited for a response. "Spriz?"

Spriz was busy shifting herself into problem-solving gear. "What should I do?"

"Keep your eyes open. And if you see anything, you call 911 first, then you call me, you hear?"

"Yeah, okay."

"I gotta go. I'll call back later."
"Okay."
"Spriz?"
"Yeah?"
"Be careful, okay?"
"I will."
"Bye."
"Bye."
Spriz absently dropped the handset into its cradle.

*Blink-blink.*

She wasn't sure she'd seen it. If she had, she'd seen it in her peripheral vision, and she couldn't be certain.

Had she imagined it? She hadn't been looking at the phone when she hung up. But she thought maybe she saw one LED button light on the phone go out, and another go out a split-second later. *Blink-blink.*

She looked at the phone. If the light for her line was the first to go out, which was the second? Had it been on the whole time?

She looked at the buttons. They were all dark now. She focused on the button she feared it would be.

The one it couldn't be.

The one it had to be.

The one for the line of the person who had just eavesdropped on her conversation with the detective.

Spriz saw the tiny LED light blink on.

A second later, all of the buttons blazed to life, as if the whole panel had just been mashed by a wide fist.

She wrenched the handset from its sticky cradle, and pressed 9. She heard what she expected: the tone that told her all the lines out of the building were in use. No call could be made. Someone had camped one phone onto all of the outside lines at once.

Spriz slammed the handset into its cradle. She ran the few steps to the table, jumped and slid across it on her hip. She grabbed Tommy's arm as her feet hit the floor, and she hustled him out the door. She did not bother to lock up.

As she pulled him up the stairs, Spriz interrupted Tommy's protestations with orders.

"I'm going for Gina. Find Maisy and get her out of the building. As soon as you have a signal, call 911."

"Call 911 and tell them *what?*"

"Anything, it doesn't matter! A gang fight, a rabid dog. Just get Maisy out and get some cops over here!"

In the hall at the top of the stairs, Tommy split off for the costume shop. Before heading onto the stage, Spriz called after him. "And whatever you do, keep away from *Conrad!*"

# 25

MENTALLY COUNTING THE SECONDS since her phone had lit up, Spriz tried to correlate the elapsed time with the top speed Conrad and his bum knee might achieve in getting out of his office, down the hall to the stairs, down the stairs to the lobby and over to the double doors that led onto the stage. If her calculations were correct, she had seconds left.

As she crossed the stage to the doors, she snatched up the ghost light and upended it, spilling its glow tape sash to the floor. Without stopping, she spun the base off the pole and let it slide down the electrical cord running through its center. She took a few steps as skips while painfully bending the pole into an L across her shin.

The ghost light's cord reached its limit and came unplugged just as Spriz jammed the bent rod behind the levers on both doors, exploding the single bulb in the process and scattering hot glass on the stage. The room was almost dark now, lit only by the spill from the light in the control booth above, where Gina was sorting gel.

In the next instant, the door levers moved, but not far enough to spring the latches.

"Hey!" Conrad called from the lobby. "Who's there? Why
are these doors not working? Hey!" He rattled the handles and
thumb levers on his side a few more times, and then stopped.

Spriz had already begun bounding up the steps to the
booth. She knew he'd go next for the only other door in, the
single door from the restroom hallway to the other side of the
seating banks. She had no way left to stop him there. She had to
get Gina.

When Spriz burst into the control booth, Gina let out a
loud peep. "Spriz! You scared me!"

"Come with me *now!*" Spriz commanded from the doorway.

"Why? I'm almost done."

"*Now*, Gina!"

As Gina stepped toward Spriz, they heard Conrad's voice
calling from below. "Who's in here? Who blocked that door?"

Spriz quickly stepped inside the booth and closed the door.
"Stay back!" Spriz ordered as she flipped the switch that turned
off the overhead light. "He can't see you as long as you stay
back from the glass."

"Why do I need to—"

"Just stay back, and keep quiet!" The booth was dark, but
the controls were glowing on the light and sound boards.

"Who turned off the ghost light! Who's up there?"

In the dim glow of the controls, Spriz noticed the god mic
Ana Maria used for announcements. It was sitting on a little
shelf above the light board.

She flipped on the little monitor speaker in the booth, the
one that amplified any sound coming from the stage. She
pushed one fader control on the light board just a quarter of the
way up. A few instruments onstage put out a dim glow, and
Conrad was briefly blinded by the sudden light after darkness.
Spriz could now see he was standing center-stage.

She squeezed the handle on the god mic, switching it on.
She spoke calmly into it.

"Hi Conrad." Her voice reverberated in the empty hall.

Conrad sheltered his eyes with his hand and looked up at the booth. "Spriz? What are you doing?"

"I'm playing a game." Spriz's voice came at Conrad from hidden speakers all around him. "It's called Three Questions. Ready?"

"Spriz, I—"

"Question one: Who sorts the mail here?"

"Spriz, what are you doing?"

Still squeezing the switch in her fist, Spriz turned the god mic and held it up to the little monitor speaker. The mainstage hall erupted in a shattering feedback squeal. Conrad winced.

She brought the mic back to her lips. "Who sorts the mail?"

"Me! Me I guess, Spriz, usually me, but what has this got to—"

"Question two: Why did you tell me Brandon had no beneficiaries? I bet every form he ever signed listed his brother as his heir."

"Spriz, let me—"

She hit the monitor again. The speakers howled like a ghost in agony.

"Stop it! Spriz, please, why don't—"

"Question three, final Jeopardy: The night Brandon died, where was your *flashlight?*"

Conrad looked down at the stage, and froze.

"You had a keychain light on Brandon in the lobby. You have a flashlight *fetish*, Conrad, you put one in my basement, and one in the costume shop. I know you had a big steel one in your office, just like mine, with three D batteries."

Slowly, Conrad lifted his face, and stared straight up at the booth.

Spriz pressed, "I used to see it on your file cabinet all the time, but I didn't think to look for it when I stopped by your office the other day. If I went to your office right now, would I see it there, Conrad?"

Conrad did not move. His eyes were burning a hole in the

glass between himself and Spriz.

"How long were you alone with Brandon after you sent Connie to the box office to call 911? Where was your big flashlight that night, Conrad? Where is it now?"

She paused. She waited, agonizing seconds. She forced herself to keep breathing. *Come on, Conrad. Tell me it's not true. Lie to me, you bad, bad man…*

Conrad inhaled quickly, paused a moment, and then spoke quietly, his soft voice floating all the way to the booth on the theatre's fine acoustics.

"It's in the river, Spriz. It was… bent. I dropped it in the pot of a fake palm in the lobby. Later I got it back and I drove to the Third Street bridge. I'm sorry, Spriz. I'm really, really sorry."

Conrad's eyes darkened. He scowled. And then he lurched for the stairs along the seating banks, throwing his bum leg forward in long strides.

"Turn it up!" Spriz ordered Gina. "Every switch on, every knob all the way to the right!"

Gina poked the power button on every audio component that wasn't already lit up, and spun every knob. The colored LEDs and level indicators in the audio rack brightened up like Vegas on a Friday night. Then she slid every slider on the sound board all the way up. The house erupted in deafening hum and feedback. Gina covered her ears. Conrad, having reached the third step, was thrown off his balance, and he staggered backwards down the steps and onto the stage floor.

Spriz used her left forearm to slide a whole row of dimmer controls on the lighting board up full, then the next row, then the next.

His eyes clamped shut and his hands over his ears, Conrad looked like he was standing on the surface of the sun.

With every power-drawing device in the theatre cranked up to its peak, Spriz grabbed the god mic, pulled it close to her teeth, and screamed. Conrad spun around and doubled over, pressing his palms hard to his ears.

A quick POP silenced every speaker and put out every light in the building. Spriz visualized all the breakers flipping at once, as she'd hoped for, and briefly thought it would be fun to be standing at the box to see it happen someday, like watching an old car odometer roll over from 99,999.9 to zero.

She couldn't see a thing, and all she could hear past the residual ringing in her own ears was Gina's rapid, husky breathing, which was just enough to help Spriz locate her and grab her hand. On instinct and muscle memory alone, she pulled Gina out of the booth and into the small upstairs corridor that led nowhere, except to the roof hatch.

Quickly Spriz climbed the tiny ladder and popped open the hatch. Streetlight poured in from above, and as Spriz descended, she saw Gina's ashen, terrified face. She guided Gina up the ladder.

From the roof, a terrified Gina peered down at Spriz. "What if he comes up?"

"Don't worry, Gina," Spriz assured her before closing the hatch. "I'm taking him down."

Just as Conrad entered the empty control booth, he heard heavy footsteps on the stairway across the theatre, on the far side of the seating banks.

The footsteps were traveling… down. She was doubling back! Conrad turned around, felt his way out of the booth, and began quickly hopping down the other stairs on his good leg, grabbing the rail on each step with his opposite hand.

As she made her way down the stairs along the seats, Spriz began to second-guess her strategy. The building's archaic multiplex system required 120-volt house current, so she had just killed all the phones except the one in Tommy's pocket, which might or might not be getting a signal today. Worse, she had also managed to erase her only advantage—in the darkness she had engineered, Conrad was invisible now, too. And stronger than she was, and twice her weight. She could easily outrun him. But if he got a hand on her, he'd have her.

The smart move was to find a way out of the building, pronto. But Gina was on the roof, and Tommy and Maisy were God knows where. If she got out, she could be leaving her friends in a dark building with a killer she herself had just poked in the eye. To be sure of saving herself and her friends, she could not enjoy the luxury of escaping the bear. She'd have to ensnare it.

Spriz made no attempt to walk softly in the total darkness. Conrad had to be in the house. He couldn't have made it to the booth yet, and he wouldn't have broken off the chase, not now. He'd follow the crumbs. The trick was moving slowly enough that he could follow, but not so slowly that he'd catch up. She tried to visualize the fastest rate at which Conrad could come down the stairs, and to match it in her gait.

From six years' experience, her body knew exactly how many steps to take and the direction to travel to reach the wide-open backstage double doors that led to the dressing rooms and the basement stairs. The latches on the heavy steel door to the stairwell made a pleasant clank when she opened it, one she hoped Conrad could hear and would recognize. He knew this old building even better than she did. But she knew the basement better. Much better.

Before descending the stairs, she stopped in the doorway to listen. Was he coming? Would he follow? His old ears might still be ringing from the concert she had played him. What if he hadn't heard her footsteps, or the door?

Spriz yelped as a huge, hairy forearm curled around her neck and yanked her away from the stairwell. She jabbed at Conrad's ribcage with her sharp elbows, but he continued dragging her down the hallway, tightening his headlock on her as they traveled.

Suddenly, Conrad's grip went slack, and Spriz fell to the floor.

As she rolled herself away, she heard scuffling feet, and a garbled growl from Conrad. She turned toward the sounds, and thought she must be experiencing symptoms of hypoxia from Conrad's embrace. All she could see was a strip of pale green light, dancing in the dark like a fat firefly.

No, she knew she wasn't hypoxic. And she hadn't been hit on the head. What *was* that light? She tried to focus her eyes, and saw a little more, in the glow. She saw part of Conrad's chin; a long firefly was stretched across his throat. And then she heard Tommy's strained voice, urging her to run.

Tommy was riding Conrad's broad back, strangling the big man with Gina's big sash of glow tape, folded over and over into a thick strap. Tommy yelled "GO!" and Spriz jumped down the stairs.

Conrad spun around twice, hoping to throw Tommy off, but the smaller man was locked tight on his neck. He gyrated wildly, and for a split-second Tommy lost his grip when the glow tape ripped in two, leaving a big loop in Tommy's left fist and a sad little strip in his right fingers.

Tommy dropped by a full foot, but held on by hugging Conrad around his broad chest from behind. Conrad hurtled backward with all his weight, slamming Tommy into a wall-mounted fire extinguisher, his head making a sickening clang against the iron cylinder.

The big man held still for a moment, and was rewarded by the sensation of Tommy releasing his embrace and slipping down to the hallway floor, unconscious. Conrad took a deep breath to regain his bearings, and then headed confidently for the basement stairs.

A few steps down, his wits returned, and he became aware of the fiery ache in his left knee. He stopped to rub it. There was no need to hurry now. He had her in a bottle.

Conrad tried to suss out Spriz's strategy. Would she go for her prop room? Probably not... The place was a lobster trap, she'd be pinned in there, she was smarter than that. No, the smart move was to try to get around him in the dark and back up the stairs. But if that was her plan, why'd she come down here in the first place?

He realized that Spriz wasn't thinking, but just reacting. A spooked rabbit had instinctively run for her warren, and now she was buried in it. She was predictable. Good.

And she was out there, in the dark. Listening for him. Hoping he'd give up and go away. He knew Maisy was in the building. She'd turn the lights back on, and there Spriz would be. All he needed was patience. He started descending the remaining steps, slowly.

Spriz leaned against a warm steel junction box at the far end of the basement, perfectly still, calming herself, trying to slow her breathing, regulating it so Conrad wouldn't hear. She wished the power was on so the box's hum would cover her gasping for air. She worried about Tommy.

Her eyes were still playing tricks on her in the total darkness. She saw blobs of blue floating across her vision, probably from the panic and the downstairs run.

As her breathing settled, the blue blobs bubbled off, but then she saw another strange light, another firefly. A tiny one, maybe far away, moving downward, falling in little stages, like a feather in a light breeze, until it suddenly stopped. She closed her eyes and opened them again, trying to reboot her retinas.

Now the firefly was still, several feet above the ground maybe, Spriz couldn't really tell how high it was. But as her eyes adjusted, she could see that it was green. Glow-tape green. *God bless you, Tommy. I hope you're okay.*

His knee on fire, Conrad sat down on a low stair, so Spriz couldn't leave the basement until he'd had his chance to explain. She was a smart girl. She might understand. He called out into the dark room.

"We were bankrupt, Spriz!"

The big man heaved a huge sigh. "I wasn't going to make payroll. I didn't know what do to. Subs were way down. We owed money all over town. Everybody else was sinking—did you know Perry Playhouse went tits-up in April? It looked like we were next." He chuckled grimly as he peered into the total blackness. "The power company was about to cut us off! And god damned *Great Expectations* cost a fucking fortune, we were losing our shirt on that goddamned play."

Conrad cried out, his frustration starting to chip away at his self-control. "He was suing us! Our friendly fucking goombah atonalist Andreo was going to sue us for breach because I wouldn't let him underscore the entire fucking play! He put me on with his lawyer after the production meeting. Hell, he wasn't gonna win, his case was bullshit, but we were still going to have to pay somebody to defend us, and I didn't have it, Spriz, the well was dry. One fucking lawyer on the board and he says he can't represent us, he doesn't do civil cases, it would be irresponsible, blah blah… I swear, Spriz, some days I'd like to take a flashlight and crack the heads of the whole motherfucking board of directors!"

The producing artistic director paused, and then spoke softly, more to himself than to Spriz. "Only hit him once. When I saw the blood pouring out of his head, I thought, 'Oh my God! What the hell am I doing? I can't do this!' But once was enough." He clicked his tongue, and shook his head.

"The old man's life insurance was a Hail Mary pass, Spriz, an impulse, I never thought of it until that bridge fell and dropped it in my lap. It was that, or go dark, and for good this time. Even then, I thought maybe cancelling *Deathtrap* would nullify the lawsuit and buy us some breathing room, but not so much. Even with our cut of the insurance money, we were gonna be lucky to break even. It's not like I got greedy, Spriz!" His voice suddenly swelled, and it cracked. "I never put a *dime* in my own pocket!"

Conrad stood and pulled the heavy steel stairwell door closed behind him. He'd hear its latch open if she tried to escape. He stepped softly into the room. She was out there, very still. What was she thinking? Was he getting through to her? She wasn't arguing...

He laughed. "The funny part is, the prick was already dead! He'd started flubbing his lines, did you know that? The last few shows, every show a little worse. He covered it so well the audience didn't know, but the cast knew, and I knew. Happens to the best of 'em, sooner or later. He couldn't remember his lines anymore, and all he had to look forward to was embarrassing himself on stage until we all stopped hiring him, and then what, Spriz? Huh? Slow death alone in a Medicare home, no visitors, no cards on his birthday and no applause, never again. I did him a fucking favor! I spared him a pathetic decline! And nobody was gonna miss him, Spriz! You were at the funeral! Did you see a single tear? I didn't!"

Conrad took a few more steps, and paused. He guessed he was about halfway across the basement. He listened hard for a response—a sniffle, a sigh, anything. Was she agreeing? Was she sneaking past him? The one-way conversation was starting to irritate him. He moved ahead, slowly, holding his arms out in front of him like Frankenstein's monster in case he lucked into her.

"I saved this company, goddammit! I saved our jobs! I saved the city—if we go, the bars and restaurants go next and the boards go back up in all the windows again. I was here last time, Spriz, you don't know what a shithole this town was. Your job, mine, Maisy's… Your buddy Tommy's! All that, all that isn't worth stealing a few pitiful, lonely years from that awful man, that waste of oxygen? Do the math, Spriz! Tell me honestly the world isn't a better place with a theatre in Galilee, you and me employed and that hateful bastard six feet und—"

He stopped his mouth and his feet when his fingertips bumped into the warm steel panel of a junction box. Shit—she was behind him.

Once he'd heard his own defense aloud, he knew how weak it was. She would never take his side. She would expose him. A wave of sadness washed over him as he made himself accept what had to be done. There were too many others who would suffer, too much else at stake. Florida needed affordable theatre. For the greater good, Spriz would be silenced. He realized he'd have to take care of Tommy, too. He was confident Tommy would keep until he was finished down here. He'd only be a few minutes now.

From across the basement, he heard the squeak of little hinges moving—the prop room door! He made for the sound as fast as he could limp.

He grunted when his face smashed into a wall of chicken wire stiffened by a shelf unit behind it. The collision spilled three nested stacks of china teacups that shattered on the prop room floor inside.

The fingertips on his right hand inspected the scratches on his face gingerly as the fingers on his left hand felt their way along the wall to the chicken wire door, which he found hanging wide open. *Careful—she wants you to go in there.* Maybe she wasn't so smart after all, if she thought she could cage him with chicken wire!

He stepped in, and waved his hands in front of him, clutching for the light pull. Damn it, where was that thing? Then he remembered the power was out.

Conrad spread his long arms wide, until he almost touched the shelves on both sides of the narrow room, and then marched slowly ahead, his arms acting like cat's whiskers, telling his brain to course-correct whenever his fingertips brushed an object. The strategy had the added benefit of keeping his head in the center of the path, where it was least likely to bang into hanging props. Spriz was tall, he thought; if she tried to double-back on him, she'd run smack into his arm in the dark.

After seven short steps, his forward motion halted abruptly as his groin painfully encountered an immovable object and he doubled over, his scratched face slamming hard against an oak tabletop.

He righted himself, and rubbed his throbbing nose with one hand while patting the tabletop with the other. What was *this* doing here? He walked slowly to the right, running his hand along the edge of the table, until he found the corner, inches away from a shelf unit full of vases—no way around to the right. He followed the edge all the way to the left, and found the left side of the table practically touching a pegboard. *Who put this goddamned thing in the middle of the goddamned prop room?* And where was she—on this side? The other side? Under the table? On top of it?

As he pondered his next move, he heard the unmistakable metallic buckling—much like the galvanized "thunder sheet" they used for making offstage storm effects—of a steel cabinet. She had opened the weapons locker at the far end of the room! He had her! He dove across the table, sliding its length on his belly, and landed face-first on the floor on the opposite side.

Then he did something Spriz hadn't counted on.

Moments earlier, as Conrad was feeling his way along the chicken wire to the prop room door, Spriz had knotted a length of black tie line to the latch of the weapons cabinet, grabbed the X-Acto knife off her workbench, and then quickly tiptoed back to her end of the dining table, where she stood taut, holding the little knife in one hand and the end of the tie line in the other, watching the glow tape as it entered the room, came toward her, stopped abruptly at the far end of the table, then danced all the way to the left of the table, and then all the way to the right. She yanked the tie line, jiggling the latch and making the cabinet buckle. Conrad would go for her at the locker.

If the glow tape came over the table, she would go under. If it went down, she would go over. Either way, she'd get to the side of the table that had the door on it.

Spriz had the padlock in her jeans pocket. She'd slip out the door, lock it behind her while Conrad was on the wrong side of the dining table, and run for the stairs, which she could easily find in the dark.

By the time Conrad had torn through the chicken wire door, groped his way to the stairs and limped up them, she would have jammed the steel door at the top of the stairwell with a chair from a dressing room. There was no other way out of the basement except the freight elevator, which was dead with the power off and sitting upstairs in its home position. After she jammed the staircase door, she'd run around and raise the wooden gate on the elevator so it wouldn't move even if the power came back. A safety feature.

When the police arrived, they would find Conrad safe and sound, and already in the dungeon. That was the plan, anyway. The little knife in her hand was Plan B.

She saw the tape come over the table, and ducked underneath it. As soon as she heard Conrad's face hit the floor behind her, she started crawling under the table, toward the door.

But Conrad jumped quickly to his feet, grabbed the table with both hands and hoisted his end of it. The opposite end dropped right in front of Spriz, blocking her way. Instinctively, she rolled to one side before Conrad threw his full weight into the underside of the upended table, like the tackle he had been, and propelled it along the prop room floor, obliterating a half-dozen hanging objects along the way, until he jammed it solidly against the open doorway, wedging it between the floor and the wooden rafters above. Spriz couldn't see, but she knew what he had done.

She was 20 feet behind him. His back was to her; she could not see the glow tape. And there was no way out now, for either of them.

Conrad turned, his back to the vertical table blocking the exit, breathing hard, his face squinting into the blackened room as though seeing in the complete absence of light was only a matter of concentration.

"So what did you get from the locker?" he laughed. "You planning to shoot some blanks and scare me into a heart attack? Threaten me with a rubber knife I can't even see in the dark? I'm theatre people, dummy, there's nothing in that box that scares me!"

No reply. He could not even hear her breathe. But he knew she was close now, she had to be. If he could make her talk—or cry, or even inhale—he'd have his target, like a submarine picking up galley noises from an enemy sub gone deep and quiet.

He took three soft steps into the prop room, and listened hard. He was rewarded with a tiny sound.

*Snick.*

What? Something cutting something? He heard it again.

*Snick.*

And then the roof fell in.

Bundles of paddles, hockey sticks, spears and other assorted rods let loose above his head, the hard, heavy poles battering his skull and shoulders as they fell on and around him. The bitch had cut the clothesline that strapped the sticks to the rafters!

Dazed by the blows to his head, and now slipping and tripping on the sticks at his feet, he fell face-first on a garden hoe. Its upturned blade dug a bloody gash straight across his forehead.

The sticks clattered and rolled under him as he struggled to get back on his feet. Still on his stomach, he stopped to listen, and some of the clattering continued—she was right there! Grabbing at the sticks! Probably trying to grasp a good one for striking him, but unable to put her hand to one that was not pinned under him.

Conrad shot his hand to his right, and purchased something hard and narrow—a flagpole? No, it was warm, and it was pulling away… He had her bony wrist! He laughed, and rolled onto his back, pulling her arm across his chest as he turned so he could free his other arm from beneath himself and get both paws on his prey.

Stars popped before Conrad's eyes as he experienced the searing pain of a short blade invading a full half-inch into the back of his hand and slipping back out again.

He released Spriz's wrist and howled as he struggled to his feet on a patch of bare floor just beyond the pile of kindling. He grabbed his shirttail and wrapped it around his hand, which was hemorrhaging badly, but not quite as badly as the gash on his forehead, which was now bleeding into his eyes.

He heard the sound of a stick—maybe two—sliding out of the pile at his feet. Shit! What did she have? Shit! He swung his good hand hard and low all around him, but made no contact.

Quickly, he crouched, hoping that if she swung at him with something she'd swing high, and with his good hand he reached blindly into the pile to find his countermeasure. His fingers discovered an irregular, knobby, polished pole, about four feet long and heavy at one end—the shillelagh, he remembered it! He'd directed *Juno and the Paycock*, and he recalled how hard and lethal the heavy Irish club felt in the hand, a deadlier cudgel than a Louisville Slugger.

He stood and swung the club hard, spinning his body in a full circle. He might get lucky. Swinging the club felt good. But he still needed a target.

"So what's the deal, Spriz?" he asked, matter-of-factly. "Why are you all alone, huh? I've wanted to ask you that for years."

He grunted as he swung the shillelagh hard to his right, annihilating a stack of Fiestaware. He listened for a gasp, a whimper. But nothing.

"You're not so mysterious as you think you are, ya know."

He took a step forward, banging his bloody head on the hanging washtub. An angry, hard swing to his left bounced a row of stuffed toys off a shelf. He listened hard. Nothing.

"I'll be honest with ya, full disclosure, I considered making a pass myself now and then, especially when I was drunk. You're not sexy, but you're confusing, and that's always been my weakness. Hope you're flattered. But even drunk, I knew I'd be wasting my time. Spriz doesn't like boys, does she? But she doesn't like the girls, either… What's that about, huh?"

Another step. Swing right. This time, he hit nothing but air.

"She doesn't wanna sleep with anybody, but there's a 'daddy' out there somewhere, a daddy she always talks about but, curiously, she never visits him, and he never visits her. Hmmm…" He listened.

*Crunch.*

Conrad caught the sound of Spriz's sneaker on the broken teacups, and swung at it. The shards of what had been an entire shelf of wineglasses exploded into the air. Jagged hailstones fell.

At least he knew she wasn't balled up in a corner. She was on the move. That would make finding her easier. There was nowhere for her to go.

"So, let's do the math, shall we?" Conrad said, putting fresh bait on the hook. "Sexually stunted, does everything she can to hide her own attractiveness, raised alone by a middle-aged man who may or may not be a blood relative, talks about him like they're *so close*, but she never sees 'im…." The volume of his voice was beginning to swell alongside his impatience.

Two steps. Swing right. An antique tin Jack-in-the-box

imploded like a Styrofoam cup.

"All those things you say he taught you... I really have to wonder, I really do... What *else* he taught you, Suz*anne*... What other lessons did that daddy man teach you, Suzy-Q, that ruined you for anybody else who ever wanted a taste?"

He didn't swing. He stood absolutely still. He'd hear her any second. He could feel her weakening.

"What else, huh?" Conrad snarled. "Come on, Suzanne! WHAT ELSE DID THAT EVIL MAN TEACH HIS BABY GIRL?"

The reply came from behind him: "Archery!"

He spun to face the sound, and immediately felt a hard knock to his chest, not forceful enough to fell him, but enough to back him up a step. Had she punched him with her bony fist? The shillelagh clattered on the floor where he dropped it.

Suddenly there was a little light in the room. His eyes reflexively clamped shut, then opened into a squint as they began to adjust. He saw red; he tried to rub the blood from his eyes. He succeeded in clearing his left eye but his bloodsoaked right hand made his right eye worse.

Conrad's photographic memory showed him an article he had read, years ago in a Sunday magazine, that said people who have died and been resuscitated often describe a heightened awareness, a perfect clarity that comes just before death. In his own final moments, he was surprised at how quickly he processed the scene, piece by piece, and understood every detail of what was happening around him, and to him.

Thirteen feet ahead, the lithe, blurry outline of Spriz was coming into focus. In her dominant left hand she held a battery-powered lantern, shoulder-high, like Diogenes. She was examining Conrad's face—his scratched, bruised, mangled, lacerated, bloody face—with an expression blending horror and pity. That made him chuckle weakly—judging by her face, his must be a sight!

Her right arm was slack at her side. She was holding

something, just above the floor. Even under the shadow cast by Spriz's long body, Conrad instantly recognized the ornate carving and beautiful paint job on William Tell's bow.

His perfect recall showed him the invoice Spriz had submitted with her receipts for that show: Replica bow, poplar & beech, 15th Century. $220.00 plus $7.50 shipping. Total Due: $227.50.

Suddenly aware of a wetness on his shirt, Conrad looked down. In the dim light, he saw a piece of glow tape on his chest. *Goddammit Tommy, what did I ever do to you?*

From the tape's dead center, a painted wooden shaft protruded. Blood was seeping around the shaft and down the front of his shirt in tiny spurts.

His eyes followed the shaft to its end, where he noticed the loveliest blue-green feathers. So beautiful! His eyes continued past the feathers, refocusing on the floor at Spriz's feet, where he saw a rubber arrowhead, an X-Acto knife—no, just the handle of an X-Acto knife—and something else scattered about... Wood shavings? Yes, tiny curls of wood. The knife handle was bloody... Where was the tiny blade that had hurt like sin going into his hand?

Conrad's jaw dropped when he put the pieces together: While he had been stomping about the room swinging a club at the dark like an Irish Neanderthal, Spriz had been down on the floor, removing the fake arrowhead and whittling the tip of the hardwood shaft to a taper, probably shaving off a bit on each of his swings to cover the sound. She'd split the shaft's tip, pulled the thin little blade from the knife handle, and jammed the stem of the blade into the split, giving the arrow a scalpel point.

While his back was turned and he was swinging away from her, she'd stood up to string the bow, and when she was ready, she called to him so he would turn toward the sound of her voice and reveal the target: the glow tape. She *was* a smart girl. He felt proud for having been the one who hired her.

He wasn't in pain, not really, but he started feeling cold,

then dizzy. He was short of breath, but he managed to squeak out his final words, "Two hundred twenty-seven fucking dollars," and then crumpled to the floor.

Spriz knew it was futile. She could tell Conrad had moments left. But she thought she should at least try to get the man some help. She grabbed one side of the oak table, and yanked with all her weight and sinew. So resolutely immovable was the table that she did not try a second time.

This was better, in a way. Had she been able to go for help, he would have experienced his final moments alone in a hot, dark basement before she could return. She didn't want that for him.

The big man lay on the pile of scattered sticks, his face up, his lower legs pinned awkwardly underneath him. Spriz set the lantern on the floor near his head, and knelt beside him. She held his good hand. He was gulping breaths. His eyes were bulging. It wouldn't be long.

She hadn't meant to kill him. She'd only meant to stop him. But she had to use the only target available. She couldn't have known the glow tape was right over his heart, any more than Tommy could have known when he slapped the tape there that Spriz would shoot an arrow though it, a hair past the sternum and into Conrad's left ventricle. Tommy was going to feel bad about that. There was a long talk ahead of her.

Where it wasn't coated by sticky runs and smears of drying blood, Conrad's face was white, as white as Brandon Wishart's face the night Conrad bashed in his skull. It was almost over.

Spriz knew only one prayer, and she didn't know whether it had a tune to go with it. So she made up a melody as she sang the prayer in a ragged whisper to the dying man, in case it gave him comfort. By "forgive us our trespasses," Spriz could see Conrad was gone. She finished her song anyway.

She covered his face with the handiest drape, a torn

Confederate flag from *The Red Badge of Courage*. Leaving the lamp with Conrad, she trudged to the back of her demolished prop room, broken glass and dishes crunching under her sneakers, to her desk. She needed no light to find her wire snips, which lived in a Chock Full O' Nuts can on a narrow shelf.

Just as Spriz was preparing to pull a shelf unit aside so she could cut an escape hole in the chicken wire wall, she heard a hard, metallic *clunk* and then the familiar hum of the breaker boxes. The power was back. The basement was still dark but for the dim spill from the lantern, and she heard Nina Totenberg, *sotto voce*, coming from her Bakelite radio. The power outage had rebooted the phone system, and Spriz's desk phone now showed every line free. She muscled the handset out of its cradle and dialed Tommy's cell.

A policeman answered. Through the dodgy connection, Spriz could make out that Tommy had raised 911 from outside after escorting Maisy from the building, and had breathlessly reported an "attempted mass murder in progress." Grudgingly doing their due-diligence in response to a call they were sure was a prank, four Galilee patrolmen had searched the building by flashlight. Two came across Tommy unconscious outside the dressing rooms; an ambulance was on the way for Mr. Gustafson. Two other officers searching in the opposite direction had come upon the breaker box.

"When Mr. Gustafson is on his way to the hospital," Spriz said, loudly and slowly, "please find the stairwell in the hallway where you found him, and come down to the basement. There's a corpse in my prop room, and I don't want him."

# 26

IT TOOK TWO BURLY OFFICERS hurling themselves against the table to push it back from the doorway far enough to allow entry to the prop room. Their heavy patrolman's shoes grinding glass shards beneath their feet, they helped the exhausted Spriz restore the badly scratched table to its berth in her furniture stacks.

One officer followed Spriz up the stairs, and the other stood guard while Conrad patiently awaited his appointment with a detective and the medical examiner.

Spriz thought if they'd paid this much attention when Brandon died, Conrad might have been taken alive, and her props might all be in one piece.

She made straight for the hatch to retrieve Gina. The officer insisted on coming along. Spriz realized he had been ordered to keep eyes on her until the detective arrived to interview her.

The hatch seemed to be stuck; Spriz couldn't budge it. She even had the policeman give it a go, but he had no more success. Finally she realized what was happening, and called out.

"Gina? It's Spriz."

A tiny voice directly above replied: "Spriz?"

"It's okay Gina, we're all safe now, the police are here. Gina, are you by any chance standing on the hatch?"

A voice peeped: "Maybe?"

After reciting her constitutional rights to her and making her affirm that she understood them, Detective Bauman kept Spriz in the box office for more than an hour, prompting her through the whole sordid tale twice and going over and over certain details, including the multiple points at which she, in his judgment, could have escaped without killing anybody, so why didn't she?

Spriz was too tired and too sad to be scared. She sat very still and answered every question, listlessly, but as fully as she could.

Finally, the inexpressible insanity of the evening's events took its toll, and exhaustion gave way to frustration. "Does Galilee have more than one detective?" Spriz asked. "I don't remember seeing you around after Brandon Wishart died."

"That was an accident, young lady," said Galilee's only detective.

"I know you know it wasn't," Spriz said. "I can prove it. If you won't reopen the case, I'm sure the *Galilee Star* would be happy to do it for you."

"Confession from a dead man, witnessed by the girl who admits she killed him," Bauman retorted. "Convenient."

"There's another witness to part of that confession, the part that matters. And I can tell you how to find the murder weapon. Hope you can swim."

Eventually they were both quiet for a full minute while Bauman reviewed his notes. "Well, Miss Prizzi," he said wearily, "This doesn't get it done. We need to talk some more at the station." He took her arm to help her to her feet.

"That's okay," Spriz said. "But we need to make a stop on

the way."

Bauman clicked his tongue. "I'm not sure you understand, miss. I'm pretty close to arresting you, I think."

"Ya know, people have been threatening to arrest me all week, but they never seem to follow through." She quoted a favorite line of her Daddy's: "Piss or get off the pot." Bauman let go of Spriz's arm.

"I'll go anywhere you want," Spriz explained as she opened the box office door, "but we need to make a stop on the way. I figured something out while I was waiting for your guys to shove the table out of my doorway. I'll explain in the car."

She held the door for Bauman. "You comin' or what?"

Ryan Mountain answered the front door at his big yellow house north of town. His kids were asleep and his wife was watching *Downton Abbey*.

When he saw Spriz, Bauman and a uniformed officer on his front patio, he said nothing for a moment. He looked past them to see the two cars on his front lawn: the detective's plainclothes sedan and the officer's black & white. He stepped outside, quietly closed the door, and greeted them all formally. "Detective. Suzanne. Officer Gresham."

He turned to Spriz. "The tax returns?"

Spriz replied, "The tax returns. The copies you gave him were phonies. The ones you actually filed had to have the right pension and dependent care numbers on them, or the IRS would've started sniffing around. Nobody could have done it but you. And you wouldn't have done it unless you were a part of the whole thing."

Ryan smiled weakly at Spriz. "You'd have made a good attorney, Spriz." He looked at Bauman. "She's right, detective. Let's go. I'll call my wife as soon as we get to the station. I'd rather she didn't see this." He put his hands together behind his back and turned away from Officer Gresham, who snapped on the cuffs.

"I want these two kept separate!" Bauman barked at the young officer. You take him, I'll take her, and we'll hook up at the station."

As Gresham started to lead the attorney away, Ryan stopped and asked, "Wait, where's she going?"

"Not your business," Bauman snapped. "Take him!"

"Wait!" Ryan said firmly. "I'm Miss Prizzi's attorney of record. I represented her only yesterday. You are required to tell me where you are taking her."

Bauman shot an exasperated look to Spriz, who nodded, then shrugged. "I have more questions," he said to Mountain.

"Let's talk, Steve," Ryan said to Bauman, and then turned his back. The detective and the lawyer took a few steps away together as they spoke quietly on the patio, the sides of their heads almost touching, their backs to Spriz and Gresham, the bracelets on Mountain's wrists glinting in the patio light. After two minutes, Bauman broke away. He looked furious.

"Take the girl home, or back to her car or wherever the hell she says!" he bellowed as he made for his car. "And then get that sonofabitch under lock and key!"


In the patrol car, Spriz sat in front next to Gresham, and Ryan sat alone in back, where he could not unlock the doors.

Spriz turned her head toward the back seat and asked, "What did you say to him?"

Ryan Mountain smiled. "It's better if you don't know, Spriz." Unseen by Spriz and Ryan, Officer Gresham smiled, too.

"I'm sorry, Spriz," Ryan said. "I didn't want to see the theatre go under. It seemed harmless enough at the time, or the lesser of evils anyway. I guess things got out of hand. I'm sorry."

Spriz turned away, and stared out her window.

"Sleep well, Spriz," the lawyer said gently. "I guess you've earned a good sleep. Everything is going to be all right." He closed his eyes, and leaned his head back on the top of the vinyl seat.

# 27

AFTER FORTY-EIGHT HOURS the police removed their
yellow tape from the prop room. The following morning,
against the advice of Tommy who was in bed at his mother's
house on doctor's orders, Spriz went down to clean up.

As soon as she pulled the string that popped on the seven
bare bulbs, her heart sank, and with it her ambition.

Half the shelves were emptied, and the tall cases had been
badly damaged. The floor was completely covered by spilled
and broken props, and underneath them, by a thick layer of
broken glass and ceramics. She could not walk anywhere
without hearing and feeling shards crackle and plink beneath
her soles.

The sticks were still a sloppy bird's nest in the center of the
room, and the middle of the pile was marked by a sticky,
brownish bullseye of Fiestaware fragments and dried blood.

Once she'd noticed the color of the blood, she became
aware of spots and smudges of it all around: on the sticks, on
the shelves, on the few unbroken dishes, on the cameras and
even on the toys. How would she ever get them clean?

A spot of dried blood on one of the seven bare bulbs began

to smoke and emit a sickly, dead odor.

On the way to the theatre early that morning, she had been to the station see Detective Bauman and the medical examiner, who showed her that he had amended his report in the matter of Brandon Wishart to read, "Probable Homicide."

But while the two men both professed that they were "not unsympathetic," Bauman told Spriz he had no intention of wasting his scant staff resources to build a case against a killer who was already A) Surely guilty, according to evidence already collected and the complete lack of another plausible suspect, and B) Dead. The case was closed, and would stay that way.

As a convincer, Bauman and the ME itemized for Spriz what it would cost just to exhume the body. Bauman asked Spriz to tell him exactly what she thought he should say to the pissant watchdogs when they asked him to show what vital public interest was served by the expense, given that there was no unknown killer on the loose from whom the public required protection.

Then Bauman made a few unsubtle insinuations about ways he could complicate Spriz's life, should she exercise the poor judgment of talking to a reporter. He told her he had received a call about her only yesterday, from an FBI special agent, no less.

"I can make you very, very sorry you ever met me, young lady, if I want to," he warned. Spriz resisted the impulse to inform him that thanks to both his personality and his breath, pretty much anybody would be sorry to have met him.

In not so many words as they parted, Bauman said he dearly hoped he was seeing the last of Suzanne Prizzi.

Spriz crunched halfway into the prop room and then slumped into her favorite Queen Anne chair, sick to her stomach. She could not decide whether to summon the will to get working, douse the lights and go home, or sit right there and cry.

She felt as though she were looking at yet another corpse, her fourth in a week counting Brandon, Conrad and the Perry Playhouse. This was one too many.

Spriz sniffled. She shuddered.

And then she buried her face in her hands and sobbed.

She'd been bawling for a full minute when suddenly startled by the sound of footsteps and hubbub coming down the stairs. She quickly wiped her eyes and nose with her fingers, and watched the darkness beyond the open doorway of the prop room.

In marched Maisy, lugging a heavy pail with steam rising from it. She was followed by Gina, laden with a spray bottle and rolls and rolls of paper towels, and Ana Maria with a broom and dustpan and a big box of green trash bags. From his sickbed, Tommy had made some phone calls.

Bringing up the rear was Master Carpenter Sandy, wrapped in a cowhide toolbelt festooned with a hammer, a cordless screw-gun and little bags of screws and nails in the pockets. He carried a box of Sham-Wow cloths under one arm and two six-packs of Yuengling in the crook of the other. When he caught Spriz eyeing the beer, he laughed and announced, "It's five o'clock somewheres, Spriz!"

After a quick breakfast toast they set to work. Ana Maria cleared a small spot for Maisy to kneel in so she could tackle the bullseye on the floor, and then went to join Sandy in repairing shelves. Spriz began picking up props and putting them away, handing the bloody ones to Gina for scrubbing—or disposal.

Led by Maisy, they sang showtunes as they worked, and they laughed. Spriz decided she really ought to have more parties down here.

Despite the disconcerting noises beneath their feet, they all recognized that there was no point in trying to deal with the broken glass until everything on top of it had been cleared off.

But Spriz worried about it. There was so much of it, and no doubt by now some glass had burrowed its way into the old wooden floor, and would not sweep away. They'd have to pull the shards out of the floor by hand, one by one, like cactus spines, and would probably spill yet more blood in the process.

As Spriz was shelving the last toy and the other four were taking a break, charging up their batteries for the final task, all five of them were startled by a deafening whir—like a jet engine.

Out of the dark basement, a twenty-gallon, six-and-a-half horsepower vacuum that had been trucked over from the scene shop rolled in through the open doorway, with Karl beside it, sweeping the nozzle expertly from side to side and practically yanking the flooring nails from their boards. Karl enjoyed boasting that this favorite appliance could suck the chrome off a trailer hitch.

His cap pulled down low over his eyes, he focused on his task until the floor was as bare as the day it had been laid, ninety-some years ago. He flipped the switch on the monster vac, and its motor slowly wound down to a whisper, then silence, as the spinning shards within ceased their rattling and came to rest at the bottom of the tank.

Karl looked up, only to catch Spriz smiling at him. He quickly turned his face away, cleared his throat and growled, "Jes' so damn tired o' watchin' you dummies do ever'thin' the hard way."

# 28

*They went on together*
*and lived happily ever after.*
*They knew, one day, the new dragon*
*would do something to please God*
*and God would let him be a boy again*
*and he would come home.*

DEL CLOSE was a minor TV and film actor with a handful of credits on his resume, mostly bit parts, often in projects filmed in his home base of Chicago such as *The Untouchables* and *Ferris Bueller's Day Off.*

But inside the legendary Chicago improv comedy scene, Close was a beloved performer, teacher, director and author. He is cited as a mentor by the likes of Bill Murray, Tina Fey and other comic actors who made their bones in the *Saturday Night Live* and Second City comedy factories.

He was also a devoted wiseass who bequeathed his own skull to Chicago's Goodman Theatre with instructions that anytime the Goodman mounted *Hamlet*, the company was to use his cranium as a prop: the skull of the late jester Yorick, the head unearthed by a comic gravedigger and caressed by Hamlet himself during a wistful speech (Act V, Scene 1) delivered lovingly into Yorick's empty eye sockets:

> Alas, poor Yorick! I knew him, Horatio: a fellow
> of infinite jest, of most excellent fancy: he hath
> borne me on his back a thousand times; and now, how
> abhorred in my imagination it is! my gorge rises at
> it. Here hung those lips that I have kissed I know
> not how oft. Where be your gibes now? your
> gambols? your songs? your flashes of merriment,
> that were wont to set the table on a roar? Not one
> now, to mock your own grinning? quite chap-fallen
> Now get you to my lady's chamber, and tell her, let
> her paint an inch thick, to this favour she must
> come; make her laugh at that.

In an act of staggering deathbed audacity, Del Close attempted to engineer circumstances through which William Shakespeare himself, in the guise of his most celebrated character, would eulogize Close before paying audiences in perpetuity and supply double-posthumous expert testimony affirming Close's belovedness and comic genius. Close even specified that he was to be billed as Yorick in the play's program.

Sadly for lovers of great theatre yarns, Close's skull never made it onstage without the rest of him. In the weeks following Close's 1999 death from emphysema, his executor was unable to find a facility willing to boil the flesh from the head and preserve the bone. So she had Close cremated, head and all.

For several years the executor passed off a skull purchased from a medical supply house as Close's, but before the Goodman ever got around to doing *Hamlet* the executor was exposed in the press. She copped to the con, which she said she had reluctantly undertaken only to fulfill Close's dying wish to achieve theatrical immortality—appearing on stage after death—and of course to earn an assist in pulling off the most permanent practical joke since Brian Epstein secretly replaced Paul McCartney with an imposter following McCartney's 1967 demise—or so rumor has it.

Where Close's executor had failed, Spriz would succeed. To Maisy, she gave Brandon's clothing, wristwatch and wigs for costumes. Convincing Maisy to accept these items was no mean feat, and was achieved through an admixture of sound argument and liberal application of guilt. Unbeknownst to Spriz, Maisy threw away the underwear and socks, and sent the hair out to be cleaned. But she racked Brandon's other togs as promised, and fully intended to use them someday to costume an ill-dressed, fat male character in a play set in the 1980s.

The police did Spriz the favor of seizing all of Brandon's papers for evidence in the ongoing fraud investigation against Kami Carroll et al, saving her the trouble of the little ceremony and bonfire she had planned to hold in the courtyard behind her apartment.

She took Wishart's prescriptions to the county resource recovery facility to be properly disposed of. She'd heard on NPR that medicines tossed in the trash were fouling the rivers, and she doubted that the gators were having prostate trouble. She did throw away his grooming tools and old makeup—Maisy reminded her it could carry germs—but she kept the playing cards and the old tackle box to use as props.

The brown leather satchel she polished with mink oil and placed atop an orderly pile of suitcases in her newly restored prop room. She had it all set to star in the very next show featuring characters who came into the story after a long journey, or packed off to parts unknown before the closing curtain.

Unlike his contemporary Del Close, Brandon Wishart would appear on stage after death, again and again, albeit by proxy and in pieces, for many years to come. Spriz the propsmistress had arranged his immortality. She must be very powerful, she thought. Perhaps she is a goddess.

His coffee mug she cleaned thoroughly with bleach and set on a small shelf above her workbench. She uses it as a caddy for her new X-Acto handle and blades. She threw the old handle away, and snuck the old blades into the sharps disposal container at the drugstore when nobody was looking.


Ryan Mountain, Esquire somehow managed to get out on bail despite pending state and federal charges against him that included insurance fraud, pension fraud, tax fraud and accessory to murder. His right ankle now decorated by a tracking bracelet, he sat home under house arrest, awaiting trial. His wife, for the time being, was standing by him.

Though technically barred from practicing law, he was working secretly through loyal associates at his firm to get Brandon's pension continued and paid to Sam. As a backup plan, Ryan and his confederates were cooking up a suit to seize Conrad's 401(k) for damages, payable to Brandon's next of kin.

Mountain's accomplices exchanged email weekly with VP Amanda Curtain, who had promised to keep the wolves at bay until something could be managed. One way or another, Sam Wishart would stay put.


EMERGENCY PRODUCTION MTG @10.

The email and text went out from Maisy the night before, and that's all anybody knew. After only three weeks off, everybody was to show up tomorrow. Were they back on the clock, or about to be told to pack up forever? They'd find out this morning.

Spriz had come in early to rearrange a few things in her prop room—she still wasn't entirely satisfied with how she'd organized it during the restoration—and to compose an important email message she'd been thinking about. She could have typed it on her laptop at home, but there were too many distractions there, including a fat cat who liked to stroll across the keyboard.

She typed the message in ALL CAPS, the better to freak out the recipient whose email address she had found in the *Great Expectations* contact sheet:

LANFORD:

AS IM SURE YOU KNOW BY NOW THEY FOUND A PATSY TO PIN BRANDONS MURDER ON. LUCKY YOU. THE SUSPECT IS DEAD SO THE CASE IS CLOSED AND NOBODYS THE WISER.

BUT YOU AND I KNOW THE TRUTH DONT WE?

FOR MY OWN REASONS IM CONTENT TO KEEP MY PEACE FOR NOW. BUT THAT COULD CHANGE. THERES ONE THING YOU CAN DO TO ENSURE MY SILENCE.

JUST THIS: BE NICE. TREAT YOUR FELLOW ACTORS WITH RESPECT. TREAT THE CREW AND DESIGNERS WITH RESPECT AND LEARN ALL THEIR NAMES. BE FRIENDLY. BE KIND. DO THAT AND YOU HAVE NOTHING TO FEAR FROM ME.

BUT IF I HEAR YOU ARE BEING MEAN OR INSENSTIVE TO CREW OR STEALING SCENES OR SPREADING GOSSIP, AND YOU KNOW I WILL HEAR ABOUT IT THRU THE GRAPEVINE, I SWEAR I WILL RENT A BILL BOARD ON I-4 TO OUT YOU. ITS UP TO YOU.

YOU CAN PAY YOUR DEBT TO BRANDON BY NOT BECOMING HIM.

BE NICE OR ELSE.

SPRIZ

YOUR PROPSMISTRESS

She BCCed Tommy.

They all sat in their usual seats in the stifling conference room, all except for Maisy, who was standing at the head of the table where Conrad had always stood. No one could see, but she was on her tippy-toes, unconsciously and futilely attempting to loom over the table because that's what her predecessor had done.

"Case you haven't heard, I'm the interim AD while the board does a nationwide search for a permanent replacement, somebody better," Maisy reported. "Let me be crystal clear about this: I do not want this job. I do not want to do it today. I do not want to do it tomorrow. I do not want to do it for an hour. But somebody set it up that way, so I'm gonna do it the best I can until somebody says different."

Already in a worse funk than usual, Karl muttered from underneath his cap, "Somebody got they math wrong."

Maisy turned slowly to Karl. "Math don't enter into it, Karl, the bylaws don't say the board has to choose by seniority." Karl had come to GaliRep two years before Maisy, and was the longest-serving employee at the table. "Maybe they wanted somebody who plays well with others, and if they did, whose fault is that?" Karl pulled the bill on his cap and slumped lower in his seat. Maisy returned to her speech.

"As of five minutes ago y'all are back at work. *Steel Magnolias* opens four weeks from Friday. Rehearsals start Monday, advertising starts the week after, and the subscribers are getting letters from me going out this afternoon." Smiles and high-fives made a lap around the table.

Ever the killjoy, set designer Sheila piped up above the celebration. "What about the lawsuit?"

Maisy smiled wide. "Well now, I had the most delightful lunch yesterday with our Mr. Andreo, just me and him, and you wouldn't know it, but the man is just a fat sack of sugar in the right company. He's dropping his lawsuit, and we're producing the wonderful opera he's just started composing, as soon as he finishes it."

Worried glances circled the room. Karl kicked the underside of the table with his knee and growled, "We ain't no opera house!" Others nodded.

Maisy gave Karl a knowing look. "As soon as he *finishes it*, Karl. Don't know about you, but I'm not planning on living that long. God forbid if he ever does finish it, he can sue us then, and maybe by then we'll be healthy enough to sue 'im back!" Laughter and cheers bounced off the table. Sheila and Spriz high-fived.

Maisy showed the group her palm. "Now the bad news," she said firmly. "Here's how we get this theatre back in the black: Sell tickets, don't spend money. Budget for the departments on this show is zero. That's Z-E-R-O dollars for set, costumes and props. Karl, Spriz, your budget is zilch. Whatever this show needs, pull it from stock or make it from materials on hand. Whatever you can't do for free, we're cutting, it's that simple. This season, we're spending every penny on actors, promotion and fundraising. And before you start feeling sorry for yourselves, we're spending zip on directors, too. Yours truly will be directing *Steel Magnolias* with my own two little hands, and y'all know I hate directing almost as much as I hate that damn play." She shook her head.

"Now, because I'm gonna be spending all my time out here herding you people, I need someone to keep an eye on the costume shop. I'm putting Tommy Gustafson on staff as assistant manager the minute the doctor lets him off the leash. Sounds like I'm spending money, but it's gonna save money, you'll just have to take my word. Spriz, Tommy doesn't know yet, you can call him after the meeting." Maisy folded her arms. "But you tell that boy he's not to set a toe in my shop without written permission from the doctor pinned to his shirt. y'hear?"

Maisy paused. She looked around the table, making sure to take a silent moment to connect with everybody, one at a time, eye-to-eye, so they all could see that she knew they could do what she was expecting of them, that she had faith in each of them.

"We're going back to the beginning, everybody. Theatre on a shoestring, like the old days. We're gonna spend nothing to make shows that look like a million bucks, and come spring we're gonna have this old cigar factory back on its feet, a new AD from God-knows-where and money in the bank. And then I'm goin' back inside the costume shop to stay 'til the Good Lord calls me home."

She leaned in toward the pouting man in the tractor cap. "Whattaya say, Karl?" Then she borrowed a favorite phrase of his, one she'd always hated: "You ready to kick this pig 'til she squeals?"

That got him. The corners of Karl's mouth sneaked upward, and he barked like a Marine cadet: "Yes MA'AM!"

Spriz was already crafting props in her head. *Steel Magnolias* needed hairdryers, those big ones ladies sat under at the beauty parlor. She couldn't rent them. She was going to have to make them. How was she going to make hairdryers? She had lots of cooking pots, maybe if she took the handles off some matching pots and painted them just right… She'd need to study some photos online, and she'd also need to beg Karl for some big air hoses from the scene shop, that wasn't going to be easy…

Oh boy, this was going to be *fun*.

NED AVERILL-SNELL is an actor of little note who works on and off in small professional theatre in Florida. He has also worked as a director, designer and propsmaster, and has written several plays you haven't seen. A Massachusetts native and graduate of Indiana University (B.A., Theatre Arts, '83), he lives in Tampa and is a father of three.

Spriz will return in *Chamber Musical Murder.*